FROM T-FORD TO T5

100 YEARS OF HAMPSHIRE CONSTABULARY TRANSPORT

STEVE WOODWARD

FROM T FORD TO T5: 100 YEARS OF HAMPSHIRE CONSTABULARY TRANSPORT

First published 2004

ISBN 1-904408-05-2

© Steve Woodward, 2004

Published by BANK HOUSE BOOKS

Printed and bound by
Lightning Source

Designed and typeset in England by
BANK HOUSE BOOKS
PO Box 3
NEW ROMNEY
TN29 9WJ

Introduction

The original concept for this book was for it to have been a pictorial history with the occasional caption thrown in for good measure. During my research I had the very great pleasure of talking to many of those people who have either been responsible for the introduction of certain vehicles into the Hampshire fleet, or who have been Police vehicle enthusiasts in their own right and have fond memories of the patrol cars they once drove. As I interviewed them it became apparent that Hampshire had done so many things first and that its avant-garde approach to vehicles was almost unique in the UK, that I thought it important that this book become as close to a definitive history as possible. There might of course be one or two people who might question the need for a book such as this, but even the most hardened and cynical of Police officers will always reminisce about certain cars, a particular pursuit and how the car coped, or more likely about some misdemeanor they committed inside the car!

The Hampshire Constabulary has become famous over the years, indeed controversial at times, over its choice of cars. It has led the way many times with its innovative approach and at the same time has been condemned in the highest of places for daring to be different, especially during the 1960s when it was the first ever UK Police force to buy foreign cars, in the shape of the Volvo 120 Amazon estates and again in the mid 1970s when it dared to purchase BMWs. Nowadays of course this is commonplace, as just about every county has non British cars on its fleet, but in years gone by, when British is Best and I'm Backing Britain-Buy British campaigns were being run by the Government, it was a different story. But Hampshire's policy has always been the same, to buy the best possible vehicle available at that time to do the job and is not governed by politics or funding. We will cover this subject more fully as we talk about individual cars later in the book.

Hampshire has also assisted car manufacturers in testing and modifying certain cars and has actually invented component parts to correct a fault where the manufacturer couldn't or wouldn't. Some of this testing was done in the dead of night in complete secrecy, whilst other testing, like that of Dunlop's Denovo tyres was more public. It would appear that car manufacturers take a more serious view of component faults now than they used to. Back in the 1960s and 70s though, if it constantly broke, the mechanics and staff at the force's vehicle repair workshops would invariably have to come up with something to fix it. And more often than not, they did. This included parts for Rover P6 gearboxes and Norton Commando exhaust gaskets. This make and do policy is now virtually redundant, partly because our cars in general are so much more reliable, but mainly because they are covered by a far better warranty and because the Police fleet market is seen by the vehicle manufacturers as a very important one and are much quicker to rectify any faults. The public does look at the vehicles the Police use and quite rightly reaches the conclusion that if it's good enough for Police use, then it must be reliable enough for his or her personal transport. This was probably never more so than in the early 1970s, when Volvos were being used by the Hampshire Constabulary. In 1965 when the first two were delivered, Volvos were about as common place in the UK as some South Korean cars are now. By the 1970s Hampshire were buying dozens of them and it didn't take long for the public to react. This trend continued right through to the late 1980s with the 240 range and again in the 90s with the 850 T5. The same could also be said of BMWs 5 series saloons, in all its guises. The public clearly believes that if the Police use it, then it must be a sound vehicle. You only had to look at the average Police station yard in Hampshire during this period, to see that there were an awful lot of private Volvos and BMWs being used by officers for their own personal transport. As a vehicle manufacturer, if your product is being used by the Police on a large scale, then you've got yourself a winner.

Before we actually look at the vehicles used by the Hampshire Constabulary over the years, it is essential that we take a closer look at the county itself. Every county in the UK is unique in some way and requires a different type of vehicle to police it. In comparison to Scotland, Hampshire is rather flat in its landscape and doesn't get much in the way of snow. Our four-wheel drive capability therefore is that much less. Hampshire has more miles of motorway than just about every other county in the country (at one time it was the highest) and it therefore has far more motorway patrol cars than say, one of its neighbouring forces like Dorset, that has no motorway at all.

So what does the county of Hampshire have? A population of some two million people, three large cities in Portsmouth, Southampton and Winchester, more than 100 miles of coastline, including the Isle of Wight and some 1000 square miles of sea to patrol, including the Solent, with the worlds busiest shipping lanes, necessitating an efficient Marine Division and Air Support Unit. Portsmouth is the home of the Royal Navy and also has the second largest European ferry terminal in the country. Southampton is the homeport of the luxury cruise ships like the QE2 and has the huge Fawley oil refinery on its doorstep, whilst the town of Aldershot is the home of the British Army. As well as the urban sprawl of our cities and larger towns, Hampshire also has a large amount of countryside, together with the natural beauty of the South Downs and the New Forest. It has some of the busiest motorways in the country in the M3, M27, M271, M275, A3M and the four lane sections of the A27, now the most congested road in the south of England. It has two big football teams in Southampton and Portsmouth, five major prisons, including the top security units at Parkhurst and Albany on the Isle of Wight. It has a large tourist trade and strong links with France and the Channel Islands. In the 1970s Hampshire became the target of the IRA, with the bombing of the Aldershot army barracks and had several other major terrorist incidents. The county is bordered by Sussex, Surrey, Thames Valley, Wiltshire and Dorset. It is a busy and diverse area to police and its vehicle fleet reflects this.

The current make up of the Hampshire Constabulary as a force has evolved over the years. Without going too deeply into the subject, the basic history of the force is as follows; modern day policing in the county can be traced back to 1839, with the formation of the Hampshire County Constabulary, although there were Watch Committees in existence prior to this. The Isle of Wight, Winchester, Portsmouth and Southampton all had their own respective Police forces during this period. The Isle of Wight County Constabulary and the Winchester City Police were amalgamated with the county force and in 1952 became the Hampshire and Isle of Wight Constabulary. In 1967, during local government boundary and structure changes, many of the old city and borough forces merged to form larger county forces. Portsmouth City Police and Southampton City Police ceased to exist and amalgamated into the all new Hampshire Constabulary. In 1974, after yet more boundary changes, the towns of Bournemouth and Christchurch suddenly found themselves being policed not by Hampshire, but by Dorset! In the first two chapters of this book we will examine the vehicles used by the two city forces, as they are an inherent part of Hampshire's history.

Many of the photographs used are from my own private collection, taken either by me or by individuals who at the time, wished to record, for whatever reason, their affiliation to a particular vehicle. Some are official force photographs, taken to provide an historical record or for publicity purposes at that particular time. It was quite commonplace in the 1950s and early 60s for example for the force to photograph every parade or inspection. These inspections were generally annual affairs and were to be recorded. Cars were also fairly scarce in post war Britain, with most Police forces having to make do with whatever they could lay their hands on. There was no fleet policy in those days. So when more affluent times arrived and Police forces started buying patrol cars, this again was a time to record the occasion with a photo or two. Today of course there are no annual inspections and we buy so many vehicles, that the Photographic Department could easily spend all its time just photographing them and nothing else. The photo then is probably the most important of historical records. Whilst I have been able to locate pictures of most of the vehicles that Hampshire has used over the years, there are some, that so far I have been unable to trace. No doubt this book may prompt someone to look in their loft or rummage through their drawers in pursuit of a lost photo or two.

But there are other records on which I have been able to extract information. Hampshire used to keep a hand written auctions book. This historical ledger listed every vehicle that the force owned or inherited from the old city forces, from 1962 to 1975. It gave the registration number, date of first registration, total mileage, date and location of auction sale, together with a general description of the state of the vehicle, prior to its sale. It also kept a similar accident book, which not only described the damage and cost to every Police vehicle involved in an accident, no matter how small, but named the driver as well! Both of these books have proved invaluable in my research, because they have given me an excellent insight into the numbers and types of vehicles used. They also revealed recurring weaknesses in certain models, like defective gearboxes or worn out back axles. Some of the mileage achieved by the early cars was quite incredible, especially when you consider that there were no motorways in Hampshire until the 1970s. How about a 1948 Morris Commercial prison van that recorded more than 139,000 miles or a Wolseley 6/99 with 142,000 miles to its credit.

Other sources of reference have included newspaper and magazine articles, some other official force documents, A History of the Hampshire & Isle of Wight Constabulary by Ian A. Watt, the Minutes of the Watch Committee from Portsmouth City and the memories of certain individuals. The information some of these people had was priceless. Anecdotes about certain cars, their crews, their pride in keeping it clean and polished are things you won't find in any official documentation and it was these stories that have probably assisted me the most. During the interviews that I conducted with these, mainly retired officers and workshop staff, I was given information about certain cars that was rather amusing. I have therefore included a 'Did You Know That....?' box in certain parts of the book and I hope they provide you with a little light relief.

This book is dedicated to the memory of PC 1703 Kevin Angus of Cosham Traffic Department, who, even on the day he died, was still
assisting me with my research.

About The Author

Steve Woodward joined the Hampshire Constabulary as a sixteen year old Cadet in September 1975, becoming a regular in January 1978. The first Police vehicles he ever drove were Austin 850 Minis, although prior to that as a Cadet, he would often have to travel in the back of a Bedford Beagle van, which wasn't even fitted with rear seats! His entire service has been undertaken in the Portsmouth area, which is where he met his wife Tricia and they have three children.

From an early age he had always had a keen interest in cars and motorcycles. This interest developed further during his career when he began to take particular note of the types of vehicles used by the force, even photographing one or two of them. But it wasn't until the advent of the national miner's strike in 1984 that he realised quite how diverse each Police force could be in the type and make-up of vehicles used. And he also came to realise just how different Hampshire was to many other forces, when he heard from other officers about how envious they were that Hampshire used cars like Volvos and BMWs as a matter of routine. From then on he decided to photograph every type of vehicle the force used and managed to obtain old photos by various means to add to a rapidly expanding collection.

About the same time he started collecting models of Police cars and thought that he must be the only person on the planet that did such a thing, until 1986 when he read a couple of letters from like minded collectors in a model car magazine. He wrote to the magazine to ask if these people and any others would like to get in touch to buy, sell or exchange models and information. He expected to get one or two replies, so imagine his surprise, when by the end of the month he had over one hundred letters, mainly from other Police officers, from all over the world! This correspondence led to the formation of the Police Vehicle Enthusiasts Club, which now boasts more than two hundred and fifty members with its own quality magazine. Such is the knowledge held by the membership that it now assists the model manufacturers to produce accurate and authentic replicas. Other members restore old Police vehicles to help preserve our heritage and they are often seen at rallies all over the country and help raise thousands for charity.

Steve has written for various car and model magazines, has organised emergency service vehicle shows and believes that we all have a responsibility to preserve what is common today, for future generations to enjoy.

Further Information

Hampshire Constabulary: www.hampshire.police.uk
Hampshire Constabulary History Society: www.hants.gov.uk
Police Vehicle Enthusiasts Club: www.pvec.co.uk

Acknowledgements

The author would like to thank the following for their invaluable assistance:

Frank Allanson, John Anderson, Kevin Angus, Keith Annals, Derek Bampton, Clive Barham, Bill Bates, John Bradley, Andy Bardsley, Sydney Booth, Bob Blake, Steve Blake, David Brown, Geoff Cadman, Nick Carter, Pete Cobbett, James Cramer, Peter R. Daniels, Christopher Davies, Chris Dugdale, David Easson, Kevin Elliott, Cyril Fellows, Roy Ford, Ron Flatman, Pete Forster, Steve Frampton, Jim Fraser, Ross Fuller, Steve Greenaway, Clifford Gray, Hampshire Constabulary History Society, Brian Homans, Matt Holmes, John Jackman, Tony Johnson, Kevin Joyner, Barry Juchau, Stef King, Ron Lilly, John Lee, Roy Middleton, Phil Moth at P.M. Photography, William Ord, Mick Payne, Len Pearce, John Prince, Alan Price, Kenneth Porter, Geraint Roberts, John Roberts, Simon Rowley, Chris Sanders, Nick Scott, David Simmonds, Andy Sparshott, Kelvin Shipp, Daniel Smith, Terry Swetnam, Christopher Taylor, John Warner, Eddie Wallace, Andy Williams, Bob Wheeler, and to my wife Tricia for all her patience and support.

Contents

Foreword

It was 11th March 1968, a crisp winter's day, as I walked across Orams Arbour in the direction of Police Headquarters, to start my first day as a Transport Storeman with the Hampshire Constabulary. As I entered the drive and looked up at the towering building, surrounded by the bareness of the trees and the echoes of voices from behind the prison wall next door, little did I realise what lay in store and after thirty three years with the department, how privileged and fortunate I am to have been involved in such a unique, challenging and diverse vehicle fleet operation.

I had been born into the motor trade, as my father owned one of the first Renault dealerships in Hampshire; H.L. Bradley's based in Staple Gardens, Winchester. Therefore I was extremely fortunate to have been brought up surrounded by a vast array of different manufacturers vehicle and model types during my adolescent years and having the opportunity as early as nine years of age to dismantle engines and gearboxes, carry out decokes and learn about the diversity of the motor trade, from engineering to customer sales and service. This held me in good stead for my future career within the Constabulary's Transport Department.

One of the first tasks I was given by Laurie Reed, the then Stores Supervisor was to dispose of the infamous Winkworth bells. If only I had realised what a sin it was to take crates of solid brass bells for scrap and particularly knowing as I do today the historic value of such devices, bearing in mind that they were the earliest means of audible warning for emergency response vehicles.

I have been fortunate to have been involved in so many Police transport related projects and operations, too many to mention, however a few do stand out in my mind; the miners strike, Operation Day Break with the travellers in the New Forest, Le Tour cycle race (Tour de France) and more recently planning for the Millennium.

The forces Transport Department has always been seen as innovative and crusading in terms of its vehicles and specialist Police equipment. We were one of the first forces in the country to purchase white vehicles, we were the first to buy a foreign manufacturers vehicles for front line policing, when the Volvo Amazon was introduced with its Ruddspeed conversion in 1965. My predecessor John Roberts was responsible for the introduction of the Federal Signals lightbar system with its integrated siren, which was another first for Hampshire. In recent times the trialling of the Ford Ecostar Advanced Electric Vehicle at Fleet Police Station and even more recently the introduction of thirty-five Liquid Petroleum Gas section vehicles, the first Police LPG fleet in the UK to be funded by the Energy Saving Trust Powershift program. This highlights our willingness to introduce new technologies where there is a benefit to our officers and the public at large. It is also with some pride that in recent years the force has won awards both at home and abroad in recognition of the standards set within the Transport Department. These have been for Vehicle Conspicuity and Corporate Image, Environmental and Fleet Management.

The transition over many years from the Sunbeam Rapiers, Hillman Minx, Austin Westminsters through to today's Volvo V70 automatic estates and BMW 325 TDS patrol cars, combined with the current technology in light bars, sirens, Tracker, Vascar and looking more to the future, with in-car data and PSRCS (new national radio system), give a clear indication of the technological changes that the force has undergone in a relatively short space of time.

Steve Woodward's energy and enthusiasm has produced a unique chronological record relating to the Hampshire Constabulary's transport operation from 1900 to 1999. His knowledge and understanding of the type and range of vehicles operated by the force and their use, combined with interesting snippets of information, both current and pre-amalgamation is truly remarkable. This book will be of great interest to both those aficionados and the layman who are interested in acquiring a definitive history of the forces vehicle fleet operation. It is an excellent piece of work for which he has to be congratulated.

John Bradley
Fleet Manager
Hampshire Constabulary

CHAPTER 1

PORTSMOUTH BOROUGH POLICE
(LATER TO BECOME PORTSMOUTH CITY POLICE)

Portsmouth City Police is recognised as one of the oldest Police forces in the UK. Records show that there were Constables in the Borough as far back as the 13th Century, but its men were not sworn in or paid wages until the emergence of the new Portsmouth Borough Police in March 1836. The name was later changed to Portsmouth City Police and at midnight on the 31st March 1967, the force was amalgamated with Hampshire.

Before the advent of motorised transport of course, there was the horse and the officers in Portsmouth were no exception in using them. Police officers of the late 19th Century used the horse to good effect to patrol the area and to help quell rioting, which was all too frequent a problem then. The Mounted Section consisted of four horses stationed at the Landport Police Station. Horses were used to pull the *Black Maria* the earliest form of prisoner transportation, to take prisoners from the courts to the nearby Kingston Prison. The prison van, as it was referred to even then, was purchased on the 1st October 1878 and cost the Borough £177 10s. It was specially constructed with partitions to house ten prisoners and its sole driver for many years was Sgt Coombs.

The horse drawn Black Maria outside Kingston Prison
James Cramer

But in the Borough of Portsmouth it wasn't just policing that was undertaken by its officers. From 8th February 1836 when the new Watch Committee was formed, the responsibility for fighting fire was shifted from the local parish and volunteer brigades onto the shoulders of the new Portsmouth Borough Police Fire Brigade. Until this time and on many occasions afterwards, the town had to rely on the military garrison and the Naval Dockyard to dampen the flames. The main hub of the Brigade was drawn from serving Police officers who were barracked at a new Fire Brigade Station in Park Road (now King Henry 1st Street) opposite the Town Hall, now the Guildhall. These officers eventually became full time firemen and were backed up by a rather precarious system of picking up policemen from their beats on route or by those same officers having to run back to the station on hearing the alarm!

By 1850 the two engines used by the Borough Police Brigade were in such poor condition that they were described as next to useless. They had been handed down by the church wardens and failed to work at all on some occasions. Eventually the town bought new ones.

14

This is one of the original hand pumps seen in 1850 and
would have been brought to the scene by horse.
James Cramer

A breakthrough in fire fighting came on the 13th December 1877, when Portsmouth took delivery of a brand new steam fire engine made by Merryweather's of Greenwich. According to a report in *The Fireman* newspaper of 15th January 1878, the new steam fire engine gave a demonstration of its capabilities on the road between St. Bartholomew's Church and Victoria Road, Southsea (Outram Road) in the presence of the Mayor, the Chief Constable Mr James Jervis and members of the Watch Committee. It was able to pump 360 gallons per minute and up to a height of 165 feet. It was commended by all who saw it. A second machine was purchased in July 1897 for the sum of £480.

The Merryweather steam fire engine of
1877.
Merryweather

15

The Brigade now consisted of 24 men with 12 of them on duty at any one time. In keeping with other fire brigades new headgear was ordered in the fashion of the brass helmet, complete with star and crescent badge.

Meanwhile PC 111 John R. Barron was employed as the Water Policeman with his boat and he patrolled the Camber Docks, Flathouse Quay and other waterways to prevent pilfering from other vessels. He took up his position on the 2nd December 1879 but eventually requested to the Chief Constable that he be relieved of his post because his brother owned a public house in the vicinity and he found the temptation too great!

The following year the Chief Constable himself obtained a dogcart in order to visit the stations under his command and on the 26th January 1892 a Bay gelding horse was purchased at £45 for the Fire Brigade. In September that year a fire escape ladder was purchased for the Albert Road Police Station at a cost of £55 from Merryweathers.

In August 1892 the Borough Police took on the added responsibility of attending street accidents using wheeled ambulance litters. These were nothing more than twin wheeled hand stretchers similar in concept to the carts used to transport the local drunks. Four were purchased at a cost of £12 1s each and they were positioned at each of the four Police Stations.

In 1896 the Police bought four safety bicycles with pneumatic clincher tyres, from Mr Allnutts shop in Fratton Road for the total sum of £47. These bicycles were to be used by members of the Detectives Branch as a means of "rapid locomotion".

In 1900 the ability to escape from a tall building was made that much easier with the purchase of a horsed hose tender from E. A. Bailey & Co. Ltd for £160. This unit came with a 55-foot extendible ladder.

The horsed tender waits outside the Police Fire Brigade Station in Park Road. Note the two sets of folding doors and in particular the smoke scorched area above the left door. This is obviously where the Merryweather came through. The archway to the far right gave access to the rear yard. The area to the left is now part of a lively pub, whilst the section to the right made way for Exchange Road.
James Cramer

On the 26th August 1902 the Brigade placed another order with Merryweathers for the purchase of something quite revolutionary. At a cost of £800 they ordered a self propelled steam driven fire engine. It was delivered almost a year later and on the 18th July 1903 the new Merryweather was paraded at a civic reception in the presence of the Mayor, members of the Corporation and the Mayor of Brighton and members of their Corporation. The steamer left the station in 20 seconds, circled the Town Hall, then proceeded down Park Road. Opposite the Public Baths, owing to a slippery road surface, the engine mounted the kerb and broke its rear axle! Merryweather's repaired the engine free of charge.

The 1903 self-propelled steamer from Merryweather.
The News

On the 1st May 1908 two motorised Merryweather fire engines were purchased. A large 40hp engine costing £889 was capable of carrying four or five men with either a chemical cylinder or air pressure arrangement and was to be stationed at the Fratton Police Fire Station in Fratton Road. The second fire engine was a smaller 25hp motor costing £488 and this was based at the Park Road Station.

In 1910 the Brigade got one of its most influential characters in Superintendent John Ogburn, who managed to organise things in a far more professional manner.

*This is the bigger of the two new motorised Merryweathers with an
impressive array of escape ladders mounted on top.
Superintendent Ogburn is standing on the right.*
James Cramer

The smaller motor engine is seen here outside the Town Hall.
James Cramer

The Police themselves though weren't quite so fortunate at this time. True there was a Mounted Section of four horses, but everyone else walked his beat. Transporting prisoners could be a problem if the horse drawn van was already engaged and drunkenness was a big problem in the town at this time. The Police therefore used a trolley for the conveyance of drunken persons to the Police station. They were unceremoniously strapped into place and wheeled away.

There was some progress however with the purchase of three more bicycles for the Cyclists Section. These bikes were shared between six officers who would ride in the town to help protect the public against the growing menace of the motor car.

An early double-nine unit at work in Portsmouth!
Collectorcard, Croydon

In 1911 reference is made to a horse drawn ambulance being used. Then on the 28th July 1913 the Chairman of the Watch Committee reported that he had seen an Austin 15hp Ambulance Wagon being displayed at the Motor Car Show at Olympia by the Austin Motor Co. Ltd. It was eventually purchased in September that year for £616 18s 9d and was based in the garage at the far right hand end of the Park Road Station. In its first six months of operation it attended 56 street accidents for which the patient was not charged. However a charge of 5s was levied at private patients who required transportation from home to hospital and in the same period made 72 trips!

In 1917 another motorised fire engine was purchased, this time from Dennis Brothers of Guildford. This 40hp engine cost £872 and was obtained to replace the now ageing steamers.

1917 Dennis outside Park Road Station with l to r; second left is PC Jack Shepherd,
PC Alfie Wright is the driver, PC Harry Colverson (standing nearest driver)
and PC Bert Prior (standing above the rear wheel).
Author's collection

In 1921 a new horse drawn prison van was purchased to replace the existing unit and yet another fire engine arrived, this time a Dennis Gwynne (TP 4113) costing £870. It was capable of pumping 400 gallons of water per minute and was at that time the most powerful engine that the Brigade had obtained. The following year a Merryweather motor turntable ladder and water tower was purchased and in 1925 a Leyland motor engine costing £1,235 arrived.

Although their vehicles were being updated on a regular basis, the method of collecting personnel from various points on route to a fire hadn't really changed at all. It was an antiquated and totally inefficient system that drew much criticism from various official sources. In 1924 the Borough Council installed a street alarm system made by Beasley-Gamewell. It was a combined fire and police telephonic and telegraphic closed circuit alarm system with 33 points around the town. At the outbreak of a fire, a glass phial could be broken at one of the points and a handle pulled down which would activate the alarm in the station. This went some way in ensuring that the Brigade got to the scene a lot quicker than had been experienced previously.

TP 4113 is seen here being used as a carnival float during a parade to celebrate a visit by the French Fleet. The driver is Inspector Gould, with Sgt Reg Smith sat beside him. Bert Prior makes another appearance on the rear corner of the machine.
Stephen Criss

On the 23rd March 1926 mention is made in the Minutes of the Watch Committee, concerning the purchase of an Essex motor car costing £190. "The Essex" as it was referred to on many occasions in the same minutes, was the official transportation of the Chief Constable Mr Tommy Davies, so in essence it is the first motor car belonging to the Portsmouth Police. Essex cars were the British subsidiary of Hudson cars in the USA. In the early 1920s Hudson were looking to expand into the UK market, but research suggested that the British perhaps wouldn't buy an American car. By scanning a map of the UK the Americans found the county of Essex and thought that sounded rather grand and therefore re-badged the car as an Essex! The parts were shipped across the Atlantic to the Essex assembly plant in Chiswick and a small network of dealerships were appointed. The Chief Constables car was a 1925 model, four-seat Tourer which had a 17.32hp, six- cylinder engine mated to a three-speed gearbox, with braking only to the rear wheels! The car would have had a TP registration number, but sadly the records of all the TP numbers issued were destroyed in a bombing raid during the war.

In the next couple of years the Essex was also used by senior detectives to go about their enquiries and in March 1930 the Chief Constable decreed that he would, from now on, use his own personal car, as it was more in keeping with the high office of Chief Constable than the Essex. In return he required an allowance of £50 per annum to use his own car, the make of which is not mentioned. The Watch Committee agreed but stated that he would have to supply his own oil and petrol! Meanwhile the Essex was handed down to the Detective Branch.

*Although this isn't the actual car, this is a 1925 model Essex
as used by the Portsmouth City Police.
Chris Dugdale*

In mid 1927 the Police Ambulance Division obtained a new 20hp Austin model, costing £620 from Haig's Motor Co. in Granada Road, Southsea. The old ambulance was taken in part exchange and a £50 deduction was made on the price. The Ambulance Division now had a dedicated driver in PC Sydney Boyland and other officers were now required to perform ambulance duties on a regular basis. They were trained by the St. John Ambulance Brigade and were required to take annual tests to obtain medallions or pendants of competence.

*The 1927 Austin 20hp ambulance is seen with its proud crew, five of which can be
identified; l to r PC Sydney 'Doctor' Boyland who was the ambulance driver
(number 2 and 4 are not identified) Chairman of the Watch Committee,
PC Bert Prior, PC Harry Colverson and PC Denny Kewell.
Authors collection*

22

The Brigade was updated further in 1927 with the purchase of three motor escape Model T Fords and these were seen as quick agile motors, capable of collecting officers from their beats and delivering them straight to the scene of a fire, whilst the actual fire engines went directly there. This helped save valuable time. The Fords, registration numbers BK 8338, BK 8339 and BK 8340 were stationed at Park Road Station, Eastney Police Station and Cosham Police Station, in Windsor Road, Cosham. The following photograph shows officers in the Cosham motor escape travelling along Cosham High Street. The photo was actually taken in 1934 and looks like it came from a Hollywood production of the Keystone Cops!

Is this Portsmouth or Hollywood?
James Cramer

In late 1928 and early 1929 the force looked at replacing the horse drawn prison van with a motorised unit. As there was no standard van to look at during this period, a suitable chassis had to be found first and the special body then built to order. A four-year-old Buick 4-cylinder car, costing £50 was looked at first, but this was disregarded when a 20 hp Austin 4-cylinder chassis, capable of carrying ten people was obtained from the Haigs Motor Co. Ltd. A purpose built body was then constructed and the whole project cost £460. The two horses used to pull the old van were then sold off.

The year 1930 was a turning point in the mechanisation of the Portsmouth Police. On the 4th February Portsmouth got its own Flying Squad and they were equipped with what has been described as a *fast patrol tender* fitted with a wireless receiving set. This vehicle would be used by two detectives to patrol the city, who would then receive information about a crime via the wireless set and proceed immediately to the scene.

But it was the introduction of the Road Traffic Act of 1930 that was to change many things on Britain's roads and Section 57 (4) was of particular interest to the Police. It provided that advances could be made out of the Road Fund towards any expenses incurred by the Police in the provision and maintenance of vehicles or equipment in connection with the enforcement of that Act. The Home Office proposed that annual grants would be paid in advance to cover vehicles running 12,000 miles a year. The grants were payable as follows; £60 per annum for solo motor bicycles, £80 per annum for combination motor cycles and £120 per annum for motor cars.

The Chief Constable Mr Tommy Davies recommended to the Watch Committee that they purchase two motor cycle combinations, as these appeared to be the best class of machine to police the roads in the city. They agreed and on the 25th November 1930 Portsmouth got its first ever motor patrols in the shape of two Royal Enfield combinations, costing £85 5s each, from Messrs Warren Brothers. They were chosen after an exhaustive search for the right type of machine, having looked at 11 different types, including a Brough Superior SS100 costing a mere £189 12s 6d!

The 500cc Royal Enfields looked very smart in their blue paintwork with matching sidecars. They bore the registration numbers RV8 and RV9. They were later fitted with fire extinguishers in case they happened to come across a small fire.

The new Royal Enfield combo's with their respective crews consisting of PC Sam Luke (rider) and PC Tubby Hawkins (observer) on the left and PC Ernie Middleton (rider) and PC Reggie Blease (observer) on the right. Inspector Sam Route looks on from the rear.
The News

In 1931 four cars were obtained for use by the Detective Branch. These were an MG Midget Sports two-seater for £154 12s 6d, a Riley 9hp two-seater with Touring body and two Morris Isis 18hp saloon cars costing £285 12s from Wadham Brothers of Waterlooville.

Also in 1931 the use of bicycles was increased with the purchase of ten Royal Enfield machines at £4 19s 6d each. Those officers who wished to continue riding their own bikes on patrol were paid an annual allowance of £3 3s.

With the increase in mechanisation came the demise of the horse, with two being sold to Edinburgh Police for £25 and the last two, aged 16 and 23 years were sold to the R.S.P.C.A for £15 each. The stables were then converted to house the detective's new cars.

Another new fire engine arrived in 1931. A Dennis rescue tender, registration number RV 8950 was stationed at Park Road and was to become known as the number 4 turbine. This was the first unit to come with pneumatic tyres and must have been something of a luxury compared to its predecessor's solid rubber ones. The new machine came fitted with an extra powerful floodlight and a large cable drum. The total cost of this package was £510.

The no. 4 turbine Dennis seen here being used in another one of those parades. Note the Portsmouth City Police Fire Brigade crest adorning the radiator and the rather humorous British bull dog mascot above it.
James Cramer

In January 1932 a Leyland fire engine, costing £1532 10s was purchased from Leyland Motors Ltd. This large machine, resplendent in its bright red paint (as all the previous engines were) was housed at Park Road Station and became known as the number one turbine and this would always be the *first away* at night to the scene of a fire.

The Police got two more bicycles at this time because of an increase in the size of their area, which now included Drayton and Farlington. Meanwhile, senior officers were given a demonstration of the new improved wireless system from the Marconi Wireless Telegraph Co. Ltd, using a Police Demonstration Van that they had brought with them.

25

The number one turbine Leyland with its crew; l to r are Fred Smith, Phil Boulter,
Harry Colverson and Bert Prior. Note the Portsmouth crest adorning the
rear wing with its motto 'Heavens Light Our Guide'.
James Cramer

On the 2nd May 1933 the Brigade got its most impressive and most expensive vehicle ever.
The awesome Leyland-Metz turntable fire escape, registration number RV 4041 cost a hefty
£3214, three times the amount normally paid for other machines of its era. It was an
impressive vehicle with its turntable ladders that could reach 98 feet and large searchlight; it
no doubt helped save countless lives in its time. And despite its high price tag it proved to be
good value for money in the long run, as it was still going strong in the 1960s having survived
the blitz on the city during the war years.

The big Leyland-Metz parked outside the Guildhall with Supt. Charles Gould on the right.
James Cramer

On the whole 1933 was rather quiet, with only the purchase of another Riley, in replacement for the first one bought in 1931, again for the Detective Branch.

Then on the 6th February 1934 came the first Police patrol motor car, in the shape of an open top Wolseley Hornet costing £234 9s from Messrs. Parker Thomas & Co. Although this vehicle was hailed as a break through in Police patrols for the city and would help in attending emergencies that much quicker, the truth is, it became the personal transport of one or two senior officers. But the patrol car was generally regarded as a great success and the true mechanisation of the force had begun. However, the two Royal Enfield combo's had come to the end of the line and were no longer regarded as suitable for Police work and were sold off.

The Wolseley Hornet outside the Guildhall, with the Chairman of the Watch Committee behind the wheel. The Chief Constable Mr Tommy Davies and PCs Ernie Middleton and George Bleach look on.
The News

Portsmouth Police Fire Brigade still had fire duties to attend to at this time and in 1935 got two more vehicles; a six-cylinder Leyland 500 gallon per minute motor pump, complete with 35 foot ladders, costing £996 10s. The second unit was a six-cylinder Dennis light motor pump with a 30-foot ladder, costing £925. An application by Supt. Gould for a third engine was refused by the Watch Committee. These were to prove to be the last significant purchases for the Brigade because in 1938, just prior to the outbreak of hostilities, the Auxiliary Fire Service was formed and assisted the City Police Fire Brigade until 1941 when both were absorbed into the new National Fire Service. From then on, the Police were no longer responsible for fire fighting duties in the city.

Did You Know That.......?
One of the old Dennis engines was kept in the garage at Eastney Police Station and even though it was one of the most powerful pumps in the Brigade it was kept mainly for the purpose of showing trainee firemen how to clean brass!

By April 1936 the Wolseley Hornet had clocked up an incredible 50,000 miles and desperately needed a major overhaul. This was done at Wadham Brothers in Castle Road, Southsea for £37 4s 6d.

On 2nd February 1937 a second patrol car was obtained in the shape of a second hand 1935 model Alvis Firebird Tourer, with 9036 miles on the clock. The force paid £235 for it, but it wasn't very well liked by the officers that drove it because the gear lever was positioned on the outside and it was difficult to use.

In 1938 Haigs Motor Co. in Granada Road, Southsea supplied four Austin 10 De Luxe models costing a mere £150 each, for the now named Criminal Investigation Department. The Police Ambulance Division got a new Austin ambulance in 1938, again from Haig's, costing £489 6s. The Austin was finished in dark blue and sported the Portsmouth City Police crest on its sides. It had an illuminated sign saying *Ambulance* above the cab and for the first time ever, we see a *Winkworth* bell placed on the front. This was the first audible warning instrument used on an emergency vehicle. These chromed brass bells became synonymous during the next three decades with all types of emergency service vehicles. One particular feature of this vehicle was that it was fitted with a map of the city on the dividing partition, between the driver's cab and the saloon. This was obviously an aid to the driver in reaching his destination quicker.

PC William A. Collins stands beside his Austin Police Ambulance during the war years. Note the headlamp covers, white wings and front bumper. You can also see the city map on the panel behind the driver's seat.
Photo courtesy of Mr Collins family

28

PORTSMOUTH BOROUGH POLICE

In May 1939 as the country prepared itself for war, the force bought two Morris 10's for the CID and a replacement for the Wolseley Hornet, a green MG TC Police model, costing a mere £300. This car was fitted with a personal address loudspeaker for the first time. Sadly there are no photographs of this particular patrol car in existence.

Portsmouth took a real battering from German bombs during World War II and like most things progress on the vehicle front came to an abrupt halt. Everybody had to make do with what they already had and this would continue for some years to come. The Portsmouth City Police though needed cars for the ARP and managed to purchase a 1933 Lanchester 10hp, a 1933 Daimler 15hp, a 1934 Austin 10hp, a 1934 Vauxhall 15hp, a 1934 Morris 15hp, a 1925 Morris 38hp van that was used as a mobile canteen, a 1937 BSA 350 motorcycle and a 1939 New Imperial 500. A second hand ambulance of unknown make was also bought for £150 from a Mr Reading!

On the 19th July 1940 Portsmouth City Police acquired the services of a new Chief Constable after Mr Tommy Davies retired, having served the city for 33 years. Mr Arthur Charles West, a former Superintendent of the Hampshire County Constabulary based at Fareham, took charge at a very difficult time. About the same time the force moved its central station to the magnificent Byculla House, in Queens Crescent, Southsea, following the bombing of its headquarters at the rear of the Guildhall.

One of the Chief Constables first initiatives was the formation of a full Traffic Division. To put it mildly he was a car fanatic, he loved them and everything about them. Those appointed to it were the cream of the crop and membership of it was truly valued. Others saw it as some kind of exclusive gentleman's club! To run a Traffic Division of course you need cars and to the utter amazement of the Watch Committee, Mr West managed to secure the purchase of four Riley 12hp saloon cars in September 1940 for a mere £200 each. They were going cheap because nobody else could afford them at this time! The Riley one-two's as they were called, were a huge success and saw service all through the war years.

Police drivers were specially selected and were seen as the best uniformed officers available. They formed the basis of an emerging Traffic Division based at the headquarters in Queens Crescent. They went on specialised driving courses at Maidstone or Preston. These two other forces were seen as leaders in the development of Police driving and their driving schools are still in existence today.

First of the Traffic Division cars the Riley 12hp or 'one-two's' as they were known.
The officers are PC 252 Sydney Booth and PC 123 Harding.
Note the white wartime bumper, although it has yet to have blackout
covers fitted to its lights. The car was later fitted with a p.a speaker.
Sydney Booth

Housing all these new cars, especially the ARP vehicles was proving to be rather difficult, but eventually the Northcote Garage in Northcote Road, Southsea was secured for a rent of £2 5s a week. It could accommodate 25 cars and there was enough room for several motorcycles. It had a rest room and washing facilities and was seen as an ideal building.

Upon forming the Traffic Division Mr West had it formally inspected on a regular basis by Government officials. This was a time for much spit and polish. The following photograph was taken in the grounds of Byculla House and clearly shows that it was taken in war time, with the addition of black out covers on the motorcycle head lamps and each officer is seen carrying his gas mask.

Annual inspection of the Traffic Division. From left to right are Inspector Sparshott, Chief Constable Mr Arthur Charles West, Councillor Privett, HM Inspector of Constabularies Colonel Hallam, Councillor Prince, with PCs Hall, Shephard, Watts, Young, Booth and Blease. The motorcycles include an AJS and a Velocette, with the Austin 10s of the CID in the background.
Portsmouth & Sunderland Newspapers

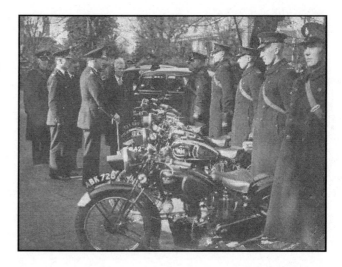

30

A rather specialist vehicle was obtained by the city Police during the war, to provide much needed refreshments to the Police and other rescue workers at the scene of bomb damaged buildings. A former Portsmouth Corporation Omnibus, a Dennis B26F Small Bus, was converted into a mobile canteen. The front of the vehicle remained the same as when it was a passenger carrying bus and the rear was converted to provide a kitchen area. It is unlikely that this work was carried out by any specialist firm, more probably the officers converted it themselves, using their own skills. The vehicle was operational by June 1941 and was capable of serving up 150 hot meals and drinks at a time. The meals were served up by the ladies of the Women's Auxiliary Police Corps and the driver was a War Reserve Constable. The only surviving record of this vehicle is the magnificent photo shown here.

Any chance of a cuppa? WAP officer James offers the refreshments.
Authors collection

Following a Home Office directive, an experiment was conducted by the Portsmouth City Police and in 1941 they became the first force in the country to have patrol cars fitted with two-way radio. The Royal Navy Communications Department was approached and a Lieutenant Commander White went with a Portsmouth City patrol car, one of the Rileys, registration number CBK 711 to Brixham in Devon, where a two-way radio was installed in the boot. Then, using a very tall aerial, they transmitted to another Riley patrol car positioned on top of Portsdown Hill, which in turn relayed the message to the radio room at Byculla House. The radio was a very large valve set taking up a great deal of boot space and the observer had a normal telephone hand set with a pressel switch on it for transmitting. This was installed in the glove box space, so the headphones and microphone system so beloved of early Metropolitan Police photographs, was never used in Portsmouth. This really must have been one of the most exciting developments for Police patrol car drivers. Following that successful experiment no fewer than eight of Portsmouth's cars, including all the Rileys got two-way radios fitted under the Wireless Scheme, paid for by the Home Office.

In June 1945 Byculla House was fitted out with 12 lock-up garages to house its vehicle fleet in and to provide maintenance facilities. It also had a petrol pump with two, 500-gallon tanks fitted and the whole yard area was concreted.

The force also started looking for replacement ambulances as those used in the war years had had a hard life and an application was made to buy two Humbers. But by 1945 Portsmouth City Council had decided to re-organise its ambulance service. This coincided with a circular from the Home Secretary to all Police Authorities, that they should no longer be providing or maintaining ambulances. Time was given to all the respective authorities to make alternative arrangements and in May 1947 the Portsmouth City Police ceased ambulance duties, with the formation of the Council operated Portsmouth Ambulance Service. At least one of the Police ambulances, BTP 194, was transferred over to the new service headquarters at St. Mary's General Hospital.

Generally speaking, vehicles in post war Britain were still scarce and for several years it was again a question of making do. It wasn't unusual for Police forces to purchase second hand vehicles and adapt them to their requirements. One such example is this 1949 photograph of a 1937 Ford V8 Model 78 Station Wagon. It is not known how or why this car was acquired, but it no doubt filled a gap until more money was made available. This huge car was used as a public address and safety car at Fratton Park, home of Portsmouth Football Club. It had an enormous loudspeaker on the roof and two more positioned on the front bumper. You will also notice that it is fitted with an aerial, because by 1949, all of Portsmouth's Police cars had been fitted with two-way radio. Now it was possible for headquarters to keep in permanent contact with all its mobile patrols.

The Ford V8 Model 78 with 'Woody' rear must have been a heavy old car to drive.
The driver is PC Frank Beckett and the observer is PC George Norman.
Author's collection

PORTSMOUTH BOROUGH POLICE

In 1946 five Ford Popular 10hp cars were obtained for the CID, two Ford 10hp vans and a reconditioned Dodge Utility Brake were purchased for general duties.

In September 1946, the Chief Constable Arthur Charles West (he was always referred to by his full name) purchased brand new traffic patrol cars. Four officers were dispatched to the MG factory in Abingdon, Berkshire where they collected brand new Riley 2½ litre RMB patrol cars. These wonderful looking cars came in black of course and were covered in a coat of protective grease. They were driven back to Wadhams, in Castle Road, Southsea, for de-greasing and servicing and were then fitted with a chrome bell, black loudspeaker and a rather unique item to the front. All Riley 2½ litre cars were fitted with twin Butler spot lamps as standard. The offside lamp was removed and the standard lens was replaced with a blue one, with the letter 'P' stencilled through it to reveal the white light. Was this the first ever-blue light fitted to a patrol car? If not, it was certainly one of the earliest examples. The light would be illuminated when the car was in a hurry, or when it was in the process of stopping another car. A small, hinged Police sign was also mounted on top of the nearside section of the dashboard and it is likely that this was also raised into position during such operations. The cars cost £1,342 each and once fully prepared they were handed over to the Chief Constable at a formal ceremony.

Every now and then there is a car produced that becomes a 'landmark' vehicle and this is probably the first such Police vehicle to fall into that category. They were greatly revered by the officers that crewed them and are still remembered today by the people of Portsmouth. With its three-speed manual gearbox, it would reach 95 mph and had handling to match. Once they were kitted out and ready to work, all four were driven to the Home Office in London to be inspected for their suitability for Police work. One can only assume that perhaps these were the first ever Riley RMB's to enter Police service and needed Government type approval, before other forces were allowed to purchase the same cars. Certainly other Police forces did buy them in large numbers and it is unlikely that they all had to travel to London to be inspected. Unfortunately, one of the four cars didn't make it to the inspection, as it crashed on route!

A Riley 2½ litre RMF (JBK 227) at speed through the streets of Portsmouth.
Authors collection

33

A total of seven Riley RM's were bought altogether, the later one's being RMF's. For the record the registration numbers were DBK 854 (this was the first one registered) DBK 956, FTP 322, FTP 541, ERV 847, JBK 227 and JBK 244. The RMF models were purchased around 1952.

Arthur Charles West was the president of the Southsea Motor Club and on the 8th August 1950, he entered drivers from his Traffic Division into the annual motor gymkhana on Southsea Common, to compete against other club members for the Faulkner Cup. In their gleaming Rileys they took part in three driving tests, watched by thousands of onlookers. The tests included the *wiggle-waggle* a slalom course of barrels, the *triple-garage* test and the *rallye-soleil* test, in which the cars had to negotiate a slippery grass course, against the clock, without spinning the wheels or losing control. The Police team consisted of PCs S. Booth, W. H. Moore, J.B. Wilkes and L. Hoad and they won the competition, much to the delight of the Chief!

The following year though saw the Southsea Motor Club win back the trophy. Entering this type of event wasn't so unusual then. Police patrol cars from the Southampton Borough Police and even West Sussex Police would come to this event to have their cars judged in the Concours D'Elegance competitions and usually went away with several of the prizes! Such was the pride in the appearance of one's patrol car then, that very little extra work was required to enter. It worked both ways of course, with Portsmouth City Police patrol cars attending similar events in Southampton and elsewhere.

Did You Know That.......?
Arthur Charles West, when questioned about the cost of the new Rileys by the press, would boast that they were quick enough to get anywhere in the city within four minutes. It was not unusual for him to telephone the control room at Byculla House from his home on Portsdown Hill, some five miles away and demand the immediate appearance of a patrol car. Having raced through the city, with bell ringing, the patrol car would screech to a halt outside the Chief Constable's house and the driver would see him turn to his dinner guests and proclaim "There you are, under four minutes!"

The lovely flowing lines of the Riley 2 ½ litre RM models are shown to great effect in this photo. Note the wooden doors to the workshops area in the background.
Sydney Booth

The Traffic Division fleet continued to grow during the 1950s, to include a large batch of Triumph 650 Speed Twin motorcycles. One of the newly acquired vehicles was a 1950 Morris Commercial van, EBK 547, used to transport prisoners. This vehicle was operated by a retired PC, Frank Chambers, who kept the van in pristine condition at all times. It had a stove enamelled finish and smoked glass side windows and was so beautifully turned out, that it became a focal point of the Traffic Division fleet.

1950 Morris Commercial prison van that covered more than 100,000 miles and still looked like new.
Terry Swetnam

In 1954 one or two of the early Riley 2½ litre cars were in need of replacement and Riley had recently released its natural successor, the Pathfinder. It used the same basic 2443cc engine, but power had been increased to give it a top speed of 100 mph. It was a modern looking motor car that promised much. However, looks aren't everything and the new Pathfinder didn't live up to its promise, with poor road holding being its biggest failing. It would wallow on bends and slide all too easily in the wet. Most officers preferred to drive the older car and only three of the Pathfinders were purchased.

The new Riley Pathfinder with Sgt Sydney Booth standing by.
This excellent photo was taken in the rear yard at Queens Crescent.
Sydney Booth.

Shortly after the cars arrived, they were fitted with the familiar Portsmouth 'P' light on the offside of the front bumper, using a straight piece of metal as a securing bracket. The warning bell was now fitted behind the grille, out of sight for some strange reason. As was now tradition of course, the cars were entered in local and regional Concours D'Elegance contests and more often than not, won several trophies. The following photograph shows one of the other Riley Pathfinders positioned on Southsea Common during such a contest. Note the 'P' light and the beautifully polished tyres, complete with white wall lettering, perfectly positioned for and aft.

Riley Pathfinder KRV 450 gleams in
the sunshine ready for inspection.
Sydney Booth.

Meanwhile the CID were having a few problems with their cars. Their small fleet of upright Ford Populars were a constant thorn in the side of the resident mechanic at Queens Crescent, Mr Les Burton. The cars were unreliable and were generally kept in a dirty condition, unlike their traffic counterparts. They were slow and unpredictable and were generally considered to be an embarrassment. They were eventually replaced by Ford 105E Anglias.

Did You Know That......?
One of these Fords had a particular problem? The oldest of these cars had a tendency to fall over onto its side when travelling slowly around a corner! Two officers had to go out in it each time, so that they could lift it back up onto its wheels. It happened so often that the car developed a severe list to starboard!

Other vehicles of note at this time were a MK1 Jaguar saloon, driven almost exclusively by PC Eric Price. This sleek 3.4 litre model had no Police markings at all and although it was used as a patrol car from time to time, it was generally used to transport Arthur Charles West to and from various engagements. He did like his cars! Now, unfortunately most of the Police forces that Jaguar supplied to no longer exist.

He wasn't quite so particular about everyone else's mode of transport however. The dog handler, PC John Tolcher had to put up with a Bedford Dormobile, whilst a second Bedford saw service as a personnel carrier. This vehicle was feared by all who travelled in it, because of its unfailing ability to induce motion sickness.

The force's photographic and fingerprint department were issued with a 1955 Fordson 15cwt van, presented in mid-night blue and this was usually the transport of PC Dick Ostler.

As the force moved into a new decade, the need for more and more transport became necessary. In 1961 a new concept was conceived, with the introduction of Lambretta 150 scooters for use by the women's branch of the city Police. In those days of course, WPCs were kept in a separate department to deal with women, kids and animals. To save them having to seek a lift from a passing patrol car, they were issued with the scooters to give them some independence. They were also used as couriers, to transport urgent correspondence between stations and Police Cadets were sometimes allowed to ride them, again as

JAGUAR CARS LTD. HAVE BEEN PRIVILEGED
TO SUPPLY CARS TO THESE CONSTABULARIES:

Angus County Police
Ayrshire County Constabulary
Bedfordshire Constabulary
Berwick, Roxburgh and Selkirk Constabulary
Buckinghamshire Constabulary
Danish Police (Denmark)
Devon County Constabulary
Dumfries and Galloway Constabulary
Dunbartonshire Constabulary
Durham County Police
Edinburgh City Police
Essex County Constabulary
Glamorgan County Constabulary
Glasgow City Police
Greenock Burgh Police
Kent County Constabulary
Kilmarnock Burgh Police
Lancashire County Constabulary
Liverpool City Police
Lothians and Peebles Constabulary
Manchester City Police
Metropolitan Police—Scotland Yard
Motherwell and Wishaw Police
Northumberland County Constabulary
Perth County Police
Plymouth City Police
Portsmouth Police
Renfrew County Police
Somerset Constabulary
Stirlingshire Constabulary
Stoke-on-Trent City Police
Warwickshire County Constabulary
West Riding of Yorkshire Constabulary
West Sussex Constabulary
Wiltshire County Constabulary
Worcestershire County Constabulary
Royal Ulster Constabulary

JAGUAR CARS LTD., COVENTRY, ENGLAND

37

couriers. The only photographic record available appears to be this newspaper article, dated the 19th August 1961, announcing the new idea. According to other records, the force had a total of six Lambrettas, XTP 759, XTP 762, GBK 91D, GBK 92D, GBK 93D and GBK 94D, all of which were transferred across to Hampshire on amalgamation. On average, their mileage totalled 12,000 miles and they were retired in 1971.

The Detective Superintendent was deemed important enough to warrant having his own car and was afforded a Humber Super Snipe in 1961. Four Austin Omnivans were also purchased around this time and were used by Divisional stations as section vans. The Photographic Department's old Fordson van was replaced by a Ford Thames van.

WPC Ivy Conybeare and WPC Ann Wigginton
astride the new Lambretta scooters.
The News

Other forms of two-wheeled transportation were a bit more masculine in the form of BSA 250cc machines. Each station in the Division was assigned a motorcycle to enable more mobile responses to general calls for Police assistance. These motorcycles were now fitted with the latest radio communications equipment that could be fitted onto the petrol tank of the machine. Like the traffic cars before them, they could be updated immediately by the control room staff, on any developing situations.

BSA 250 showing the new, smaller radio equipment. This photo was taken in
Somers Road by Police Photographer PC Ron West, who later
became Chief Superintendent of Portsmouth Division.
Terry Swetnam

In 1961 the Traffic Division's beloved Riley RMs and the not so well liked Pathfinders were either gone or in desperate need of replacement. The force opted to buy the MK2 Austin A110 Westminster, with its three-litre, straight-six engine, this was a big, powerful car, well suited to the demands of traffic patrol work. These cars were fitted with a new piece of equipment not seen on the streets of Portsmouth before, the revolving blue light, fixed to the roof. Like the old Riley RMs, these cars had a presence about them, they looked the part and performed accordingly.

This splendid looking Austin A110
Westminster is seen parked outside
Cosham Police Station circa 1963.
Author's collection

A new unit was formed in the mid 1960s to help fight more organised crime and they too needed their own cars. In April 1966 the Regional Crime Squad were gifted three new cars, an Austin A40 Countryman and two Austin A60 Cambridge saloons. They must have terrified the opposition!

The Dog Section meanwhile took delivery of two Morris Minor 1000 Vans, which for some strange reason were delivered in almond green. The Morris Minor range was already a hugely successful car, because of its excellent ride and handling, coupled to a tough, durable and immensely reliable engine. The vans were fitted with a single blue roof light and an illuminated Police sign, front and rear. Inside the rear of the van, a cage was fitted to contain the dog and a rotating ventilation unit was fitted to the roof. The two vans were GHO 406D and GHO 407D. The latter was used by PC Terry Swetnam and his German Shepherd dog Greif, which is the German word meaning 'to bite'.

Portsmouth City Police Dog Section Morris Minor van.
Terry Swetnam

In 1967, at the time of amalgamation, the Portsmouth City Police vehicle fleet numbered 52 vehicles. Most of these were transferred across to the Hampshire Constabulary and continued to be used, much as they were before. Those that were deemed surplus to requirements were auctioned off. A once proud and innovative Police force had now ceased to exist.

Perhaps we should close this chapter with one last look at the pride of its fleet. In 1993, Classic Car Weekly, a newspaper style classic car journal, used a photograph of Sergeant Sydney Booth standing next to his favourite car, the Riley 2½ litre RMF, to help advertise the paper. Both man and machine look immaculate, as well they should, because that particular photo was taken in 1955, on the day both of them went to Portsmouth railway station to escort Prince Charles and Princess Anne during a Royal visit to the city.

"No Classic Car Weekly sir? You'd better accompany me to the newsagent....."

Make sure that you don't miss out on all the latest news and
bargains brought to you by Britain's biggest Classic Weekly.

EVERYTHING CLASSIC. EVERY WEDNESDAY.

CHAPTER 2

Southampton Police crest
Author

SOUTHAMPTON BOROUGH POLICE

(LATER TO BECOME SOUTHAMPTON CITY POLICE)

Southampton Police first came into being in 1836, seven years after the formation of the Metropolitan Police and one year after the passing of the 1835 Municipal Corporation Act, requiring provincial boroughs to organise police forces. Southampton has always been a docklands city, so it is no surprise to learn that the force's first form of transportation should be a boat. In May 1873, the Borough Council asked the Watch Committee to "consider appointing river Police for the better protection of waterside premises". The Chief Constable of the time, Mr Thomas Breary allocated three officers to the new department and spent the grand sum of £10 on the purchase of a rowing boat.

In 1889, a new Chief Constable, Mr Philip Clay was appointed and he introduced mounted Police to the town. The first Police horse was not owned but hired and the mounted patrol was used for the supervision of law and order on Southampton Common, a place frequented by rogues, vagrants and vagabonds. The horse cost two guineas a week to hire (£2 10p) from a man in Bevois Town and when he asked for an increase of ten shillings a week (50p) the Watch Committee promptly told Mr Clay to find someone else to hire a horse from, at the old price!

SOUTHAMPTON BOROUGH POLICE

In 1893 came the first horse drawn Black Maria, again used mainly on Southampton Common to help convey the aforementioned rogues to jail. They would be handcuffed to a long chain inside the wagon, driven to the local railway station, where they would be placed on a train and escorted to Winchester prison for incarceration.

By 1904 Southampton had acquired another Chief Constable, Mr William Berry and he decided that he should have a horse and trap and that he should be paid an allowance for it. This led to questions in the Town Council, but the Watch Committee stood firm, declaring that a horse and vehicle were necessary for the Chief Constable and payment of an allowance for it was the most economical arrangement.

By 1910 Mr Berry had been replaced by another Chief Constable, Mr William Jones and the H.M Inspector of Constabulary, Captain Herbert Terry, recommended that the Chief Constable should have for his sole use "a horse and cart, with a Police groom". The Watch Committee at that time decided to defer the matter because they were considering a proposal to amalgamate the Police with the Fire Brigade. Perhaps they had visions of the Chief Constable hitching a ride on the back of a fire engine! The merger between the two forces did not materialise and unlike Portsmouth, fire fighting was left to a dedicated unit.

In 1915 a proposal was put forward to replace the ageing horse drawn Black Maria with a new motorised version. This idea was shelved until after World War I had ended and so in 1920, Southampton Police purchased its first motor vehicle, a Pierce Arrow van, which was used as a prison van until 1928. This former military vehicle was probably supplied under the USA/UK Lend/Lease scheme at the end of the war. Many of these chassis passed into civilian and Local Authority ownership during the period 1918 to 1920.

*The Pierce Arrow prison van of the 1920s was the first motorised
transport of the Southampton Police.
Authors collection*

The first real motor patrol vehicle arrived in 1925, when Southampton Police purchased an AJS combination, with the registration number TR 4. How much is that number worth today? Sharing the newly acquired means of mobility, riding in shifts, were specially selected men. PC Frederick Saunders, later to become an Inspector and the first head of the Traffic Division, Sergeant John Hill and PC Sydney Emery, both of whom later became Superintendents. Within the force they received the nickname *The Three Musketeers*. Five years later a grant from the Road Fund, "for the better supervision of traffic and detection of traffic offences" made it possible to purchase three more machines. The motorised era had truly arrived in Southampton.

In 1928 the Pierce Arrow was replaced by a Star, which was made in Wolverhampton. This vehicle was again used for prisoner transportation, but may also have doubled up as a temporary emergency ambulance.

The Star prison van of 1928.
Author's collection

By 1933, the force had yet another new Chief Constable, Mr J. T. McCormac and he made comment that the force was somewhat lacking in mobility, to answer urgent calls for assistance from the public. After a great deal of debate, the force bought eight pedal cycles and these were distributed among the various stations.

One year later, Southampton Police finally bought three cars for the purpose of providing mobile patrols. Two Austin 10 Coupes and what has been recorded as a saloon car were purchased to set up what became known as the Southampton Mobile Patrol. These Austin's had a canvass hood and were often referred to as rag-tops. They became instant celebrities in the town and borough, where drivers of other cars now needed to be on their guard.

The two Austin 10 Coupés are seen outside of the Headquarters at the Civic Centre. Inset the new Police/Stop box.
Hampshire Constabulary

In 1935, the Southern Daily Echo reported that members of the Southampton Mobile Patrol had invented a device and fitted it to their cars. The officers concerned were PC R. Hannon and PC S. Pearce and what they invented appears to be the first ever 'Police-Stop' box. The device consisted of a wooden frame with a glass front, measuring ten inches by six inches on spring guides inside the rear window of the car. Cut in stencil were the words Police and Stop. The signal was invisible from the rear of the car until it was brought into view through the window by the driver or his observer, pulling a short length of flex over a pulley. At the end of the piece of flex was a switch, which operated an electric light inside the frame, enabling the signal to be illuminated at night. A similar device was invented by two other Southampton officers, PC F. Thompson and PC G. Payne. Their effort was a dark painted brass box, measuring six inches, by four inches, by four inches, fitted to the rear bumper. The box contained a strong electric light that illuminated through two pieces of glass, one blue, the other frosted, with the words 'Police' and 'Stop' stencil cut through an aluminium sheet placed on top.

Both inventions were said to be an improvement over ideas used in other parts of the country, but it is not clear whether the force ever continued with the idea, or whether it lay dormant for several years, until the advent of slightly more modern boxes made an appearance in the 1960s and beyond. Whatever the case, it was many years ahead of its time.

Like Portsmouth, Southampton bore the full force of Hitler's Luftwaffe during World War II and much of the city was reduced to rubble. It was during this time in May 1942, that radio communications were installed throughout the force. All stations were linked and an experimental radio was even put in one of the Mobile Patrol's vehicles. The installation was inaugurated by Colonel W. B. Vince, D.S.O, O.B.E, M.C, from the Home Office, but was removed following an unsuccessful trial period. It wasn't until after the war that full two-way radio was installed in all of Southampton's cars.

At least four new cars were purchased either just before the outbreak or shortly after the war had started. These cars were Dagenham built Ford V8's and were given to the Mobile Patrol, whilst the Austin 10's were given the status of Divisional Cars and were made responsible for local area policing. The big Fords were powered by 3622cc V8 motors producing 30hp, a powerful and robust car in its day.

About the same time the people of Guelph, Ontario, Canada presented the Southern Civil Defence Region with a single axle caravan, to be used as a mobile kitchen at bomb scenes, to provide much needed refreshment.

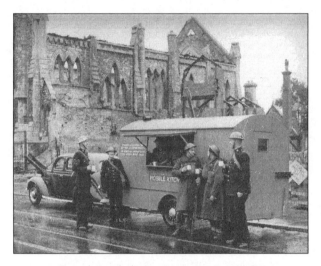

The big Ford V8 coupled to the mobile kitchen
donated by the people of Ontario, Canada.
Hampshire Constabulary

Another early wartime purchase was a replacement prison van, in the shape of a Morris Commercial CV Type, registration number BOW 805. No doubt this vehicle doubled up as an ambulance, stores transport unit and had a hundred other uses before the end of the war in 1945.

The Morris Commercial CV prison van was probably used
for all manner of jobs during the war years.
Authors collection

In 1947, following a large increase in thefts from river front warehouses along Southampton Water, a 38-foot single-screw launch was purchased by the Southampton Police for the sum of £1,300, from the yacht builders, Camper and Nicholsons. The vessel, named *Versatile* was already 35 years old and had seen duty during the war as a supply tender, carrying gas bottles from Southampton to Cowes Roads in the Solent, for barrage balloons. *Versatile* was fitted with a rather old petrol engine, giving her a top speed of just under ten knots, one of the earliest of VHF radio's, complete with a rotary converter and a small, three-sided wheel house to give the crew some degree of shelter in the winter. It became part of the Mobile Patrol and its first crew consisted of PC Tom Cullen, PC Jack Pile and PC Alex Freemantle.

In later years, *Versatile* was fitted with a larger enclosed wheelhouse and a four-cylinder Ford diesel engine.

*The Southampton Police launch 'Versatile' on patrol in
the busy waters around Southampton Docks.
Hampshire Constabulary*

On the 2nd October 1948 the force purchased another replacement prison van in the shape of an Austin K3 chassis with coach built body, registration number FTR 750. This vehicle covered more than 16,000 miles in its first year of service, conveying more than 457 prisoners to Winchester prison and 292 other prisoners to and from various other establishments, including two to the docks for deportation. In total, this vehicle covered more than 140,000 miles and it was driven almost exclusively by PC A. Page. In fact he was the sole driver for the three previous Southampton prison vans and must have known his way around quite well after 30 years on the road.

*Austin K3 prison van driven, as
always by PC A. Page.
Authors collection*

On the 1st January 1949, it was decided to expand the Mobile Patrol and the Chief Constable, Mr Charles Box bought four brand new Wolseley 18/85s with 18hp engines. These 2322cc engined cars had a top speed of 80mph. The registration number of the first one was GHO 90 and these vehicles patrolled an ever increasing area and population. In November the same year, a further four cars were purchased, not Wolseleys this time, but 18hp Vauxhalls and the Mobile Patrol had its name changed to the Traffic Division. The cars were fitted with two-way radio and each of them drove more than 40,000 miles in their first year. The 25 Constables of the Traffic Division had all undergone advanced driving courses at either Brighton or Preston in Lancashire.

Like many other Police forces', the Traffic Division was the only department with motorised transport, the station's having to make do with the hoof or shoe leather! However, one or two specialist vehicles started to creep in, with the purchase in July 1951 of a Ford Utilicon, registration number JCR 106, for the newly formed Dog Section.

Meanwhile, the old mobile kitchen used in wartime was re-furbished and given a new lease of life as a mobile Police Enquiry Office. This unit would be towed out to Southampton Common, or other area being used for a large public event, where it would be used as a contact point for the public. This caravan was used for many years for this purpose and was still in the back yard at the driving school at Hulse Road as late as the 1980s!

"No son, we don't do tea here anymore"
Authors collection

49

In 1955, the Borough Council, on the recommendation of the Watch Committee, finally decided to abandon the use of horses for patrol. All six Southampton Police horses had in fact been evacuated to Stockbridge at the outbreak of the war, but they were occasionally brought back into service to patrol Southampton Common and two of the outer divisions. The last time they were used was in November 1941, thereafter they returned to Stockbridge where they were pensioned off. The reason for the delay between actually not using the horse and making the decision to abandon the system was because there were those opposed to the whole idea of disbanding the mounted units.

It seems incredible now that whilst the powers that be were making decisions about the use of the horse, the force itself went out and purchased six, shiny black Wolseley 6/80 saloons for its Traffic Division. The purchase date of May 1955, several months after the cars went out of production, tends to suggest that perhaps they bought the end of the line products at a reduced price. Who said value for money was a modern phenomenon? With its 2215cc engine and three-speed manual gearbox, this car had a top speed of around 80mph. The cars were fitted with two-way radio, but had no markings on them to otherwise distinguish them as Police patrol cars. These cars were obviously very well used and in just over a year, two of them had completed over 90,000 miles each.

These two cars were then replaced with two new models from the Wolseley stable, the 6/90. These wonderful looking cars came with a bigger 2600cc engine and a top speed of 96mph. As with the 6/80, the cars were basically unmarked, except for a large aerial placed in the centre of the roof. It doesn't appear that they had any form of audible warning device either, so attending an emergency situation must have been a bit slow at times. In 1956, one of these cars was entered in the Concours D'Elegance contest held on Southsea Common and won the Wadham Trophy for the best Nuffield car. That must have upset the boys from Portsmouth City! By 1958 the force had bought a total of six 6/90s and disposed of the last one in October 1962.

This 1958 model Wolseley 6/90 was one of the last of the line purchased by Southampton
Police. Driving it in breeches and riding boots must have been an experience!
Authors collection

SOUTHAMPTON BOROUGH POLICE

In 1956, Southampton Police needed more than just a Traffic Division to cope with a growing number of calls and responsibilities and they devised a new concept in mobile policing that is still used to this day. The concept was called Team Policing and involved the use of locally based series 1 Hillman Minx estate cars with a 1390cc engine, giving a top speed of 79 mph. The cars, commonly called Team Cars, were placed one on each sub division and were responsible for attending emergencies, outside the remit of the Traffic Division, such as public disorder, domestic disputes and other incidents requiring an immediate response. The cars were painted in a dark grey, with a light grey roof, but still did not have any form of Police markings, except for the telltale roof mounted aerial. To get through the traffic, the crews would just put their headlights on and that would be enough in those days, to ensure that the public would oblige and move out of their way! As well as the six Team Cars, the CID were also given a new Hillman Minx estate to use on enquiries, although this was not fitted with a two-way radio. The Team Car experiment was a huge success and in later years the word *Team* was dropped in favour of a new term and the Area Car was born.

The original line up of Team Cars at Hulse Road, a concept that lasts to this day.
David Simmonds

Four Triumph 500cc motorcycles were also purchased in 1956 and one of them was fitted with two-way radio for the first time. This enabled the motorcyclist to assist the Traffic Division cars at important functions in the Borough or when escorting VIP's to the docks, a job they found themselves doing quite often, as cruising ships like the Queen Mary and Queen Elizabeth attracted the rich and famous to the area.

The River Patrol, aboard their vessel *Versatile* had a busy year in 1956, retrieving two bodies from the water and assisting at various other rescues. But perhaps their most intriguing job, from our point of view, looking as we are at the past, was having to pass information to Aquilla Airways, about floating objects which could have endangered the flying-boats whilst coasting along the surface of Southampton Water!

The vehicle fleet remained rather static until 1960, when natural wastage meant that certain vehicles were due replacement. On the 1st July one of the Wolseley 6/90s was replaced by a rather grand looking Humber Super Snipe. This series 2 saloon, with its 2965cc, six-cylinder engine could reach 94 mph and in rather grand style too, with its leather upholstery and burr walnut trim. Yes, going on a shout in YOW 600 must have been a salubrious experience. Needless to say, it was quite often taken away from traffic duties to convey the Chief Constable to and from public engagements. There were still no markings or audible warning instruments fitted, although this car did come with a loudspeaker cone for the public address system now fitted.

The luxurious Humber Super Snipe fit for inspection
by the Chief Constable Mr Alfred Cullen.
Authors collection

The following month, on 1st August another new type of car arrived for the Traffic Division, a Wolseley 6/99. Engine capacity had now risen to 2912cc and the car boasted a top speed of 98 mph. At last it was fitted with a chrome Winkworth bell to the front, a black cone speaker and a small sign placed above the number plate saying Police. This was modern indeed and a big step forward for the Southampton Police. Two officers were assigned to the car, PC Jack Chalk and PC Norman Chalk. They weren't related, but no doubt they came in for some serious ridicule from colleagues.

*Wolseley 6/99 was Traffic Divisions first patrol car to be fitted
with bell and sign to warn the public of a fast approach.
David Simmonds*

Later that year the CID Hillman Minx estate was replaced by a Ford Popular and two of the Team Car Hillmans were sold in exchange for a pair of Austin Omnicoaches. During the next two years all the Hillmans were replaced by such vehicles or by the Commer Workabus. A total of four Austins and nine Commers were purchased altogether and averaged 70,000 miles each prior to replacement.

On the 4th June a full motorcycle section was formed as part of the Traffic Division, comprising six Constables using the four old Triumph 500s and two new Triumph 650 Speed Twins. In their first year they covered a total of 52,000 miles between them.

On the 1st September 1961, the force diverted from the usual crop of Wolseleys and took a trip on the wild side with the purchase of a Series 111A Sunbeam Rapier, in black with a red side stripe inside the chrome strip. The 1494cc engine took the new Traffic Division car to a top speed of around 93 mph. It was fast, agile and had far better handling characteristics than the now dated Wolseleys and Humbers. It was modern looking and has to be classed as one of the landmark cars in the history of Hampshire's Police transport. There are many people who still remember this car and the bigger engined 1725cc Series IV fixed head coupes that came over the next four years. These later cars were even faster and could top 100 mph. They were all equipped with Winkworth bell, Police sign and cone speaker, with the later ones being fitted with a roof mounted blue light. Southampton Police had definitely moved up a gear. Seven of these fine cars were bought altogether and the last four were transferred across to Hampshire on amalgamation.

*1961 Sunbeam Rapier Series 111A was the first of the breed. This photo was
taken at the Southsea Concours D'Elegance where it came second.
Authors collection*

In November 1961, Southampton Police purchased the first of a whole batch of 14 Triumph
650 Speed Twin motorcycles, to expand the motorcycle section of the Traffic Division still
further. These proved their worth time and again, because of the increase in traffic on
Southampton's busy streets. For the first time they were all fitted with two-way radio, which
was placed on top of the petrol tank. An Avon fairing was also fitted to afford the rider a
degree of weather protection and this had the word Police emblazoned across the front of it.
The riders themselves would wear open faced, cork helmets with goggles, large white
gauntlets, breeches and leather boots. Otherwise the uniform was pretty much the same as
their colleagues on foot patrol.

*PC 264 Fred Cleverly assists a lost
motorist with directions. Note the radio
pack with hand set on the petrol tank.
Hampshire Constabulary*

54

By September 1964 one of the Wolseley 6/99s and the Humber Super Snipe were replaced by two Triumph motorcycles and a Humber Hawk, registration number AOW 580B. This series 111 saloon had an engine capacity of 2267cc and a top speed of 86 mph. This effectively increased the Traffic Divisions strength still further and motorcycles were clearly seen to be a cost effective and efficient method of traffic policing, especially when you see that according to the records, there were some 535 abnormal loads escorted through the city that year!

Back on divisions, the strength of the vehicle fleet continued to grow with the purchase of Commer Cobs and a Ford Popular for CID use. The various Commer Workabus vehicles used by each station were now fitted with two-way radio, but perhaps the most significant development concerned the fitting of blue flashing lights to all patrol cars and motorcycles for the first time. The modern age had surely arrived in Southampton? Not quite, because as all the cars were being fitted out with blue lights, the force went out and purchased 34 pedal cycles as well! All this work was carried out by three civilian mechanics for the first time, thus relieving the officers, who until this time had undertaken most of the general maintenance of their vehicles.

Meanwhile the River Patrol crews had been busy rescuing no fewer than 12 persons from the water, together with two bodies. *Versatile* though was starting to become an expensive vessel to maintain, with two major overhauls and various other minor repairs and adjustments needed in one year.

By 1965 the fleet consisted of no fewer than 38 vehicles and included the purchase of a MK1 Austin Mini 850cc van, registration number COW 408C, for use as a Dog Section vehicle. This car was fitted with two cages, to house the German Shepherd dogs used on the section. The Mini of course was to become one of the most famous of all cars and found a variety of uses in Police guise throughout the country. A second Mini van, HTR 395D was added in 1966.

One of Southampton's Mini vans used by the Dog Section. Authors collection

In early 1966, the Southampton Borough Police changed its name to the Southampton City Police. In September 1966 the old Austin K3 prison van, purchased in 1948 and with a total mileage of over 140, 000 miles was finally replaced with a new Commer van, registration number HTR 616D. A Ford Anglia van, HTR 224D was purchased for use by the CID and then in October a batch of eight Triumph 650cc Saint motorcycles arrived to replace the ageing Speed Twins.

These were the last vehicles obtained by the Southampton City Police, before amalgamation with the Hampshire Constabulary in 1967. The entire fleet was then transferred across to Hampshire ownership and although most stayed in the Southampton area, a few were distributed elsewhere, including three of the Sunbeam Rapiers, one of which found itself transferred to the Isle of Wight.

CHAPTER 3

Hampshire County Constabulary helmet plate

HAMPSHIRE COUNTY CONSTABULARY 1900 TO 1959

Like the cities of Portsmouth and Southampton, the two counties that currently make up the force of the Hampshire Constabulary were once policed by several different forces, according to boundary. Winchester, the old capital of England had its own force, the Winchester City Police until it merged with the County in April 1943. The Isle of Wight at one time had three separate forces. Newport Borough and Ryde Borough both had their own Police forces until they merged with the Isle of Wight County Constabulary in 1890 and 1922 respectively. Then in 1943, the island merged with Hampshire to form a two County force. At first it was given the name Hampshire County Constabulary, but in 1952, following the publication of the Police Act of 1946, the force was renamed the Hampshire and Isle of Wight Constabulary. This name stayed until the major amalgamations took place in April 1967, when it was changed again to the Hampshire Constabulary.

In the early days, Hampshire's officers had to rely on the horse, the bicycle or foot to get around their beat. In the latter part of the 19th Century, officers who could afford bicycles were paid a small allowance of 15 shillings (75p) a year for the maintenance of their machine. This allowance commenced on the 1st January 1898 and was payable quarterly. The Chief Constable of the time, Major Warde later secured authority from the Standing Joint Committee for it to be increased to 30 shillings (£1.50p) per year. This was on condition that officers in charge of divisions inspected the bicycles, to ensure that they were kept in serviceable order. Precisely what interpretation was placed on the term *serviceable* is open to debate, because in 1902 an order was published, insisting that all cycles ridden by Police officers were to have brakes fitted!

Mounted and cycle patrol officers outside Whitehill Police Station circa 1906.
Woolstone Bros, London

Great use was made of the bicycle it seems. In 1899, First-Class Constable Jennings was commended for his prompt action in a case of theft from Meonstoke. He traced the two men suspected of the offence on his bicycle and arrested them both in Guildford, still with the stolen property in their possession. But that effort pales into insignificance when you look at the efforts of two officers in 1904. Sergeant Eades and Constable Pope were highly commended for "their praiseworthy perseverance" in tracing a stolen horse, cart and harness from Aldershot. These two officers continued their enquiries on bicycles for several days, finally arresting the thieves and recovering the stolen property in Birmingham!

In the same year the cycle allowance was increased to £2 per year and a few years later all Police bicycles were equipped with rear reflex red lights, which were to be attached to the back stay of the machine. These lights had been supplied to Police bicycles and carts throughout the County by the Automobile Club (later called the RAC) in order to advertise the value of such aids in the dark.

Hampshire County Constabulary officer and his bicycle.
Hampshire Constabulary

The horse though was the main means of transportation at this time for anyone who could afford it. Each Superintendent was paid an allowance for the use of a horse and cart, usually hired from a local stable. The allowance was to pay for its upkeep and food. The Police 'driver' of course came free! The horse and cart allowed the Superintendent to travel to and from the various stations or beat houses in his division, to inspect his men.

Superintendent's horse and cart of 1900
Hampshire Constabulary

Hampshire also had its own Mounted Section from around 1900 to 1929, when it was disbanded. The section was used to help quell rioting in Winchester and Andover over the years, but was also used to help in general patrol of rural areas. At the time of its disbandment, the section consisted of nine horses, ridden by one sergeant and eight constables, but at one time consisted of more than twenty-one officers and steeds.

The Mounted Branch circa 1910.
Hampshire Constabulary

Whilst the local Superintendents made do with the horse and cart, the Chief Constable, Major Warde purchased the first ever motorised form of transport for the Constabulary. In 1904, a Napier 6-cylinder motor car, registration number AA 118, was bought and was actually registered to Major A. B. Warde of West Hill, Winchester. This vehicle would have conveyed him around the county in grand style and would obviously have been chauffeur driven. However, it was also used as an early patrol car and was apparently fitted with a large Claxton horn and a powerful electric warning light, in the middle of the bonnet, above the radiator. The cars other lights would have been gas and oil powered. The following photograph shows the Napier at the George Hotel crossroads in Middle Wallop, at an early speed trap. On the rear of the original print is the caption *Wallop Motor Trap* and you can just see an officer sat on the running board on the nearside of the vehicle. The officer's engaged on such a trap would use stop-watches to time the vehicles over a set distance, a system similar to today's method.

The Napier AA 108 at the Wallop motor trap in 1904.
Peter R. Daniels

By 1907, Major Warde appears to have acquired another vehicle, in the shape of a Panhard 12/14 hp landaulette model, with chain driven transmission and oil fired driving lamps. The liveried chauffeur and lack of any form of audible warning instruments as on the earlier Napier, tends to suggest that this car was used exclusively by the Chief Constable. Two things about this car remain a mystery though. It is London registered and the letter 'B' has been painted onto the passenger door. Perhaps Major Warde purchased this vehicle second hand or it was on loan from another source, perhaps for some special occasion? The photograph comes from Hampshire's own archives and it was obviously thought important enough at the time, to warrant photographing it.

Panhard 12/14 of 1907 was
probably the Chief Constable's car.
Hampshire Constabulary

The Panhard was replaced in the early 1920s by a Wolseley, but it is not known what model and in 1925 the Superintendent's horse and carts were replaced by Ford Model Ts.

Towards the end of 1926 the Standing Joint Committee sanctioned the payment of an allowance of £12 per annum, for the use of motorcycles for Police purposes in circumstances where the Chief Constable considered the payment of the allowance to be justified. Such circumstances existed where large areas had to be policed and the allowance was to be made to inspectors and sergeants in charge of such sections and at the headquarters of such divisions. In all cases the grant was to be subject to the officers concerned producing each year, a satisfactory policy of insurance covering not less than third party risks! This motorcycle allowance was in lieu of the previous bicycle allowance and marks a steady advance in the motorised society. Aldershot division had at least one solo motorcycle under this scheme.

This early 1920s photo shows the officer with a New Hudson motorcycle, complete
with hand gear change, which must have made it interesting to ride!
The photo is taken in Mark Lane, at the entrance to Basingstoke Police Station.
Hampshire Constabulary

Meanwhile, on the Isle of Wight it wasn't until 1929 that they obtained their first means of mechanical transport, a BSA twin motorcycle combination, which was used on motor patrol and other duties. The first mobile officer on the island was PC Francis George Rugman, who was issued with breeches, leggings, a mackintosh, peaked cap with goggles and a British Warm (overcoat). PC Rugman went on to become an Inspector in charge of Ryde sub-division.

PC Francis Rugman aboard his
BSA combo circa 1929.
Hampshire Constabulary

In 1931 the island got its first patrol car, a Ford and this was later replaced by a Morris and then in 1939 by a Wolseley, although there are no records available to describe what models were actually used. All of these vehicles were based at Newport and it wasn't until the early part of World War II that vehicles were provided for sub-divisional stations and even then it was motorcycles that were purchased. Seven Aerial motorcycles saw service at various stations across the island.

Back on the mainland, the Hampshire County Constabulary purchased several Austin 7 motor cars for use as divisional patrol cars and this did both motor patrol and other duties on alternate days. In 1931 motorcycle combinations were brought into use on divisions. The first such machines in Bournemouth were V-twin Royal Enfields, one of which bore the registration number LJ 3400. Its crew consisted of PC Bryon and PC Rowe, who's job it was to time speeding drivers by using a combination of stop-watch and speedometer mounted on the front of the sidecar. Aldershot station had a similar set-up.

1934 Austin 7 with a top speed of 60 mph.
Hampshire Constabulary

By 1936 slightly more powerful cars were on the market and at least one Division had the good fortune to have the services of an Austin 12/6, with a 1535cc engine, giving 12hp and a top speed of some 65 mph. In 1937 several Austin 10hp open two-seaters were purchased and by 1938 MGs were also being used.

1936 Austin 12/6 Superintendent's car.
Authors collection

As in the rest of the country, at the outbreak of the war, everything was turned upside down, with vehicles requisitioned and emergency powers introduced. The following three photos show vehicles used by Hampshire during the war years, but not necessarily owned by them. Note that all of them have black-out covers on the front headlamps and that the first two are also fitted with a mobile air-raid warning horn to the front wing. This device would be operated in a similar way to the land based units, by winding an electric motor to produce that spine chilling sound that enemy aircraft were on their way. The car would tour an outlying village or small town area that didn't have the benefit of a full size air raid siren.

The first photo is of a 1939 Austin Norfolk 18hp, 2510cc six-cylinder, side-valve motor with five seats on board. This huge car was probably donated or loaned to the local beat man at the time, Police War Reservist 925 H. (Bill) Carter, whose area included Sparsholt, Harestock and Littleton. The photo was probably taken in 1943 at the bottom of Dean Hill, near Sparsholt, close to the house now called the Old Police Cottage, which is where he was living in 1943.

65

Austin Norfolk with Police War Reservist 925 H (Bill) Carter.
Note the air raid warning siren on the front wing.
Clive Barham

Austin 12 taken during the war years. Note the siren attachment
and the sandbags packed high against the walls of
the old Headquarters in Winchester.
Authors collection

This 1938 Ford Model 81A de Luxe Fordor Sedan, with 3622cc V8 motor
producing 30hp, was one of only 1200 built in right hand drive form at Dagenham.
The original photo, taken in 1945 stated that the car had been borrowed from the USAF,
although there are no further details.
Authors collection

At the conclusion of the war in 1945, there was still no Traffic Department as such and in a directive from the Chief Constable, Mr R. D. Lemon, to all Superintendents' it was decided to form a "Traffic and Communications Department under Superintendent Wright". This new department would be set up at headquarters and was intended to co-ordinate traffic problems, accident prevention and motor patrol's maintenance. It was hoped that all new patrol cars would eventually be equipped with two way radio and each Superintendent was asked to supply detailed information on the number of patrol cars he thought would be required to police his particular area. By the start of 1946, the nucleus of a Traffic Department had been formed, but they continued to use whatever vehicles they had available at that time, as new car production in post war Britain was still somewhat limited. By 1948 the strength of this department consisted of one Superintendent, one Inspector, four Sergeants and twenty-eight Constables and for the purposes of traffic policing, the County was divided up into four areas, with a Traffic Sergeant in each area, at Headquarters, Aldershot, Fareham and Ringwood. In 1949 the department at last obtained a quantity of brand new patrol cars and motorcycles, befitting such an establishment. A total of 13 Wolseley 12/48s fitted with 1548cc engines giving them a top speed of 62 mph were purchased. All of them were identically fitted out with illuminated Police signs placed above the front windscreen, two-way radio and a public address system, incorporating a black cone speaker placed on the front bumper.

The motorcycles were Triumph 500cc Speed Twins, with coil sprung seats and drum brakes. They were all over black in colour and their riders wore standard issue peak caps with the chinstraps down, breeches and boots. Ten Triumphs were purchased initially and these were placed at various stations throughout the County, but were for the sole use of those designated traffic officers.

For the first time in its history, the Hampshire County Constabulary now had a properly equipped, purpose built fleet of cars and motorcycles specifically for use by the Traffic Department.

This excellent photo of one of the Wolseley 12/48s, shows PC Ken Piper
as the driver and PC George Kirby using the two-way radio.
Hampshire Constabulary

To celebrate this momentous occasion, an official inspection of the department was held on the parade ground at the nearby Winchester Barracks. As on all these occasions, an official photograph or two were taken by the force's Photographic Department. Apart from the two photo's reproduced here, there is a further shot taken of all the Wolseleys, their respective crews, the four Sergeants and Superintendent Wright.

In 1952 the original Wolseleys were replaced by the much more modern 6/80 saloon, with its faster 2215cc engine, it had a top speed of more than 80 mph. The same illuminated, roof mounted Police sign was fitted, together with the public address cone on the front bumper. These modern cars were much more suited to the expanding roads network in the county and with the increase in vehicular traffic, so the Traffic Division (as it was now called) had to expand to. No fewer than 20 of the new Wolseleys were purchased to replace the old model and these now averaged 50,000 miles each per year.

The original Triumph 500 Speed Twins of 1949 line up for inspection at Winchester.
Hampshire Constabulary

The Wolseley 6/80 became synonymous with traffic patrols throughout the country and is still regarded as the archetypal Police car of its era, by a public that remembers them with a fondness not given to other cars. With its illuminated Wolseley badge adorning the top of the front grille, the cars would quite often be seen in films and early television dramas as late as the mid 1960s. As such, the 6/80 has to be regarded as a landmark car in Police vehicle history and will forever be remembered by people of that generation as *the* Police car, even though I'm sure some will have confused it with other makes and models of the time.

Did You Know That..........?
The officers of the Traffic Division were so proud of their cars, that they would spend two hours a day cleaning them and in order to ensure that theirs was the best kept, they would go to extraordinary lengths to go the extra mile. For example, they would strip off the paint from the top of the radiators and some of the coolant hoses, to reveal the brass underneath. This would then be polished to a gleaming finish.

This 1953 photo shows the 20 new Wolseley 6/80s lined up, prior to the annual inspection of the fleet at the Winchester Barracks.
Hampshire Constabulary

This 1954 photo gives us a close up view of a Wolseley 6/80 used at Andover.
The car was crewed by PC Sam Black (left) and PC Snowy White (right).
Someone at HQ obviously had a warped sense of humour, putting those two together!
Authors collection

The vehicle fleet remained rather static during the mid to late 1950s, the force having spent rather a lot of money on the Wolseleys for the Traffic Division. Each station was eventually equipped with its own van, usually a Morris or Commer, to help with prisoner transportation or moving large items of stolen property. Generally speaking though, most Police work was still being done by foot patrols or on bicycles.

The motorcycle though was gaining in popularity; it was a fast and responsive piece of equipment that could attend to car accidents where traffic had built up as a result, far quicker than anything else. By 1958 there were six traffic motorcyclists in the County, PC John Wavell at HQ, PC Keith Battle at Aldershot, PC Pat McCarthy at Andover, PC Peter Gibson at Gosport, PC Eric Brown at Eastleigh and PC Nick Carter at Christchurch. They all rode identically equipped new style Triumph 500 Speed Twins, finished in amarath red.

These bikes were fitted with all the latest equipment, including leg guards, leather panniers, Perspex windscreen, wing mirrors and the radio system, now an essential policing item, was neatly housed in a metal box, behind the single seat. The riders now sported open faced cork crash helmets with goggles, white gauntlets and full-length boots. The Triumph Speed Twin was good for 90mph, with handling to match. With the ever-growing traffic problems, even a bike would sometimes have difficulty in getting through heavy traffic and the motorcyclists needed something extra to assist them. Sergeant Harry Webb from the workshops at Winchester, eventually produced a black metal box, with an ingenious pair of flashing amber lights on it. These were electrically powered and would flash alternately to alert the public. A white 'Police' label placed on the box and liberal use of the bikes headlight ensured that the motorcyclists reached their destination even quicker. Was this the first ever flashing emergency light used in this country? Quite possibly. Sadly, the following year the system was deemed illegal, as using twin orange flashers on the move was not yet an acceptable practice.

PC 408 Nick Carter on his Triumph 500 Speed Twin outside Christchurch Police Station, showing the flashing orange lamp unit. This particular bike was displayed on the Triumph stand at the 1958 Earls Court Motorcycle Show.
Nick Carter

In 1959 the motorcycle section of the Traffic Division was increased in size by another nine bikes. The Speed Twin was replaced by Triumphs big new 650 Thunderbird and was again finished in amarath red. This confused the local tearaways on their café racers, who thought the new bikes were still 500s and couldn't understand how they could no longer get away from the law! The bikes were all identically equipped with just about the same items as on the Speed Twins, except that the panniers were now colour matched metal boxes. The radio set was contained within the rear box and could be heard via a cone speaker, placed on the left side of the handlebars. It wasn't uncommon for a group of people to stand around a Police bike at this time, listening in on the radio, whilst the officer was busy attending to an incident.

PC John Wavell from Headquarters Traffic with his new Triumph 650 Thunderbird.
This excellent photo shows the illegal flashing amber box to good effect.
Hampshire Constabulary

Following the decision that the newly invented flashing light system was illegal, they were of course all removed. The bikes stayed in a naked state for some considerable time. The following four photos all show the same Triumph Thunderbird in four different states, in a matter of eighteen months, following the removal of the offending item.

They get younger everyday! Actually this is PC Nick Carter's son aboard
THO 425, Triumph Thunderbird showing off the bikes modern new equipment.
Nick Carter

THO 425 now stripped of it's flashing lights.
Nick Carter

THO 425 being ridden by PC Nick Carter, dressed as a sailor, at a 1959 Traffic Road Safety Display Team exhibition at Gosport Naval Base, showing the sailors how <u>not</u> to go home at Christmas. The kit bag and Christmas tree are about to depart company from the bike! Note that the windscreen has now been removed.
Nick Carter

By 1960 THO 425 had gained a rather streamlined, fibreglass Avon fairing.
Nick Carter

At the close of the decade, the now ageing Wolseley 6/80s were replaced by the bigger, sleeker and faster 6/90 model. With its 2639cc engine, it had a top speed of 96 mph and the force purchased 27 of the all black saloon cars. Equipment levels remained very much the same as before, although the addition of a boot mounted Police/Stop box appears to have now become a standard fitment on Hampshire cars and the Traffic Division had once again had to expand to keep pace with a growing workload.

This classic Wolseley 6/90 (RCG 585) is seen in the rear yard at Fareham Police Station. It had the call sign C.20. Note the Police/Stop box on the boot lid.
Roy Middleton

The following photo shows the Traffic Division at its annual inspection at the Winchester Barracks with an array of Wolseley 6/80 and 6/90 saloons, together with the Triumph motorcycles.

The Traffic Division annual inspection of 1959/60 showing
the all new fleet of Wolseley 6/90 patrol cars.
Hampshire Constabulary

CHAPTER 4

HAMPSHIRE & ISLE OF WIGHT CONSTABULARY 1960 TO 1969

As the force moved into a new decade, no-one could have forecast the huge changes that were about to take place over the next ten years, not just in automotive technology, but in Police vehicle design and demand. By 1969, the vehicle fleet of the new Hampshire Constabulary would bear little resemblance to that of 1960 and certain new initiatives were inspired that would last for several decades yet to come. The 1960s saw fast and furious change.

But it all started rather quietly, with minor changes or additions to an ever-expanding fleet, including a Morris van, registration number YAA 906 purchased for prison duties. This vehicle was kept for seventeen years and covered more than 100,000 miles before being sold at auction for a mere £80. Other vehicles included an Austin Omnicoach, an Austin van and a couple of Commer Cobs, but there are no further details available as to what their exact role was.

In May 1960, the force purchased several Lambretta 150cc scooters, primarily for use by the Women's Police Department. These blue and cream coloured scooters would be used to carry out enquiries and to transport correspondence between stations. A total of 23 machines were bought and six more that were transferred from Portsmouth City, supplemented these on amalgamation.

Some of the Wolseley 6/90s were already up on mileage toward the end of 1960 and its replacement was the new Wolseley 6/99, a faster, better handling modern saloon car, it came with a 2912cc engine giving it a top speed close to 100 mph. New Police vehicles of course were still quite a rarity and the manufacturer didn't very often deliver them. Instead, individual officers were sometimes tasked to travel to the factory by train, armed with a set of registration plates, to collect the new car. They would then drive them back to Hampshire, where they would spend as long as two weeks 'running it in' before taking it to Winchester workshops, where it would be kitted out with its Police equipment. New items on the 6/99 included an illuminated Police/Stop box on the boot lid, Police sign at the front of the roof, a p.a. system and for the first time ever, an audible warning device in the shape of a chrome Winkworth bell, placed on the front bumper. Emergencies could now be attended to that much quicker and the public soon got used to the sound of an electric bell, which signalled the approach of a fast moving emergency vehicle.

The officers that crewed these cars still took immense pride in the fact that they were driving a class car and that they were amongst the best drivers in the world. At least one hour per tour of duty was spent washing the car down and cleaning the inside. It wasn't unusual to place extra layers of carpet in the foot-wells, to prevent the original carpet from becoming soiled. Every week there was a four-hour *servicing period* when the car would be thoroughly cleaned and polished, using Simoniz Wax; the hard stuff! Every month the car would be taken to HQ workshops where the officers who crewed it, would assist Sgt Harry Webb in servicing it. Major repairs generally went to an outside garage.

The Chief Constable, Sir Douglas Osmond, also used a Wolseley 6/99, registration number WOT 230, as his official car. This vehicle was equipped with a two-way radio, p.a. system and bell, because when it wasn't being used for official functions it was utilised as a travelling crime car.

Did You Know That........?
During Traffic Division inspections, it wasn't unusual for the inspecting officer to wipe his finger around the inside of the Winkworth bell to ensure that it had been cleaned!

The Chief Constable's official car had the call sign 38. It was only driven by two officers, PC George Kirby and PC Dennis Bulpit.
Hampshire Constabulary

In 1961, some of the motorcycles were due replacement and newer style Triumph 650 Thunderbirds were purchased, this time in gloss black. A white fibreglass Avon fairing was fitted and for the first time, the radio set was fitted to a specially made box, placed on top of the petrol tank. This was to aid the motorcycles stability and placed the heavy weight of the radio equipment toward the centre of gravity. The following photograph was supplied by Nick Carter, who had to take his pride and joy back to the Triumph factory because it vibrated so badly, it shook three radio sets to pieces. It was eventually discovered that the wrong bias flywheel had been fitted and this had caused excessive vibration and engine wear. The correct item was then fitted, together with higher compression pistons, performance camshaft and two small bore exhausts, instead of the Siamese pipe that was originally fitted. The vibration had also split the front mudguard and the only black ones that Triumph had in stock at that time, were those used by the French Police and these came with a gold leaf centre line. Therefore, Nick Carter's bike was not only the fastest in the county, but also the smartest. Some years later, during his retirement, Nick managed to track the bike down, with a view to restoring it back to original, but was horrified to find that its current owner had turned it into a chopper bike!

*PC Nick Carter on board the fastest Triumph 650 Thunderbird
in Hampshire, complete with gold leaf mudguard.
Nick Carter*

By 1963 the fleet had grown considerably with the introduction of more cars for use by CID officers. Gone were the days when only the Detective Superintendent had access to a vehicle, now, day to day enquiries could be made by detectives, using a variety of cars, including the Ford Anglia 105E, Hillman Husky and the series 3 Commer Cob.

Each station now had at least one 'section car' again in the shape of the Hillman Husky, a green estate car with red interior. They had no Police markings on them at all and were not for use as emergency vehicles. They were equipped with two-way radio though, to allow for better communications whilst out on patrol. Some of the county's larger stations had more than one of these cars, together with a divisional van, usually a Morris or Commer to transport prisoners with. Again these were painted either black, blue or dark green and had no markings on them.

The Dog Section was another department that was expanding rapidly and by 1963 the force had eight dog vans, all Morris 1000 5cwt types. These were fitted with a wire mesh grille between the load area and the driver's cab, to prevent the dog from climbing into the more comfortable passenger seat! Again these vehicles were not marked in any way.

One significant purchase in May 1963 was a short wheelbase, Series 1 Landrover, registration number 290 HCG. This dark blue, four-wheel drive utility vehicle was based at Winchester HQ and was used by the workshops staff to collect spares from suppliers and for other general-purpose duties. It's main function though, was to tow the force's brand new mobile enquiry office, a twin axle caravan to be used at the scene of a murder or other major incident. It also doubled up as a mobile exhibition unit and recruiting office. As can be seen from the following photograph, the caravan was rather long, very heavy and despite the fact that it had four wheels, was extremely unstable. Legend has it that you couldn't drive it any faster than 15 mph, before the caravan started to swing from side to side! It earned the

81

unfortunate nickname of *The Blue Elephant*. You will also note that the caravan has a force crest placed on the side of it. This is the first time we have seen any form of force identity being put onto a Hampshire vehicle and it comes in the shape of the star and crown type, so familiar with other UK forces. This is the only vehicle to have been liveried in this way and we have to wait until 1977/8 for the force to identify most of it's vehicles in this way, using the more familiar Hampshire rose and garland crest.

Hampshire's blue elephant, otherwise known as a
Series 1 Landrover and Mobile Enquiry Office.
Note the extendible wing mirrors on the Landrover.
Len Pearce.

When it wasn't being used at major crime scenes the caravan
was converted into an exhibition and recruiting unit.
Hampshire Constabulary

The country beat policeman was also brought into the modern age at this time, when his trusty pedal cycle was exchanged for the Velocette LE 150 (LE stood for *Little Engine*). These single-cylinder, two-stroke machines enabled him to cover a wider area in quicker time. They came equipped with a fibreglass handlebar fairing, leg shields and aluminium panniers. A radio set was placed behind the single seat and the whole thing was painted a rather dull light grey colour. Top speed was a heady 60 mph, but with drum brakes fitted front and rear, stopping took an eternity. Between 1964 and 1970, Hampshire purchased 132 Velocettes for rural beat use, with the last one being retired from service as late as December 1976. The average mileage sustained was 25,000 miles, although one Isle of Wight bike covered more than 39,000 miles!

*PC Frank Allanson, who covered the Wootton beat on the Isle of Wight
for many years, is seen here aboard his Velocette LE 150.
Frank Allanson*

By July 1964, the concept of relying on local garages to undertake anything more than routine servicing was way out of date and the force set up regional Police workshops at Aldershot, Totton, Gosport, Newport and an updated base workshop at HQ Winchester. Staff for these workshops consisted of a Transport Officer, a chargehand mechanic, a storeman and nine skilled mechanics. The mechanical condition of the fleet rapidly improved because the work and repairs were carried out to a much higher standard than had previously been experienced. Another Landrover was purchased in April 1965 and this was fitted with a Harvey Frost crane on the rear deck, to facilitate the recovery of broken down patrol vehicles back to the workshops. Finished in dark blue paint, this long wheel based model was a real asset to the workshop staff and stayed in service for nearly 15 years. In later years an orange side stripe was added, together with the word Police and an amber beacon was placed on the cab roof.

Workshops recovery Landrover, photographed in the latter part of its service.
Kenneth Porter

Some of the Wolseley traffic cars were now due for replacement and over the next three years Hampshire purchased no fewer than 32 MK2 Austin A110 Westminsters, fitted with the same basic 2912cc, six-cylinder engines as the old 6/99. The Austin was slightly faster and handled better than its predecessor. All the cars were fitted with an illuminated Police sign on the roof, p.a. system, Police/Stop box at the rear, a Winkworth bell and for the first time, a revolving blue light, of the Lucas *acorn type*, was placed on the roof, to help warn other road users of the vehicles approach in an emergency situation. This small innovation was of course one of the major improvements to the safety of all emergency service vehicles throughout the country, in fact world-wide. In the Hampshire vehicles, a Lucas 31696 illuminated switch, was positioned on the dashboard, to remind the crew that the blue light was in operation.

Did You Know That.......?
The workshops staff used to paint the engine blocks on the Westminsters in green engine paint, everytime they came in for a major service, to make it look like they had got a replacement engine!

MK2 Austin A110 Westminster of the Traffic Division
in the rear yard at Eastleigh Police Station.
Clifford Gray

By 1964, the CID had obtained a new means of transportation, the Austin 850 Mini. The ingenious front wheel drive, transverse engined little car, was to prove very popular with the detectives that drove them. They were reliable, quick and fun to drive, although some of the force's larger officers may have found them rather cramped. Austin Mini vans were also bought for Scenes of Crime and Photographic Departments to use and were equally well received. Most of the urban sub-divisions were now equipped with a Commer J4 series van, as it's prisoner transportation unit. And a new system of fighting cross border crime came in the development of the Regional Crime Squads, whose first two cars in Hampshire were Morris Minor 1000 saloons!

But reliability with some of the traffic cars was becoming a major problem. There were constant problems with gearboxes on the Wolseley and Austin Westminsters for example, compounded by a poor spares service from the manufacturers. Even cars that were fairly new in service were proving to be very expensive to run and maintain. This wasn't a new problem and patience in some quarters was starting to wear a bit thin. Representations were made to the Chief Constable and in early 1965, following a series of meetings, the Deputy Chief Constable, Mr Broomfield instructed the Chief Inspector, Traffic Division, Len Pearce, to undertake a project to produce an Accident Emergency Vehicle. It had to be capable of carrying a large amount of equipment to be used at accidents, but in all other respects had to remain a normal traffic patrol car.

Chief Inspector Pearce formed a team of people to assist him and these included Inspector Jack Hamblin and Sgt Les Puckett of the Traffic Division, the Transport Officer, Tommy Atkins, the workshops Admin Officer, Cliff Thorn and the workshops Foreman, Jim Fraser. Between them, these people held a wealth of knowledge and experience on car design, engineering and performance. They looked at the various options open to them in the estate car market in the UK at that time and found that most were either too small or vastly under powered. They ended up with just three contenders, the Series 3 Humber Super Snipe estate, with its six-cylinder, three litre engine, the Citroen DS19 Safari estate, at sixteen feet in length and powered by a four-cylinder, two litre engine and the Volvo 121 estate, with a four-cylinder, 1780cc engine.

Arrangements were made for demonstrator vehicles to be supplied for road trials and a blue Volvo 120 (as they were commonly called) was borrowed from Rex Neat Volvo Distributors at Hedge End, Southampton. Volvos in 1960s Britain were about as commonplace as South Korean cars were in the 1990s and there weren't that many people who knew much about them. Cliff Thorn also managed to acquire a sample gearbox from Ken Rudd, another Volvo supplier in Southampton. It was examined very carefully and was described as a masterpiece in engineering and was finished to a very high standard.

After a few weeks trial period, the big Citroen DS Safari was found to have the capacity, but not the weight carrying capability. It was also unstable at high speed when fully loaded and so this car failed to make the grade. Everybody liked the Volvo, but its 1800 engine lacked power. A second 120 estate was obtained, in white this time, because Volvo didn't have a black one. It had a Ruddspeed conversion fitted to the engine and this consisted of twin carburettors and an increased size manifold and this helped the acceleration and top end. On a quiet dual carriageway, with three passengers on board, Inspector Jack Hamblin DFC, an ex RAF Lancaster bomber pilot took the Volvo past the 100 mph mark and on to a claimed 116 mph. According to legend, only Jack Hamblin was allowed to drive the car at this speed, because he was the only person who had ever travelled at over a 100 mph on a regular basis, whilst thundering down the runway aboard his Lancaster!

In all departments the Volvo won hands down. It was a good quality, solidly built motor car that had a good turn of speed and handled well, even when fully loaded. The mechanics liked working on it and it was good value for money. But it was foreign. No Police force had ever bought foreign cars before and Hampshire knew that they would probably be criticised for even thinking about it. Nervously, the team approached the Chief Constable with the result of the trials and requested permission to buy the Volvo. His reply was "You're the experts, if it's the best car for the job, then go out and buy it".

And so in June 1965, CHO 621C became the first foreign Police vehicle to patrol the streets of the UK. But, just in case the force received too much flak from the media, it also bought the Humber, registration number COT 778C and it was decided to place both cars on a further six-month trial basis, only this time with the Traffic Division. Basingstoke got the Volvo, whilst Eastleigh trialled the Humber. After three months, they swapped over and reports were submitted to Len Pearce.

CHO 621C the first foreign Police vehicle in Britain.
Hampshire Constabulary

Prior to going out on regular patrol of course, these cars required the necessary kit to turn them into the Accident Emergency Vehicles that was the original brief. The team scoured the country looking for lightweight signs and lamps to use at the scenes of accidents, but to no avail. The only signs available were heavy metal plate signs, placed on steel fold up frames. Ply wood compartments were therefore built into the rear load compartment, above the back axle, to help spread the weight. Plastic cones were found, together with No-Tech flashing blue lamps, broom, spade, blankets and first aid kit, all went into making this a fully operational accident unit.

Consideration was given to respraying the cars black, as had been the tradition with all Police vehicles of course, but a decision was taken to leave them in white, as they would be easier to see at the scene of an accident during poor visibility. Another new concept on these cars was the introduction of an illuminated, roof mounted fibreglass box, incorporating the Police/Stop sign at the rear and the Lucas blue light. A blue panel across the front of the box had the word Police stencilled in white on it and they were manufactured by Wadham Bros of Waterlooville. The Winkworth bell was positioned out of sight, behind the radiator grille, on the nearside. The public were left in no doubt that this state of the art Police vehicle meant business.

After the six month Traffic Division trial, the Humber was deemed to be unstable at high speed when loaded and was noticeably heavy on corners. All concerned preferred the Volvo and in early 1966, a second 121, FOR 298D was purchased. This coincided with two important factors. First, the heavy steel accident signs were replaced by roll up cloth and vinyl items that buttoned onto fold up metal frames. This weight saving idea allowed for the provision of a petrol driven generator to be carried instead. This powered two Mitra-Lux floodlights, carried on tri-pod frames, to help illuminate accident scenes on dark country roads. The second and more important matter concerned the removal of the Winkworth bell, which was replaced by the all new two-tone horn. These electric air horns, made by Fiamm were much louder than the old bell and proved popular with the crews that drove the Volvos as they appeared to help clear the traffic that much quicker.

Did You Know That........?
One of the Volvos was put on display and used for publicity purposes at the opening of Britain's biggest Volvo dealer of the time, Rudds of Southampton.

The second Volvo 120, FOR 298D showing off its array of new equipment.
Len Pearce

But the introduction of the Volvo wasn't welcomed by all. There were mutterings in the local press about it and some members of the public wrote in protest to the Chief Constable. In the October 1st 1965 issue of Autocar magazine a Mr A.M.F.Gillan of London SW1 wrote to complain that he had seen a Volvo patrol car in Basingstoke and that it was a crime that the Police were 'living it up'. In a future edition on the 29th October a Mr Michael Cram from Glamorgan reciprocated the argument by sending in a photo he had taken of a British built Ford Zephyr 6 being used by the Polis in Stockholm and wondered whether a strongly worded letter had been sent to the Swedish equivalent of Autocar! They were all somewhat pacified when informed that this was still only a long-term evaluation of the product and as if to reinforce the point, two MK1 Triumph 2000 estate cars were purchased! Sadly there are no photographs of these two vehicles available. All we know about them is that they were CWK 769C and GHO 655D and that they were equipped the same way as the Volvo's and the Humber.

The public unrest about buying foreign cars was only a foretaste of what was about to come. What we can say now is that the Volvo 120 is definitely one of the landmark cars and laid the foundation stones of a relationship that has so far, lasted for more than 35 years.

The concept of using white patrol cars was greeted with such enthusiasm that the decision was made to order all new traffic cars in white and to respray the current fleet in the same colour. Another batch of six Austin Westminsters, in white this time were ordered and equipped with the new Wadhams roof box, Lucas acorn blue light, but with the Winkworth bell, in favour of the horns, as these were still at the experimental stage.

PC John Prince standing next to one of the new white Austin Westminsters.
John Prince

Motorcycles were also updated and increased in number, at this time. The new Triumph 650 Saint was equipped with a full Avon fairing, which had a flashing blue light incorporated in the screen and one or two were fitted with two-tone horns as an experiment. Between 1965 and 1966, the motorcycle section rose in number to 32 and all the machines were equipped in the same way. According to records, the force also purchased three BSA 250s and three BSA 650 machines, but their role is not identified.

Meanwhile, the Regional Crime Squad got two new cars in the shape of the Austin A60 Cambridge and three new Commer vans and two Morris vans were purchased as prison transport.

Did You Know That.......?
In 1966, when the new Headquarters at Winchester was opened by HRH Princess Margaret, that an apprentice at the vehicle workshops had to paint all the wheel nuts on the two Landrovers with silver paint, to make them look shiny!

The Triumph 650 Saint, with its new style fairing and
blue light, is shown next to the first of the Volvos.
Standing proudly between the two is PC Roy Ford.
Len Pearce

The wind of change concerning policing methods and therefore the vehicles it used to carry out those tasks, was now reaching gale force. Until now, most emergency situations were attended to by the Traffic Division, but as more and more demands were being placed upon the Police for a speedy response to calls, so the need for more vehicles increased. Since the beginning of the decade to 1967, vehicle registrations in the county had risen by a staggering 67%, to almost half a million. A scheme similar to that of the Southampton Police Team Car system was adopted, by issuing most urban stations with a sub-divisional emergency response car, or area car, as it became known. The force had already spent a huge amount of money on its Traffic Division and funds were therefore at a premium. Twenty Bedford Beagle estate cars were bought, as they were cheap to buy and run. They were finished in black with a white coachline side stripe. Each car was fitted with a number plate style Police sign to the front grille and for emergencies a plug in, magnetic *Francis* blue light could be placed on the roof. Some of the cars issued to busier areas were fitted with two-tone horns. The Bedford Beagle was the estate car version of the 1057cc Vauxhall Viva HA and was intended as a cheap and cheerful runabout. They were basic in just about every department and tended to be a bit 'shake, rattle and roll' to drive! Even so, one of them still managed to record more than 145,000 miles! Nevertheless, they achieved their objective, by providing an immediate response to local emergency situations. Between 1967 and 1976, Hampshire purchased 110 Beagles and the later defined HA model, initially for area car use, until better vehicles came on stream when it then found a new role as a country beat unit.

The Bedford Beagle being used as an early area car is seen on Hayling Island.
Note the magnetic blue light.
Kenneth Porter

April 1st 1967 of course meant amalgamation with Portsmouth and Southampton forces and with it came a whole host of vehicles to adopt. Although most stayed where they were, some were relocated, to make more efficient use of them. One vehicle of note concerns a Morris 10-cwt van, which was fitted out by staff at the Winchester workshops, shortly after it was acquired by Portsmouth City. The vehicle was a dual role section van and prisoner transportation unit. A double cage was fitted, complete with partition and door between cab and load area. It had blacked out side windows and even a port-a-loo, to be used on those long trips to Brixton or Holloway prisons!

Morris prison van seen in the rear yard at Portsmouth Central Police Station.
Terry Swetnam.

Inside the rear of the prison van, showing the mobile toilet on the far right.
Terry Swetnam

By early 1968 the force took a rather large step backwards and purchased a batch of ten Wolseley 6/110 saloon cars for traffic patrol. These were the end of the line products from the Abingdon factory and came at a vastly reduced price! A Wadhams roof box and blue light were fitted, but even the addition of two-tone horns didn't do too much for morale amongst the officers that had to drive them. The design of the car was now fifteen years old and it showed.

However two more Volvo 121 estates were also added to the fleet. LOR 187F and NCG 236F had larger 1986cc engines, uprated brakes and other improvements and were stationed at Basingstoke and Aldershot Traffic Sections respectively. Both these vehicles covered more than 140,000 miles in their lifetime.

*The Wolseley 6/110 was the last of the line. This one was photographed
in the rear yard of the old Aldershot Police Station
and had the call sign Bravo-01.
Roy Ford.*

This is the fourth Volvo 121 estate at the scene of a plane crash at the 1968
Farnborough Air Show. Note that it now has Police signs on the front doors.
Kenneth Porter collection

Another acquisition, for a rapidly expanding force, was a new mobile control unit. An ex-Ministry of Defence, Bedford S Type 4x4 lorry, bought at an MOD auction, was repainted white and fitted out inside as a mobile communications unit, for use at major incidents. This vehicle was one of several vehicles once used by the Police Mobile Column and the Auxiliary Fire Service and many of them found similar homes amongst Britain's Police forces. It was a large cumbersome vehicle to drive, but was fitted with a range of useful equipment, including a generator and an extendible stem light, incorporating a flood light system and blue light.

Bedford S Type Mobile
Control unit.
Hampshire Constabulary

95

Scenes of Crime Officers weren't being neglected either. As technology advanced to assist these officers in their work, so the amount of equipment they needed to carry also increased. Bigger vehicles were needed and a number of Commer J series vans were purchased and fully kitted out with drawers and cupboards to house it all in. Some of the bigger equipment was similar to that used in the Accident Emergency Vehicles, like the generator and lighting units. The vans were quite a success, albeit they gave a very bouncy ride and it wasn't long before they were being used as section vans. Another new vehicle to arrive at this time was the MK1 Ford Transit van. Hampshire purchased four between 1967 and 1969, but sadly there are no photographs or records available to assist us with what their role was.

A Scenes of Crime Commer J Series van and some of the equipment carried.
Len Pearce

The Regional Crime Squad meanwhile got slightly better cars in the shape of two Vauxhall Victor FDs and a couple of MK2 Ford Cortina saloons. The early Bedford Beagle area cars were now being superseded by Hillman Hunter 1725 saloon cars. These 90 mph vehicles were far more suited to the type of work that they were required to do. Fitted with two-tone horns and the now familiar blue light and roof box set up, they became synonymous with attending emergency calls. An additional item of equipment now fitted to area cars and traffic cars, included a calibrated speedometer, made by Smiths of Nottingham. These were to become a standard attachment to most traffic/area cars throughout the country, in the fight against speeding motorists. To test the accuracy of this instrument it was checked using a stop watch over a measured mile, at the start of a tour of duty, a system similar to that used way back in 1904 at Middle Wallop.

All area cars were now designated as *five-one* units, preceded by the station code lettering, so for example, the Southampton Central unit shown in the following photo had the call sign, Foxtrot Charlie Five One. This system remains to this day.

96

*This Southampton Central Hillman Hunter area car was driven by
PC David Easson and had the call sign FC-51.
David Easson*

*This excellent interior shot of the Hunter shows the
calibrated speedo in the centre console.
David Easson*

Hillman actually produced two near identical cars at this time and the Hunters sister car was the Series 7 Minx, fitted with a twin-carb, 1725cc Sunbeam Alpine engine. The only visual difference between the two cars was that the Minx came with a different grille and round headlights. Between 1968 and 1975, Hampshire bought no fewer than 44 Hunters and Minx saloons as area cars, with the last one being disposed of as late as 1979.

Hillman Minx area car from Gosport in 1968 had the call sign HG-51.
John Jackman

Of all the innovations that came to the fore in the 1960s, there is one that stands head and shoulders above all the others. In 1965, in Kirkby, Lancashire, a system called 'unit beat policing' was devised, whereby an officer was given a large area to police, whilst driving a distinctive car, that the public would immediately recognise as their local beat car. The Lancashire County Constabulary bought hundreds of Ford 105E Anglia's (although the first two cars used were actually Ford Zephyr 4s) in a turquoise blue colour (commonly called Bermuda blue) and painted the doors and front section of the roof in white. The 'Panda car' was born.

Forces throughout the UK quickly adopted the idea, using basic cars like the Anglia, Austin Mini and more commonly the Morris Minor 1000. This vehicle alone became synonymous with the panda car concept. On 1st July 1968, Hampshire took the idea on board and the first four panda cars, all Austin 850 Minis were issued to Basingstoke. Each car was identically fitted out with a Wadhams roof box and Lucas blue light, two tone horns and a few items of equipment capable of being used at the scene of an accident, to help protect the area until a traffic or area car arrived. A large blue sticker with the word Police on it was placed on both the doors.

The very first pandas used at Basingstoke are seen here outside Headquarters.
Hampshire Constabulary

As soon as Basingstoke had received their complement of cars, the system was expanded to Gosport, Bitterne, Andover and the three stations within Portsmouth. In the first year of operating the unit beat scheme, the force purchased 42 Minis and over the next ten years or so they bought no fewer than 530 of them, including the later Morris and BLMC variants. Although many of these were for CID use, the vast majority were used as pandas and within two years the scheme had been extended across the entire force. This method of covering a larger area with fewer officers quite literally changed the face of policing in Britain forever. In Hampshire, just about every station now had an area car and a couple pandas, to respond to public demands even quicker and this was aided still further by the introduction of the personal radio to each officer on patrol.

Even though the blue and white colour scheme was eventually killed off (see Chapter 6) the term *panda car* still remains today and the system of unit beat policing, in its basic formula, also continues. The Mini panda therefore has to qualify as one of the landmark cars.

Gosport's first Mini panda cars, showing just how much kit you could get in the boot!
John Jackman

One of Southampton's Minis with a Francis blue light which was so dim,
it was described as worse than useless.
Hampshire Constabulary

By late 1968, Hampshire had a vehicle fleet second to none and this is reflected in the following photograph, taken during the opening of the new Basingstoke Police Station. From left to right you can see two traffic cars, a MK2 Austin Westminster and the third Volvo 121 estate, a Hillman Minx area car, Austin Mini panda and CID unit, Triumph 650 Saint, Velocette LE 150, Bedford Beagle rural beat unit, Bedford HA dog van, Landrover workshops recovery unit and a Commer J Series section van.

This aerial photograph shows the average stations vehicle fleet to good effect.
Roy Ford

In 1969 new cars were in production and some of these found favour with Hampshire. The RCS obtained the services of three MK2 Ford Cortinas and a MK1 Ford Capri 3000 V6. Two more Ford Transits joined the fleet, as did a Triumph T100F and four Triumph TR6P motorcycles. Basingstoke Traffic Section took delivery of a fully marked MK1 Ford Capri 3000 XL V6 patrol car, UHO 139H, which was enjoyed by all who drove it. Some of the Mini pandas were replaced by the new MK1 Ford Escort 1100 saloons, which were also painted in blue and white and the Chief Constable, Sir Douglas Osmond, who had overseen all these developments, obtained a blue Rover 3500 P5B, WYL 985H as his official transport. It is unfortunate that none of these vehicles appears to have been photographed, either by the force or by individuals.

In August and September 1969, Hampshire bought a performance car that became a legend in its own lifetime, in the shape of the MK2 Lotus Cortina. Quite simply, this vehicle scared people! With its 1558cc, twin-cam, twin-carb engine developed by Lotus, it had a top speed of 105 mph with acceleration to match. In comparison with the Volvo's, Westminster's and the old Wolseley, it was a racing car, made for the road. Hampshire managed to obtain ten cars for traffic patrol and two more for use at the force's driving school. Unlike civilian versions of the Lotus which came with a green side stripe, Police spec cars were finished in white without the stripe, but did sport the Lotus badge on the rear wing. As a drivers car they were brilliant, but as a reliable workhorse they were a nightmare. The engine needed constant tuning and it wasn't unusual for crews to take their car to workshops once a week to get this done. There were also problems with water pumps and cracked cylinder heads and on average the cars were disposed of after just 75,000 miles for a mere £500 at auction. Ford also lent Hampshire a MK2 Savage Cortina, with a 3.0 litre V6 engine, on long-term evaluation. Again there is no photographic evidence to support this, but there is no doubt that such a vehicle did exist and that it was an interesting car to drive!

About the same time, ten of the new Volvo 144 DL saloon cars arrived. This new design from Volvo came with a 1986cc, four-cylinder engine, giving it a top speed of 105 mph. A Wadhams roof box and blue light were fitted, together with two-tone horns and a Police label on the front doors. It wasn't as fast as the Lotus, but it was always there.

Did You Know That........?
The body on a Lotus Cortina flexed so much that if you drove it hard enough through a bend, the doors would pop open!

The MK2 Lotus Cortina is seen here in the yard of the old Aldershot Police Station together with a MK2 Triumph 2.5 PI (on test) and one of the new Volvo 144 DLs. The officer is PC John Prince
John Prince

A better view of the new Volvo, this one belonged to the Petersfield Traffic Section.
John Jackman

So, by the end of the 1960s, we had seen the introduction of foreign cars, the blue light, two-tone horns, white cars instead of black, illuminated roof boxes, area cars and the panda and most of that came in the latter half of the decade. It was, without doubt, a period of great change and much of it has stood the test of time. As the force moved into the 1970s it had a fleet of 564 vehicles, travelling more than 10 million miles a year.

CHAPTER 5

Hampshire Constabulary helmet plate

HAMPSHIRE CONSTABULARY
1970 TO 1979

If the 1960s were a decade of rapid growth and development, then the 1970s would be seen as a time of dispute, delay and frustration. Britain was being plagued with industrial disputes, especially at its car factories, where the quality of the final product was so low that we rapidly became the laughing stock of Europe. The Middle East oil crisis meant that petrol was in very short supply and at one point rationing was introduced. This fuel shortage resulted in higher inflation, which at one point reached 26%. There was the three-day week to save electricity, which during the miners strike, also meant power cuts.

In 1970, Hampshire continued to expand its vehicle fleet, even if it was experiencing real difficulties with British manufacturers over delivery dates, which were sometimes between three and five months overdue. This was clearly not acceptable and led to many older vehicles going way beyond their economic mileage. The force had already set up a Vehicle Working Party to observe and report on the vehicle replacement policy and also to study servicing programs and to devise an incentive bonus scheme for vehicle workshops staff. Owing to a poor County Council wages structure, many of the force's mechanics had left during the previous three years for better paid jobs in the private sector. This had left the various workshops in a state where they were not able to cope, especially as the force seemed to be buying more and more vehicles. An improved rate of pay and a bonus system were introduced and eventually this halted the flow of resignations. The big influx of new vehicles had also created a problem at the main workshops at HQ. They all required fitting out with radio and other specialist equipment and there simply wasn't enough room. Plans were therefore put forward for an alternative site to be found. A similar problem had arisen at Portsmouth, where wooden garages in the grounds of the old Portsmouth City Police HQ at Queens Crescent, were clearly inadequate.

Upon amalgamation in 1967, Hampshire acquired the Southampton Police launch *Versatile*, which was now sixty years old, lacked any real speed and was not sufficiently seaworthy for use in unsheltered waters. The force was awarded a grant from the Home Office for £22,000 towards the cost of a replacement and an order was placed with Auto Marine Engineering of Bembridge, Isle of Wight.

Following the introduction of the MK1 Ford Escort the previous year, Ford then followed this up with a van version and this quickly found favour with many forces, including Hampshire. They were used by Scenes of Crime and Photographic Departments to transport their equipment, but were more readily seen as ideal dog vans. These vehicles were ordered in the same blue as used on the panda cars, but their doors were not repainted white. A roof box and blue light were added, together with Police signs on the doors and front of the roof. Inside, the load area was caged to house the dog and wooden flooring was added to help the animal keep its grip whilst in the back. The force Dog Section was growing steadily and now consisted of 15 units.

Mk1 Ford Escort van of the Dog Section.
Clifford Gray

All main stations were now issued with their own section vans for the safe transportation of prisoners. Owing to the increasing violence being shown by some prisoners, it became necessary to provide some means of protection for all concerned. Instead of fully enclosed vans being used the force bought Commer J series buses, with wooden slatted crew seats placed down either side. The side windows allowed visual access to be gained, prior to opening the rear doors to extricate the prisoner. To prevent the prisoner from breaking the glass and making good his escape, metal grilles were riveted to the inside of the window frames and doors, together with a screen to separate the cage from the cab area. The Commer came with a 2500cc engine and was fitted with a blue light and Police signs to the front and rear. Early examples were finished in dark blue or black, but in keeping with the new force policy, 1970s versions were painted white.

Commer J Series section van showing the cage in the rear.
Kenneth Porter

Some of the Hillman Hunter and Minx area cars were now due replacement and an order for 15 MK2 Ford Cortina 1600 GTs was placed. Ford failed to deliver on time and this meant increased expenditure on spares for the old cars, which wasn't popular. When they eventually arrived, the cars were fitted out the same as they had been previously and they were generally quite well liked. The big weak point though concerned the car's gearbox and most of them needed replacement after 50,000 miles. On average the MK2 Cortina lasted for about 100,000 miles and they were all retired by mid 1972. No photographs exist.

Another replacement problem arose due to the Velocette motor cycle going out of production. At first it was thought necessary to replace these rural beat machines with small cars or vans, which would have caused difficulties in connection with garage accommodation at detached beat houses. In the end it was decided that the BSA 250 Gold Star motor cycle would make a good replacement. Orders were placed, but again difficulties arose with delivery dates and the machines didn't arrive until June 1971. A total of 35 were obtained and no sooner had they arrived, then BSA went into receivership and eventually closed its gates forever. All the Hampshire bikes were fitted out with a small Craven handlebar fairing, leg guards, panniers and radio set. Quality control and reliability was a major problem with the BSA and many of them had seized engines after just 15,000 miles!

The ill fated BSA 250 Gold Star, seen here in the rear yard of Newport Police Station.
Frank Allanson

Two cars of note that arrived in 1970, concern a Morris 1300 saloon, WHO 922H that was issued as a panda and an Austin Mini Cooper, YAA 486J that was given to the RCS, which was probably very popular.

But Hampshire had other concerns at this time, with the opening of its first stretch of motorway. The M3 was going to require a whole new system of traffic policing, with cars to match. A delegation of officers went up to Hertfordshire for several days, to learn from officers who had been patrolling the M1 since 1959 and who had a wealth of experience on the subject. They came home with a host of ideas and by the end of the year four new cars had arrived and were kitted out in a striking new livery. The cars were MK2 Triumph 2.5 Pi models, finished in white, with an orange side band, bordered in reflective blue striping. The *jam sandwich* had arrived in Hampshire. The origins of using a reflective side stripe are unclear, but Staffordshire Police started painting the boots of their MK2 Jaguars in fluorescent red paint, following the death of two traffic officers in 1967. They had stopped at the scene of an accident and their patrol car was hit from behind. The old East Sussex Police are reputed to be the first force to have actually used reflective side stripes, again in 1967 and one or two others followed in 1968, but it is not clear where the idea originated. A new system called the 'stand off position' meant that officers would place the car at an angle, or echelon fashion, to help protect the scene of an incident. This ensured that as much of the car as possible could be seen from a distance and the addition of reflective stripes, meant that it could be seen even further away, especially at night.

The cars themselves were 2.5 litre, six-cylinder motors with petrol injection. This was a new idea for production cars and helped push the big saloon to 110 mph. New, sloping style roof boxes, made by Ferrie Plastics of Blackpool, with a more powerful Lucas blue light attached, were placed on the roof, whilst new VHF communications equipment, with a dedicated motorway channel, was fitted inside. Generally speaking, the Triumphs proved to be a reliable workhorse and all four lasted for 120,000 miles before replacement.

Triumph 2.5 Pi seen here during the construction of the new M3 motorway,
with Sgt Sid Claridge (left) and PC John Prince.
John Prince

The new Traffic livery was then retrospectively applied to some other Traffic cars within the fleet to gauge reaction to its effectiveness. The experiment was deemed to be a huge success and within months all new Traffic cars were fitted out in the same way.

The following official force photo shows how different the new livery looks on a MK2 Lotus Cortina, when compared to its now rather plain looking predecessor. This Isle of Wight car was based at Newport and must have been one of the fastest vehicles the island had ever seen! See Chapter 9 for further details on this particular car.

This excellent photo of the Isle of Wight's MK2 Lotus Cortina shows off its new side stripes together with its proud driver, PC Peter Hillier
Hampshire Constabulary

Did You Know That........?
In 1970, a certain young transport stores assistant by the name of John Bradley, was given the job of collecting up all the discontinued Winkworth bells and taking them to the scrap yard to be melted down. An entire tea chest of brass bells fetched just £2!

As the force moved into 1971, it was about to be criticised at the highest levels about its vehicle policy. Although there were mutterings in the press about Hampshire buying the

Volvo 120s, this was always deflected by replies that it was just an experiment and that the vast majority of the fleet was British built. As has already been stated, a few of the newer 144 models arrived in the latter part of 1969 and these were added to in 1970 and 1971, with another 30.

This was headline news, not just locally, but nationally and questions were even asked in the Houses of Parliament. Pressure was put on Hampshire by the Home Office, who in turn were being bombarded by pressure from the media. The fact was, the Volvo was the best car available at the time and unlike the more traditional British built cars, it was delivered on time, was reliable and had an efficient spares back-up. Things came to a head when the Home Office discovered that Hampshire had ordered another batch of Volvos and insisted that the order be cancelled.

Volvo then intervened and complained that the decision was in direct breach of the then European Free Trading Association (EFTA) trading agreement, of which Britain and Sweden were both members. The Home Office backed down and Hampshire kept its Volvos. But the Chief Constable, Sir Douglas Osmond continued to receive huge amounts of criticism and eventually issued the following statement.

"The Volvo is regarded by patrol car drivers as the most outstanding high performance vehicle that has ever been used by this force and there is no British vehicle in the same price range available which stands up so well to the excessive demands of road patrol work. Quite apart from its superior performance, there is no doubt that it is an economic proposition and results in financial saving to the ratepayers.

"My Police Authority has agreed that we must continue to purchase a number of these cars but at the same time we also purchase and assess every new British car that is of the same power, speed, performance and price range. This policy has been rigidly adhered to, but we have so far come across no British model, which in this respect, compares favourably with the Volvo. The suggestion that it is in some way unpatriotic to invest in the Volvo and not a British product should be seen in light of the facts.

"There are a great number of factories in this country producing components for export to AB Volvo and the value of the components exported for use in Volvo cars all over the world is far in excess of the value of the complete cars imported. It is in the interests of the British industry therefore that the good will of the Volvo Company towards the use of British components should be maintained and the embargo by public authorities on the use of these cars might well have adverse effects on the balance of payments".

Brave words indeed. Hampshire stuck by its policy of buying the best vehicle for the job and changed the face of police vehicles in the UK forever. Almost overnight the names Volvo and Hampshire Constabulary, became world famous.

Slowly but surely, other forces followed suit and bought the Volvo 144 as a patrol car, although nowhere near as big a number as Hampshire. Norfolk, Cambridgeshire, Derbyshire, Lincolnshire and Durham all experimented with them and each force purchased a couple on 'long term evaluation'. But for one reason or another they failed to catch on and it would be several years yet, before the rest of the country was politically ready to accept foreign police vehicles on a large scale.

FROM T FORD TO T5

One of the early Volvo 144 DL patrol cars is seen here with dark storm clouds gathering on the horizon, a feeling Hampshire got to know quite well.
Clifford Gray

So what was the Volvo 144 like as a patrol car? What made it worth all the political flak? Its engine was basically the same 1800cc, four-cylinder unit used on the 120 series. Improvements to the chassis, suspension and gearbox meant better performance all round, although in their basic form they only had a top speed of 107 mph. The cars later received Rudd Speed conversions and this increased top end to around 115 mph. They were solidly built and had a quality feel not experienced with home grown products. Above all they felt safe and gave the driver an air of confidence at speed that few other cars had ever achieved. They were equipped with the newer style roof box and blue light, two-tone horns, reflective red side stripes and a reflective Police sign on the doors. The white panel on which it was placed would almost glow in the dark, when light was transferred onto it from an approaching vehicle.

Between 1969 and 1974, when the 144 went out of production, Hampshire used no fewer than 91 models, in all its guises, the highest ever number of patrol cars from one manufacturer to date. The average mileage for the cars was 130,000, with one of them notching up 144,015 miles. Better than this though was the resale value at auction, where the cars fetched more than £1000 each, in comparison with about £500 for most other makes.

The Traffic Division was still expanding in the early 1970s and took delivery of a new motorway accident unit for use on the M3 in 1971. A MK1 Ford Transit Custom van on a long wheel base chassis, with a 3.0 V6 engine was loaded with a huge number of orange cones, signs and other equipment for use at motorway incidents. Painted white with reflective orange side stripes, it also had roof box, blue light and two-tone horns to get it to the scene as quickly as possible. The words *Police Motorway Patrol* were added to the sides and the vehicle was operated from Basingstoke. The concept was brilliant, but in practice the idea quickly fell

110

from favour amongst those that had to use it on a daily basis. To utilise the vehicle properly meant that it had to be on the road 16 hours a day. It had no power steering and with the additional weight it was carrying, it was a slow and cumbersome vehicle to drive. Eventually, officers found new excuses not to drive it and it was only brought out to attend major accidents and then taken back again! It was eventually retired from traffic patrol duties, de-kitted, repainted in grey and used as an observation van.

This is the only known photo in existence of the MK1
Ford Transit Motorway Unit used at Basingstoke.
Bob Blake

The motorcycle section of the Traffic Division also got new machines towards the end of 1971. Triumph as a manufacturer was dying, there were no new models in the pipeline and spares were becoming difficult to obtain. The Norton 750 Commando Interpol seemed like the natural replacement and an initial batch of 16 bikes were obtained. The Norton was famed for its excellent handling qualities with its featherbed frame and suspension set up. The 750cc, twin-cylinder engine was capable of 105 mph and sounded great with its reverse megaphone silencers! Stopping was a bit of a problem though, as it was fitted with drum brakes, front and rear. Each bike was painted white and fitted with an all white Avon fairing, with a single blue flashing light positioned above the headlamp. A pair of Fiamm two-tone horns were poked through holes made in the lower half of the fairing, to help project the sound forward. Police signs were placed across the front of the windscreen and on the lower half of the fairing. The radio set was bolted to the petrol tank and behind the single seat, a fire extinguisher was neatly clamped to the rack that also housed the Craven panniers. These also had Police signs attached and another one was positioned above the rear light. The motorcycle section had now increased its establishment to 76 officers and machines.

111

Norton 750 Commando Interpol in 1971.
Clifford Gray

The aforementioned problems with lightweight motorcycles came to the fore again in late 1971, when supplies of the BSA all but dried up. The only British made machine left in existence now was the Rickman Metisse 150cc, single-cylinder, two-stroke. An initial batch of 56 were purchased and over the next two years or so, a total of 110 saw service with the force, averaging 20,000 miles each. The two stroke engines became the target of much mirth amongst officers in Hampshire, because they would produce so much blue smoke that the station yard would be left smog bound for several minutes after the bike had left to go on a call! Each bike was fitted with a handlebar fairing, panniers and radio set. Like many other British products of the time, the Rickman was plagued with reliability problems, in particular the gearbox which tended to seize up on a regular basis.

A MK3 Ford Cortina 1600 GT area car, call sign KS-51, outside of the old Southsea Police
Station in Victoria Road South, Southsea.
Kenneth Porter

Did You Know That......?
According to legend, the reclining front seats in the MK3 Cortina GTs were removed by HQ
workshops and replaced by non-reclining seats from the 1300L model, because it was felt that
such luxury items were not necessary in Police cars!

The Rickman Metisse produced lots of smoke from its two-stroke engine.
Kenneth Porter

It wasn't all bad news in 1971 though, because the new Central Workshops at Bar End, Winchester were opened and this had an immediate effect on staff morale. There was plenty of space for servicing, repairs and fitting out, together with radio workshops and administrative offices. Storage space for new and old vehicles was plentiful and to this day, Bar End still serves the force well.

But perhaps the biggest news of the year belonged to the Marine Division, who took delivery of their new launch *Ashburton* on the 3rd March. It was named after Lord Ashburton, who was the Lord Lieutenant of Hampshire at the time. *Ashburton* was a Nelson 40 twin screw patrol vessel, built of glass reinforced plastic with a wooden superstructure. She was powered by twin Cummins V504 V8 diesel engines, each delivering 205 hp, giving her a top speed of 20.5 knots on her official acceptance trials. Halmatic Ltd of Havant moulded the hull and Auto Marine Engineering at Bembridge on the Isle of Wight fitted her out. In the meantime *Versatile* was sold to Itchen Marine Towage and continued to work as a yard launch in the Southampton area for some years. She was last seen in the 1980s at Milford Haven, still going strong after more than 60 years of varied service.

Ashburton was based at Cowes because of the excellent marine maintenance facilities in the area and because it is geographically, the centre of its patch. The work undertaken by its crew of 12 officers is basically the same as any land based unit, to protect life and property, to prevent and detect crime and to prosecute offenders. However, there are one or two aspects that are somewhat different, in that they also form part of the local Search and Rescue teams under the co-ordination of H M Coastguard and investigate accidents on the water. Given the huge amount of marine traffic that there is in the Solent and its surrounding waters of over 1000 square miles, they are often very busy.

To assist the crew with its work, *Ashburton* was fitted with radar, echo sounder, Decca navigator, two marine VHF radios, force VHF and UHF radio, fire and salvage pumps, resuscitator, first aid kit, survival bags, shallow water breathing apparatus and an Avon rigid inflatable dinghy, with 10hp outboard motor.

The Ashburton patrols the Solent.
Hampshire Constabulary

In comparison with previous years, 1972 was rather quiet on the vehicle front. Industrial action in the country was still a major problem and affected the force with regards to its fleet, with constant delays in supplies of new cars and spares. The RCS got its first foreign cars in the shape of two Renault 16TSs and two VWs, although the records do not record exactly which model, it was possibly the K70, a front engined, water cooled, front wheel drive saloon, similar to the early Audi 100.

The force driving school, based at Hulse Road, Southampton took delivery of two Morris Marina 1300 saloons, for 'improver driver training courses' to enlarge their fleet, which until then had consisted of Minis and MK1 Ford Escorts. Driver training was becoming more and more important as the fleet expanded. Damaged vehicles were costing huge amounts of money to repair and the Police also had a responsibility to the public to show that their drivers were of an above average standard. These courses were designed for drivers of panda cars and CID vehicles, to improve their general standard and ability. For those officers looking at going on to area car or traffic duties, this was the first step on the ladder. As well as road driving, the course involved exams on the Highway Code and reverse and parking tests, to ensure that they wouldn't damage the Police vehicle in the station yard, where most of the damage to police vehicles seems to occur!

A MK1 Ford Escort of the force driving school seen here in 1972,
doing the slalom test through the poles, in an area behind
the old Hampshire County Cricket ground in Southampton.
Roy Ford

Bedford ceased production of the Beagle estate and transformed the vehicle into the HA 110 van. The force continued to purchase these cheap vehicles for use by the Dog Section, Scenes of Crime and Photographic Department and in some rural areas, as beat vehicles, where the use of lightweight motorcycles or pandas was not thought appropriate. The Isle of Wight and parts of the New Forest were two such places that took the vast majority of these vehicles. Finished in white, with a single blue light on the roof and Police signs on the doors, these cars were not intended to be used as emergency vehicles, but of course were, when the need arose. A total of 47 were purchased, the average mileage was 80,000 and they fetched around £600 at auction with the last one being retired in October 1979.

This later Bedford 110 HA van shows its basic style.
Kenneth Porter

Perhaps one of the most important developments at this time was the purchase of a completely new type of vehicle. Landrover, long famed for its rugged, off road vehicles, entered the 'luxury' car market in 1970 with the Range Rover. This 3.5 litre V8 with four-wheel drive and a top speed of 100 mph, was seen by many forces as the ideal motorway patrol car. By 1972, when Hampshire showed an interest, several forces already had them on their fleet and they had been tested and reviewed in many motoring publications of the time. It was a remarkable car and quite unlike anything that had come before it.

On the 22nd June 1972, Hampshire took delivery of two Range Rovers, GOT 996K and GOT 997K. One was posted to Basingstoke, where it quickly took over the role that the Ford Transit van had been assigned to and the other went to Eastleigh. The cars were generally equipped the same as any other traffic car, with orange side stripes, two tone horns, p.a. system and Police signs on the front doors. In addition, a new item of equipment was installed. A Dale Stemlight, was placed on the roof and this system allowed the blue light, affixed to the top of the unit to be projected about six feet higher than the car, on an extendible, rolled metal

116

pole, powered by an electric motor, housed inside the vehicle. Immediately beneath the blue light were two floodlights, which could be used to illuminate the scene of an accident. This system replaced, to an extent, the old generator fired floodlights carried in the Volvo 120 estates. The idea of extending the blue light skywards would be that approaching vehicles would be able to see it from a lot further away. The Range Rover was also capable of carrying extra kit for use at accidents and also came with a tow bar; to drag accident damaged vehicles out of the carriageway. Both of these new cars were used as a base for experimental roof boxes made by Ferrie Plastics in Blackpool. GOT 997K was equipped with a huge triangular shaped box that showed the word Police from two different angles at the front. At the rear it could show Police/Stop or a series of other messages like *divert* with a directional arrow. A large blue light was placed on top. This system took the place of the stem light during the experiment. GOT 996K got a similar triangular box but it was much smaller and didn't come with a blue light and was positioned behind the retained stem light system.

This is GOT 996K positioned on an observation ramp
on the M3 near Basingstoke.
Brian Homan's collection

GOT 997K, the Eastleigh based Range Rover is seen
sporting the latest in roof box technology.
Brian Homan's collection

Three more cars, VCG 667N, VCG 668N and VCG 670N were purchased to replace the original two, with the third one being sent to Havant. These three cars were equipped with the stem light system and a standard Wadhams roof box. The original two cars travelled a total of 149,057 and 178,272 miles respectively, before being sold at auction for £1800 and £2200 each.

The Range Rover could and should have been everybody's favourite traffic car, but reliability problems reared their ugly heads again and the cars were frequently being taken off the road for niggling little faults that rapidly caused frustration amongst their crews and the mechanics that had to fix them. Even so, the car had a dramatic impact on the Police service in general and deserves to be recognised as one of the landmark cars.

One of the 1974 Range Rovers, call sign HM-01, seen here at the
old Fareham Police Station, being driven by Sgt John Jackman.
Note that this one is fitted with a blue repeater light
on the leading edge of the bonnet.
John Jackman

If 1972 were deemed to be fairly quiet, then 1973 would prove to be the exact opposite, with some significant cars being introduced. The forces ageing fleet of Commer J series section vans were replaced by the Bedford CF. These were powered by 2.0 litre engines and had a top speed approaching 90 mph. They were fitted out at Bar End in the same way as before, with wooden slatted crew seats and riveted mesh grilles. A single blue light adorned the roof and city based vans were equipped with two-tone horns. These vans were also used as personnel carriers, to transport officers to and from public order incidents, like football matches. One of this vehicles endearing features was its huge, bus like, flat steering wheel, which seemed to take up most of the room in the cab!

A 1973/4 Bedford CF section van.
Kenneth Porter

Volvo updated the 144, with a 2 litre, fuel injected engine and even without a Rudd Speed conversion fitted its top speed increased to around 115 mph. This was quite impressive for a big car, but it did lack decent acceleration in reaching that speed. Once there, it would happily sit at that speed all day, but some officers were now beginning to question the car's suitability for traffic patrol, especially on the motorway.

A Volvo 144S of the Petersfield Traffic Section, call sign J-01 seen at speed.
John Jackman

Excellent interior shot of the Volvo shows the force VHF radio on the left, with a Wipac map light to the right. The receiver from the two piece Pye personal radio is clipped onto the ashtray! The speedo was a Smiths of Nottingham calibrated unit, whilst the additional plate on the centre console, houses the Lucas illuminated switches for the two-tone horns, blue light, Police sign and Police/Stop sign.
John Jackman

In an effort to stem the tide of Volvos entering Police service in the county, one or two mainstream manufacturer's made an attempt at forcing Hampshire's hand, by loaning the force a number of cars, with a view to purchasing them at a vastly reduced rate, if after 12 months, they had proved satisfactory. For the first time ever, we were seeing a British motor company actually making an effort to secure orders from the Police, which it obviously now recognised, was a prestige market.

In May 1973, Ford loaned the force a Ford Consul 3000 GT. This large four-door saloon, with its powerful V6 engine and excellent handling characteristics was very popular. With a top speed of 115 mph, it also had the acceleration to outpace the Volvo, adding more fuel to the debate that Volvo was starting to lag behind in the performance stakes. Ford had done its homework and the cars came ready equipped with additional battery, stronger alternator, wiring for the added electric's and items like spot and fog lamps, already wired into the emergency lighting switches. All Hampshire had to do was stripe it up, fit it with a radio system and send it out to work. The Consul was also fitted with a revised style roof box, made by Ferrie Plastics. This aerodynamic, triangular box, with single blue light on top, helped cut down on wind resistance at speed. Because there were two Police signs on it, placed at an angle, the word Police could also be seen if the car was viewed from the side. At the rear of the box, was the standard blue and red illuminated Police/Stop sign. It looked great and helped make the Consul look sleek and very purposeful. The car passed its 12-month trial and was purchased. It covered more than 145,000 miles and was retired in July 1976. Fords offer to buy more was refused, not because the Consul GT wasn't up to the job, but because in the meantime Hampshire had also been testing the Rover 3500 V8 P6 (see Chapter 8).

This is the only known photo of the Ford Consul 3000 GT used by Hampshire.
Kenneth Porter

The other manufacturer to sit up and take note was Vauxhall. In August 1973 they delivered three Vauxhall Victor FEs, fitted with the more powerful 3.3 litre, six-cylinder engine from the Ventora. The Vauxhall was a big car and although it had the straight-line speed and ability, with a top speed around 110 mph, its handling was described as vague and woolly. It also suffered from some recurring mechanical defects, particularly the gearbox and rear axle. Nonetheless, the cars were fitted out as per the Consul and saw service for two years, clocking up an average of 90,000 miles. One of these cars, VXD 569M was posted to Basingstoke Traffic, where it performed on the M3 for a while. It wasn't deemed quick enough for motorway patrol and after a year or so, it was sent to Newport on the Isle of Wight, to be used as a joint traffic/area car. The Traffic Division on the island at this time performed a joint role, as per the old days on the mainland and was responsible for attending all emergency calls.

One of the Vauxhall Victors photographed on the Isle of Wight, circa 1974.
Pete Cobbett

The year 1973 is likely to go down in force history, as the year it made one of its biggest automotive errors. Still plagued by political pressure to buy British, it succumbed and ordered a batch of Morris Marina 1.8 TCs, as replacement area cars. The Marina was a last ditch attempt by Morris at staying afloat and being seen to be used as a Police car was obviously an important market to them. Unlike most of the twin-carb versions offered to the public, which were two door coupe's, the Police variants used the four door saloon body shell, but with the faster engine, giving them a top speed of about 100 mph. The cars build quality had sunk to an all time low, bits would just fall off them and workshops invented an ingenious device to keep the engine cool, when sat at idle for any length of time at an incident. To stop the car from boiling over, an additional water bottle, with the aid of a small electric pump, was fitted under the bonnet and when the cooling fan was activated by the thermostat, it would blow water all over the engine block, in an effort to keep it cool! But it wasn't the cars inability to stay in one piece that gave it its legendary place in history, but it's handling or rather, a distinct lack of road holding. The Marina would roll and lean over at some incredibly unnerving angles, whilst negotiating the average bend or roundabout. Push it hard through a faster bend and the body roll, in conjunction with massive understeer, would ensure that the driver would be fighting the wheel for supremacy. Every now and then, the car would win and the driver was looking at the possibility of a re-test!

Over the next 18 months, Hampshire bought 25 Marina TCs; most of which were defected with only 80,000 miles on the clock, with a variety of engine and gearbox faults. They all received standard area car equipment, except two, which were striped up and issued to Traffic Division senior officers, as a Traffic Supervisory unit. Well, if the front line officers had to drive them, why shouldn't the Chief Inspector!

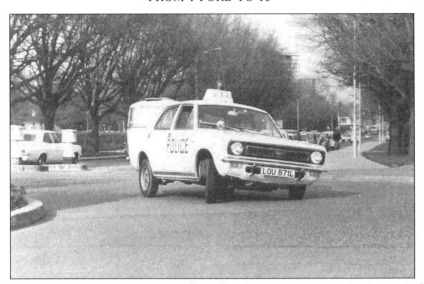

A Morris Marina 1.8 TC in typical pose! This area car was based at Portsmouth Central, call sign KC-51 and PC Derek 'Wishbone' Bampton is the officer struggling to negotiate the roundabout outside Clarence Pier.
Derek Bampton

The Traffic Division meanwhile had a much more impressive toy to play with. The much acclaimed Rover P6 saloon, which had been around since 1963 in 2000 and 2200 variants, gained a 3500 V8 lump in 1968 and was tested a couple of times by Hampshire during this time. But it wasn't until 1973 that a number of 3500S models were purchased for traffic patrol use. An initial eight cars were acquired and fitted out in the now standard traffic livery, complete with the new triangular roof box and with the Smith's of Nottingham calibrated speedometer, housed in a special binnacle on the dashboard. Over the next two years, Hampshire purchased 30 Rovers for traffic patrol and they became one of the better loved cars, purely from the aspect of their drive ability. On the reliability front they had their weak points too, like the Morris Marina gearbox that was fitted, continually seizing when placed in reverse. The problem appeared to be that the unit was splash fed oil when put into reverse and if this were done in a hurry, as is often the case with Police vehicles, then it would lock solid. A firm in Maidstone was eventually found and they did a roaring trade in fixing Police Rover gearboxes from all over the country! It obviously didn't cure all the problems though, because according to records, at least seven of the cars went to auction with defective gearboxes, upon retirement. Most of the cars clocked up 120,000 miles and fetched £1000 resale.

*Rover 3500S V8 of the Petersfield Traffic Section. This later 1975 model
is J-05 with its driver PC Derek Bampton.
Derek Bampton*

The Rover V8 was an impressive car, with a top speed of 125 mph; it was by far the quickest patrol car ever used at that time. As a motorway patrol car it was ideal, except for one thing. On the M3 crews would experience something that was both frightening and very dangerous. As soon as the Rover hit 90 mph, it would change lanes all by itself! The officers at Basingstoke complained bitterly to the Transport Manager, Mr Patrick who in turn passed on their comments to the Rover factory. Their Fleet Sales Manager, Stan Faulkner stated that he had been selling Rovers to Police forces all over the world and that no-one had ever complained about poor handling in the past and that it wasn't the car, it was Hampshire's drivers who were at fault. Sgt Nick Carter took exception to this verbal lambasting and challenged Stan Faulkner to come down to Basingstoke to witness the problem for himself.

A few days later he duly arrived, together with a Rover engineer and Nick Carter took them out onto the M3, where at an area known as Blackdam the car suddenly veered from lane one, across to lane two at 90 mph. Mr Faulkner was invited to try it for himself, but declined and stated that the tyre pressures must be wrong. They were checked and found to be correct. The front suspension was then inspected to ensure that the correct units had been fitted and these to were found to be in order. The rear suspension was then scrutinised to see if it had been set up correctly and that too, passed the inspection. The car was then taken to a weigh bridge, where it was found that the front axle weight was half a hundredweight (28k) lighter when the car was loaded, than it was when unloaded. Further tests were carried out and it was discovered that when all the kit was placed in the boot, the front of the car was raised by three inches! The three of them concluded that the combination of speed and excess weight, probably meant that at 90 mph or more, the front wheels would actually leave the ground, hence the car would have little or no steering!

The men from Rover went back to Longbridge scratching their heads and the traffic boys took all the kit out of the boot and dumped it on the back seat. A few weeks later, Stan Faulkner returned to Basingstoke with an orange Rover 3500S V8, which had been fitted with the most hideous steel spoiler, right across the front of the car. It had been welded to the front apron of the car and almost touched the road surface. Loaded with kit, the car was taken out and was found to handle very well indeed, with none of the previous handling problems being apparent. The car was left with Basingstoke Traffic Section for a month and they were asked to play around with the spoiler to obtain a compromise between aerodynamic efficiency and reasonable looks. Over the next few weeks the spoiler was cut back until it looked reasonable, but still allowed the car to handle well. The result was that Rover then produced the spoiler in glass fibre and fitted them to all production V8 models, including those Police issue cars that had previously been sold without them.

The orange Rover 3500S with prototype spoiler fitted to the front, being driven by
Sgt Nick Carter, with Stan Faulkner of Rover in the passenger seat.
Hampshire Constabulary via Nick Carter

The Rover P6 became infamous for another reason to. The tyre manufacturer Dunlop, in a deal with Rover, produced a run flat tyre system called Denovo and Hampshire traffic cars trialled the system in 1973 prior to it being offered to the public the following year. The Denovo was a low profile tyre, which could sustain a complete loss of air pressure at high speed, with almost no effect on the stability of the car. The tyre was then capable of travelling limited distances at speeds up to 50 mph in deflated condition and after repair, would be fully operational again. Its secret was a special lubricant carried in canisters attached to the wheel rim inside the tyre, which was released automatically when the tyre deflated. This lubricant reduced friction, kept the tyre temperature down, sealed any small punctures and partially reinflated the tyre, all in the space of a few seconds. The tyre had to be fitted to specially made two piece wheels fitted with plastic trims, with a radial spoke design that made them easy to recognise. That was the theory anyway. In practice, the actual system worked very well,

126

almost too well, because the Police drivers that experienced high-speed deflation's on the M3 were completely unaware that anything had happened and continued to drive the car at speed. Dunlop of course recommended speeds no greater than 50 mph, which is all very well if you know what's happened. The first most Police drivers knew of any problems, was when the tyre disintegrated and pieces of it were seen flying passed the window! On one occasion the impact was so great, that the front wing on a patrol car was ripped right off!

Dunlop supplied Hampshire with the Denovo tyres free of charge, which was just as well, because they worked out at twice the price of a standard tyre and even if they didn't get punctured, they tended to wear out a lot quicker anyway. But the biggest problem as far as the force were concerned was that every time one of the devices was activated, the wheel had to go back to Dunlop and a new one fitted in its place by a Dunlop fitter. This meant that some considerable delays were experienced during out of hour's periods, like night shifts. After testing the tyres for 18 months, Hampshire reverted back to standard road tyres. Dunlop continued with the Police link, when it paid the just retired Metropolitan Police Commissioner, Sir Robert Mark to endorse the product on television and in various magazines, by stating that he "believed the tyres made a significant contribution to road safety". But, by 1977 Dunlop had to admit defeat, the public weren't buying the Denovo tyre and it was withdrawn.

*A Basingstoke Rover 3500S (KBK 167P) call sign BM-04,
showing the Dunlop Denovo wheel and tyre system.
Bob Blake*

Other cars of note at this time included a Vauxhall VX4/90 loaned to Hampshire by Vauxhall for a trial period. Like the Savage Cortina, this was fitted with an uprated engine from a tuning specialist. The Bliedenstein 3.3 litre Vauxhall was a beast and great fun to drive, but like it's adversaries it kept going off tune and the novelty factor soon wore off. Regrettably there are no photos in existence.

The idea of giving senior officers in the Traffic Division their own cars soon caught on and as well as the Morris Marinas previously mentioned, two MK1 Ford Escort 1300 XL saloons were utilised. These cars were fully marked up as traffic patrol cars, with red and blue stripes, triangular roof boxes and with a limited amount of emergency equipment in the boot. They would only ever be used by senior officers to attend the scene of a fatal accident or other major incident and this idea meant that there was always a car ready for them to use, without the need to call one back in. Sadly no photos have survived.

In 1974, Norton updated its 750 Commando Interpol to an 850 by the same name. It was a little quicker than its predecessor was and suffered from many of its inherent problems, like oil leaks and worn crankshafts. Hampshire though had one distinct advantage over the rest of Britain's Police forces when it came to obtaining spare parts for its bikes. Norton had a parts depot in the north of the county at Andover and Bar End's storeman at the time, John Bradley was quite often smuggled into the back of the premises to obtain parts for Hampshire's bikes ahead of everybody else's! A total of 21 850s saw service with Hampshire, but the writing was on the wall for the British motorcycle industry. It was slipping into decline with out-dated products facing stiff competition from Japan and parts of Europe. Even with the formation of the Norton Villiers Triumph (NVT) collaboration the following year, the days of seeing the British policeman on a British made motorcycle were numbered.

This excellent photo of the Basingstoke Traffic Section, circa 1974 shows the newer Norton 850 Commando Interpol, the Rover 3500S V8 fitted with Dunlop Denovo tyres, a Volvo 144S sporting the new Ferrie Plastics roof box and the two door Range Rover 3.5 V8 4x4.
Hampshire Constabulary

The force continued to buy the Mini in large numbers during the 1970s for both CID and Panda car use. On the Pandas, to help reduce costs, the frontal area of the roof was left in its

128

original Bermuda blue colour and only the doors were repainted in white. This made a significant saving in both time and money at the fitting and decommissioning stage. Morris Minis were now being used, but there was little difference between them and the Austin version. Each Mini Panda was fitted with a rather crude looking aluminium plate, about six inches in length, on the right of the dashboard shelf. This plate housed the illuminated Lucas switches that operated the two-tone horns, blue light, Police sign and Police/Stop sign.

A Mini panda parked on Southsea seafront, shows its slightly revised paint scheme.
Kenneth Porter

Did You Know That…..?
If you the driver of a Mini panda car, you had to lift up the hinged driver's seat each time you took over the car from the previous crew, to ensure that they hadn't left a glass phial stink bomb behind! Much mirth was had when the seat was sat upon and the glass broke, ensuring that you had a very unpleasant and smelly day!

Despite the numerous problems with the Morris Marina, the force purchased six Marina vans for use by the Dog Section and Scenes of Crime Officers. The RCS obtained the services of a Triumph Dolomite, a Vauxhall Magnum 2.2 saloon, a Ford Consul 3000 GT and two of the new MK2 Ford Capris. Hampshire's Police Cadet Training School at Bishops Waltham also got three vehicles to assist with the movement of its trainees, a LWB Landrover and two MK1 Ford Transit Minibuses, SHO 198M and SHO 199M. No doubt there are many ex-Cadets who remember sitting in the rear of one of those, on route to a dreaded expedition across Dartmoor!

The operational cost of the fleet was being seriously affected in 1974 by inflation, particularly with regard to the purchase of new vehicles, which was subject to no less than four increases during the year. Cars delivered late in the year cost as much as 33% above the original quotation and there was a corresponding increase in the cost of spares. At the same time the force had to make stringent cuts in its mileage to make the best use of fuel during a severe shortage, which at one time led to petrol rationing. Patrol cars had to adopt a method of sitting at certain points until they received a call, instead of patrolling the streets.

Always mindful of the need to keep apace of the times, the staff at Bar End decided to look at the most economical means of transport available at that time, in an effort to help save fuel. Their answer? The Reliant Robin! That's right, Reliants three-wheeled, 'plastic rat' was chosen as the next Panda. The 750cc car was capable of more than 45 mpg and a top speed of 70 mph. It was kitted out with a roof box and blue light, together with a radio system and all the necessary Police signing. It was ready for work. The trouble was, no one would drive it! Every officer who was asked to test it, refused point blank! The idea therefore, was rather short lived and regrettably, no one took a photograph of it.

There was growing unrest amongst many traffic officers that the Volvo 144 was no longer capable of mixing it with more modern vehicles. In comparison with many other cars it was too slow to be used on the motorway. It struggled on acceleration and many smaller cars were out classing it on top end. Most officers preferred to use the Rover and the Volvo tended to get left behind in the garage. Legend has it that eventually, the Transport Manager Mr Patrick lost his temper during a heated debate with a group of officers at Bar End. Fed up with what he classed as ingratitude, he took hold of a lose bit of striping on a nearby Volvo, ripped the whole lot off and declared "Now it's an area car!" And so it was, that the Volvo found itself relegated to the role of area car. But in so doing, Mr Patrick inadvertently created an icon amongst area car drivers that few cars have ever come close to, let alone match.

A big bumper model Volvo 144 DL outside Aldershot Police Station.
Kenneth Porter

About the same time, Volvo gave the 144 a major facelift, with a 2.0 litre, fuel-injected engine, a four-speed manual gearbox with an overdrive switch placed on a new short gear lever, a completely new interior and huge bumpers, front and rear. The car was already suffering from the indignity of being labelled a tank in parts of the motoring press, an expression that was to haunt the range for years to come and the big new bumpers didn't help. They were intended to absorb low speed impacts and were an added feature on an already safe car. Area car crews loved them; they were solid, dependable, reliable and safe. Traffic's loss, was definitely their gain.

Not to be outdone by their four-wheeled compatriots, the motorcyclists got their bikes updated with the same striping arrangement used on the cars. This aided their safety and helped make the machines more readily identifiable to the public. The Traffic Motorcycle Section had grown significantly over the years and now stood at 113 officers and bikes. A far cry from the original six!

Norton 750 Commandos of the Petersfield Traffic Section showing their smart new livery.
The officers are PC John Warner and PC Mick Hart.
Note that they are wearing the latest safety feature, the reflective bandolier!
John Warner

Sgt Nick Carter's previous association with Stan Faulkner developed into a very good, friendly relationship and in late 1974, he turned up at Basingstoke Police Station and asked Nick if he would like to test drive a prototype Rover, on that notorious stretch of the M3 known as Blackdam. Nick was driven to a quiet lay-by on the A30, where he saw a trailer with a rough looking American pick-up truck on it. The Rover technicians then pushed the truck off the trailer, undid some wing nuts and removed the front. They then removed the rear canvass cover to reveal a very sleek looking car, finished in matt black, with no name badges or identifying features on it, except for the Jensen Interceptor rear window that was fitted. Inside the car it looked like a mobile laboratory with dozens of gauges and dials, to test every component. This was the prototype of the Rover SD1. Nick thrashed it up and down the M3 to test the cars handling characteristics in the strong side winds, whilst the technicians checked their instruments. The new car passed its test drive, but it would be another two years before the public caught a glimpse of the finished product.

By 1975 Britain was in an economic recession, with sky high inflation, rising unemployment and continued industrial disputes, many of which directly affected the motor industry and in turn, the Police. The previously proud manufacturers of Austin, Morris and Rover cars were merged, to form the British Leyland Motor Corporation (BLMC) in a last ditch effort to save them from disappearing forever. The same cannot be said for the British motorcycle industry though, which suffered the indignity of virtual collapse. The availability of even basic spares for Hampshire's fleet of Nortons, could sometimes take six months to arrive, during which time the bikes would generally be off the road. In his annual report of 1975, the Chief Constable Sir Douglas Osmond, made special mention of this situation, stating that if the industries problems were not resolved in the very near future, then

A later model Honda CB 200 motorcycle seen in 1978.
Hampshire Constabulary

Hampshire would be forced to look at buying foreign motorcycles, which he personally found very sad. It was already too late for the lightweight motorcycle industry though. Having suffered major problems in sourcing a reliable small motorcycle for the last few years, the force turned to Japan and bought 27 Honda CB200 motorcycles. Some saw this as sacrilege, but those in the know, saw it as the only solution.

The Hondas were powered by a proven 200cc twin-cylinder engine, giving them a top speed of 85 mph. They were oil tight, smooth and quiet to ride and came with the added bonus of an electric start! Above all they were very reliable. Each bike was fitted with a full length Rickman fairing and panniers. A radio set was positioned on the rear rack, together with a Chubb fire extinguisher. The Honda 200 was only ever made available in red or green and Hampshire opted to take all its bikes in green. They were not repainted. There are no records available detailing the number of Honda CB200s purchased, but as they were to replace other rural beat motorcycles, it is likely to have been a considerable number.

Ford unveiled the MK2 Escort in 1975 and a gradual replacement program took place within the force, with the phasing out of the old MK1. The newer Escort was quicker and handled better, although the back end did tend to step out rather too easily, especially in the wet! Hampshire purchased the 1.1 Popular, which was the base model in the range. It had a top speed of 85 mph and made an ideal Panda. They were finished in the now familiar Bermuda blue with white doors. A Wadhams roof box and Lucas blue light were fitted, together with two-tone horns and radio system. The car's worst feature, by far, were the vinyl-covered seats, which tended to collapse under the weight of heavy policemen! After several months use, this state of collapse became permanent and it felt like you were sitting on the floor, straining to look over the dashboard! Hampshire continued to buy the MK2 Escort in large numbers, until 1980 when the replacement MK3 was introduced.

This Southsea based MK2 Ford Escort 1.1 Popular had the call sign
Panda-9 and is parked outside Cosham Police Station.
Hampshire Constabulary

Ford also released the Escort van variant of the MK2 and this to was brought in to replace the MK1 vans used by the Dog Section, Scenes of Crime and Photographic Departments. The previous dog vans had been ordered in the special blue colour, as used on the Pandas and this was now dropped in favour of white. It was cheaper and was more in keeping with the rest of the fleet and helped make the Panda car more distinctive.

The first of the BLMC Mini 850s came on stream in 1975 and other than badging, there was very little difference over the previous car. The force continued to buy them in large numbers for both CID and Panda car use.

Volvo announced the replacement for the ageing 144 range, in the shape of the 244. The same basic cabin shape was retained, but it got an all-new sloping front and redesigned rear end. Engine size was increased to 2.1, with an over-drive gearbox and a new interior. Top end was now a credible 105 mph with better acceleration and increased road-holding abilities. For a car of this size it also had an incredibly good turning circle of just 32 feet (or twice its body length), which a patrol car of this nature will always find very useful. They were fitted with a Ferrie Plastics roof box and blue light, two-tone horns, calibrated speedo and a range of cones and signs, for use at any incidents. In comparison with the Morris Marina they were a positive luxury, but above all, the officers driving them felt confident and safe and the car itself appeared to suit the *Police System* of driving perfectly.

An early Volvo 244 DL area car.
Kenneth Porter

Even though mainland Traffic Sections stopped using the Volvo, on the Isle of Wight it remained the number one option for use with its unique Traffic/Area Car Section. This was LP-11 based at Newport.
Stef King

This brilliant photo shows the interior of one of the early Volvo 244s. Note the Smiths of Nottingham calibrated speedo, which occupies a large hole cut into the dashboard and the VHF radio speaker mounted above it. The car is travelling west along the Military Road towards Freshwater on the Isle of Wight.
Stef King

Throughout the rest of 1975 and early 1976 the fleet remained fairly static, with a steady replacement program of panda cars and area cars being implemented. Then in June 1976, Rover introduced the new 3500 SD1 V8. This beautifully styled, five-door fastback with five-speed gearbox, looked like a natural replacement traffic car for the old P6 series and it wasn't long before Police forces across the country got their hands on one. Rover bosses saw the Police market as an important endorsement of their product and were quick to ensure that each force got what they required.

In fact Hampshire didn't get theirs until later in the year, but it was worth the wait. The car was very fast, with plenty of torque and rapid acceleration. Top end was 125 mph and there was plenty of cabin and boot space. The only real complaint concerning the design was that the gear lever and handbrake were positioned too far away to the left and that the rather strange looking *quartic* square steering wheel was awkward to use, especially on these early models because they were not fitted with power assisted steering. But the performance was such, that these design quirks were soon forgotten about and Hampshire therefore placed a large order for the car. The honeymoon was short lived though, when the cars build quality was called into question yet again. Like the Marina, items of trim would just fall off or break, water pumps would pack up and the problems associated with the gearbox on the old model didn't appear to have been cured either.

An early Rover 3500 SD1 V8 of the Fareham Traffic Section
with Sgt John Jackman at the wheel.
John Jackman

All the Rovers were identically equipped with Ferrie Plastics roof box, two-tone horns, reflective orange striping and a host of emergency kit. In addition the cars were also fitted with the Vascar speed detection unit as well as a calibrated speedo, housed in its own separate binnacle on top of the dashboard. The SD1 became one of those archetypal traffic cars, remembered by many, with either fondness or frustration.

In September 1976 Ford replaced the MK3 Cortina with the MK4 version and almost immediately Hampshire bought two as trial area cars, but instead of buying the usual 1600 model, opted for the uprated 2.0S instead. This rather clean looking car came with sports wheels, front spot and fog lamps, smart matt black trim, inside and out and a top speed of 105 mph. It was a lot lighter than the Volvo 244 and was considered to be better suited to area car work within the city, where turning points were sometimes at a premium. Southampton got the first two cars and the following year two more were purchased and sent to Southsea and Portsmouth Central. Two further cars were striped up for use as Traffic Supervisory cars, replacing the Marinas.

Standard area car kit was fitted, the only difference being that the Southampton cars were adorned with an older style roof box, whilst the Portsmouth cars and Traffic Supervisories got the newer triangular box.

Southampton Central's MK4 Ford Cortina 2.0S,
call sign FC-51 is seen close to the Docks.
Kenneth Porter

The force purchased a vehicle in 1976 that quickly gained the reputation for making everybody feel ill! A custom built mobile canteen called the *Chefmobile* was a self-contained mobile kitchen that would accompany officers engaged on large-scale operations, to provide hot food and drink.

The vehicle was a MK1 Ford Transit parcel type van with bodywork alterations carried out by Messrs C F Taylor of Wokingham. It was equipped with an electric convection oven and water boiler run from a large generator of 25 KVa rating. However this generator was so heavy that it could not be transported within the vehicle and had to be taken to each site in another unit. The meals would be pre-packed in foil dishes and then heated in the ovens and it was possible to feed up to 200 men at a time. The food however wasn't of the best quality and was frequently either burnt or not cooked at all. The vehicle quickly acquired the name of the *Force-Feeder* and became the butt of many jokes.

Not to be outdone by all the new vehicles within his force, the Chief Constable Sir Douglas Osmond had his old Rover P5B saloon replaced by a dark blue MK1 Ford Granada 3.0 Ghia with automatic gearbox in September 1976. This splendid looking car would be chauffeur driven by a senior class one traffic officer, to convey the Chief to and from various formal functions. The car, NOT 382R led a varied and interesting life. After serving Sir Douglas and his successor, Mr John Duke, the car was retired from chauffeur duties in 1980 and posted to the Driving School at Hulse Road, Southampton. There it was used as a deceleration car on standard and advanced driving courses. The idea, was to allow those officers who had been on these high speed courses for the last four weeks, a chance to come back down to earth and drive a sedate automatic, at no more than 30 mph. Anyone who drove faster than that had to buy everyone else in the car a doughnut at the next coffee stop! It cost some drivers an absolute fortune!

The Chief's former MK1 Ford Granada 3.0 Ghia is seen here at the Hulse Road Driving School being used as the deceleration car.
Mick Payne

The Chief Constable's former car, the Rover P5B wasn't retired though. Instead, it was transferred to the Isle of Wight where it became the official transport of Earl Mountbatten of Burma. He would visit the island on a regular basis and stay at Osborne House in East Cowes, the residence of his late grandmother, Queen Victoria. He loved the island and would spend a lot of time there, but on occasions he required the services of an official car. The Home Office contacted Hampshire and it was made clear that the force *would* provide a suitable car! When Mountbatten was away from the island, the car became the official transport for the Chairman of the Isle of Wight County Council.

The first section of the M27 motorway, between junction 9 and junction 12 was opened and placed additional burdens on the Traffic Division in the south east of the county.

Hampshire, like many other forces at this time, was forced to look elsewhere for its large capacity motorcycles. No criticism was levelled at the force on this occasion, because buying foreign had been thrust upon it. The thought of taking further Japanese bikes for its Traffic Division wasn't really an option at this stage, given the fact that many people blamed cheap Jap imports as one of the main reasons for the collapse of the home market. The only real European candidate was the BMW R/75 boxer. The horizontally opposed, 750cc twin-cylinder bike, with shaft drive was about as far away from a Norton as you could get! It wasn't quite as fast as the Norton, but it was smoother, handled better, albeit in a very different manner, was a lot more comfortable and above all, reliable. They were an instant success and it wasn't unusual for officers with Norton's to suddenly start finding additional faults with their bikes!

BMW R/75 a new breed of traffic motorcycle.
Hampshire Constabulary

These early *Beemers* or *BM's* as they were affectionately known, were fitted with an Avon fairing and Craven panniers, a pair of blue lights, two-tone horns, tank mounted radio set and an illuminated rear Police/Stop sign. They were striped up and had Police signs added to the screen, panniers and handlebar covers. Within a year of their release, updated versions, badged as the R/80 arrived, with an 800cc engine, but they were basically the same bike. Another change came as a result of a very nasty accident in another force area, when the rider suffered serious injuries after colliding with the radio set positioned on the tank of the motorcycle! A Home Office directive then ordered that all such radio sets should be repositioned at the rear of the machine.

These motorcycles were also the first vehicles to be fitted with a new identifying logo, in the shape of the force crest. Many other forces in the UK had used their force crest as an integral part of the vehicle livery for years, but for some inexplicable reason, it had taken Hampshire a long time to catch on. The design showed the red rose of Hampshire surmounted by a crown and outlined with laurel leaves. The County motto *Com Southton* was scrolled along the bottom and the name *Hampshire* placed beneath that. At first, only Traffic Division vehicles were deemed eligible to wear the crest and it wasn't until 1979 that area cars got the same treatment.

An early style Hampshire Constabulary vehicle crest.
Author

Sir Douglas Osmond retired in 1977 and Hampshire gained a new Chief Constable, Mr John Duke. The Fleet Manager Mr Patrick also retired and the force took on the services of a new Fleet Manager, Mr John Roberts. New workshop facilities were also opened in Basingstoke, but Portsmouth and Southampton continued to struggle on with sub standard facilities.

Ford managed to off load three MK1 Granada 3.0S saloons onto Hampshire and these were no doubt purchased at a vastly reduced rate, as Ford introduced the new MK2 model about the same time. The MK1 3.0S came with Ford's renowned Essex V6 engine and twin Weber carburettors, giving it a top speed of 115mph. The big saloon could be hustled along at great pace and handled particularly well, unless pushed too hard in the wet. With no power steering though, they were very heavy to manoeuvre at parking speeds. Inside, the car was finished in all matt black, even the fascia.

The sleek looking MK1 Ford Granada 3.0S area car from Alton, with its driver
PC 1999 Bill Ord. This is the only known photograph of any of the Granadas.
William Ord

The cars were issued to Alton, Romsey and Fratton and were used as area cars and equipped with triangular roof box, two-tone horns and all the necessary items required for such work. In addition, the Romsey and Fratton cars were deemed to be motorway back-up units, to assist the Traffic Division in times of urgent requirement. The Romsey car would cover the newly opened western section of the M27 and the soon to be opened M271. The Fratton unit would be responsible for assisting on the new M275 motorway leading into Portsmouth.

Perhaps one of the most significant new vehicles to come out in 1978 was the Southampton built, MK2 Ford Transit van. Although the force had used the likes of the Commer and Bedford for its section vans, it wasn't until the advent of the MK2 *Tranny* van that the concept really came into being. In short wheel base specification, it was fitted out with side window and rear door grilles, blue light and wooden slatted crew seats along the sides. The rear glass was replaced with Perspex, which was a lot tougher to break than standard vehicle glass. The Transits secret was that unlike any of its rivals at the time, it looked like a car from the cab and more importantly, it drove like one to. Although a bit heavy on the steering at slow speeds, the 2.0 litre engine gave it a very flexible performance and many officers actually preferred to drive the van, than a panda. As had been the case for a couple of years now, all section vans were known as *double- nine* units and this helped simplify matters during urgent requests for a van over the radio! Just about every sub-division was supplied with its own van, although some of the smaller, more remote sections still had to call upon one from another area if needed.

In all its forms, the Ford Transit was to play a major role in the policing of this country, from aforementioned section van to major motorway accident unit, from personnel carrier to mobile police station, it fulfilled every requirement. As such, it fully deserves to be recognised as one of the landmark vehicles.

This MK2 Ford Transit section van, call sign KS-99 is parked
outside the old Southsea Police Station.
Author

142

In February 1978, the crew of a traffic car in Basingstoke arrived for work one morning, to find that their beloved Rover 3500 V8 P6 had gone missing! PCs Neil Fox and Roy Williams drove HBK 875N, call sign M-3 everyday and had done since it was new. Despite numerous enquiries around the station they were unable to locate the car, until a phone call to Bar End revealed that it was there and that they wouldn't be getting it back. For reasons never disclosed, this car had been chosen for grander things. All its traffic kit was removed, as was the striping and anything resembling Police accessories and the car was shipped across to the island, where it was to replace Mountbatten's old Rover! The car had been fully valeted and looked magnificent. The Earl was not impressed though because the car was white. Official cars should be black! Therefore, the car was taken away and resprayed gloss black and became the second Hampshire Police vehicle to be used for the Royal visitor. But the cars new career was relatively short lived, because on 27th August 1979, the IRA committed one of its most heinous crimes in murdering the Earl, by placing a bomb aboard the boat he was sailing on in Ireland. Romsey and the Isle of Wight in particular were in mourning.

The Rover was eventually returned to Bar End in May 1980 and sold at auction. It has since resurfaced and has been returned back to its former traffic patrol glory, by an enthusiast (see Chapter 9).

Earl Mounbatten's Rover V8 HBK 875N has now been restored back to its original specification by Police vehicle enthusiast Terry Wells.
Christopher Taylor

Also in 1978, all traffic and area cars were fitted with a new item of equipment called the Coded Tone Generator (CTG) made by a company in Farlington, Portsmouth. This device was a small black box placed inside the cabin, with two knurled wheels, which revealed numbers when turned. The cars call sign was pre-programmed into the device and by turning the wheels to a set number, say 10-5 and by pressing an adjoining green button, a coded signal was sent to the Force Control Room at Winchester, that that unit had just arrived at an incident. This alleviated the need to use radio transmissions for minor messages. Hampshire had recently adopted the American Ten-Code radio system and the CTG was ideally suited to this form of radio language. There was an additional red button fitted, which if pressed, gave the crew a 30-second clear speech window. This meant that in the event that they were hijacked, they could alert control room of their situation without the need to pick up a handset. It was a brilliant idea in principle and was thankfully never truly put to the test. But, the red button was accidentally activated on many occasions and it was always a joy to listen to the officers concerned, who were usually in the process of talking about someone at the station! The CTG system lasted for about two years and was eventually removed, because they had proved to be unreliable.

Another item that was removed at this time was the two-tone horn from panda cars and section vans. This infuriated the frontline officers concerned, but they were reminded that these vehicles were never intended to be used as emergency response vehicles and as such didn't need audible warning devices. In a perfect world of course, this statement would have been true, but the fact is, in most city areas especially, two-tone horns were a definite advantage to all. Officers were left in the rather silly situation whereby they would have to constantly use the cars standard fit horn!

Elsewhere in the country things were changing. Other forces, who had watched Hampshire's commitment to buying foreign cars, if they were the best things available at the time, were now starting to realise that perhaps they were right after all. By the late 1970s the industrial situation was just as bad as it had been throughout the rest of the decade and in some instances, was actually worse. There were still unacceptable delays with vehicle and parts deliveries, with rising inflation and spiralling wage demands. By late 1978, Britain was in the depths of what later became known as 'the winter of discontent'. Fed up with the whole situation, other forces were now looking at foreign imports. Forces like Thames Valley, Derbyshire, West Mercia and even the City of London were seriously contemplating the wholesale purchase of BMW cars for their traffic fleets. Thames Valley actually became one of the first to do so and bought several BMW 2500 saloons in 1975 and were very pleased with the cars reliability. To really rub salt into the wound, Thames Valley infuriated the Home Office, by allowing one of its cars and a BMW motorcycle to be used in a glossy BMW advert, which stated *It takes one to catch one!*

After testing a BMW saloon for a month (see Chapter 8) Hampshire took the plunge and purchased four BMW 525s in early 1979. At the same time, the force decided to change the entire look and sound of its traffic fleet. But let us start with the car itself. The BMW came with a 2.5 litre, straight-six engine giving it a top speed of around 120 mph. Acceleration was good, once it was up and running and the cars handling was described as excellent. It was a quality built car, with excellent reliability and a spares back-up that would shame anything in the UK at that time. They really were an instant success and officers could be heard for miles around boasting of unheard of speeds and tales of heroic cornering antics! Their excitement was apparently, almost child like.

The BMW 525 parked in the car park at HQ Winchester.
Brian Homans

The cars were fitted out in an entirely new way. A large dome light was placed directly onto the roof, because the Police/Stop lights had now been placed in a smart new, boot mounted black spoiler. They were the fashion accessory of the late 1970s and early 1980s; Ford fitted rear spoilers to the Escort XR3i and the MK2 Granada, whilst the after market sales of such items reached new heights. Hampshire Police spoilers were manufactured in glass reinforced plastic by Ferrie Plastics. The idea behind using the spoiler was to give the car more down force at high speed and to help reduce wind resistance, by removing the roof box.

145

The all-new boot spoiler is shown to good effect here.
Hampshire Constabulary

The BMW was also decorated with a new side stripe in saturn yellow, bordered in blue. This new material was supposed to be more reflective than the orange and gave the cars a whole new look. Blue Police signs were positioned on the front doors, together with the Hampshire crest. But it was the new audible device that really gave the car its new identity. A Premier Hazard Tri-Sound system, gave it three distinctive sirens, with *wail, yelp* and electric *two-tone* sound. New York had arrived in Hampshire! The cars looked and sounded so futuristic, they were very different to anything that had been tried and tested in the past, that they became a talking point wherever they went. The American style sirens weren't to everyone's liking and letters were sent to various local newspapers deploring the hideous sound and whatever happened to the good old days when police cars were painted black and had bells fitted!

A LWB MK2 Ford Transit personnel carrier based at Fratton Police Station.
This is a later 1980 model.
Author

It wasn't all space age technology though, as there were rather more mundane items to be addressed, like the purchase of several MK2 Ford Transit long wheel base minibuses. These large scale personnel carriers were fitted with forward facing seats, capable of seating 12 officers, including the driver and were a lot more comfortable than being crushed in the back of a section van. Early models were fitted with a 2.0 litre engine and no power steering, making them rather slow and incredibly heavy at slow speed. A single blue light was mounted on the roof and a blue Police sign positioned across the leading edge of the bonnet.

Another major change took place in 1979 that was so low key, that hardly anyone noticed and nobody ever questioned. Fleet Manager John Roberts was under pressure to reduce costs and had to make cuts somewhere. In looking at the huge fleet of panda cars he concluded that having to order them in a special shade of blue obviously cost more. Then the force had to respray the doors white to produce the panda scheme and when it came to retiring the vehicle, the doors were repainted back to blue! Just painting and repainting the doors cost £80 per car! He therefore ordered plain white Escorts and Minis, sent them out as replacement panda cars and nobody said a word, not even at Headquarters! In one stroke of the pen the original panda concept was gone. Fleet Managers obviously talk to each other on a regular basis about various things and it wasn't long before other forces, under similar financial constraints, followed Hampshire's lead and abandoned the idea for good. But the name and in some respects, the concept lives on. Even in the late 1990s, young officer's who had never actually seen a real panda, still refer to their section cars as such! A year or so after the colour change was introduced, the vehicle call signs were changed and the word *panda* was dropped and replaced with the word *car* so that *panda 9* became *car 9*.

One of the early all white panda cars based at Fratton Police Station.
Author

Following on from the introduction of a new livery for the force's traffic fleet, some cars were recalled into Bar End to have the new graphics applied. This included a few of the now ageing Rover 3500 P6 saloons, Volvos, MK4 Ford Cortinas used as Traffic Supervisor's cars and the SD1 Rover.

Old car, new livery. This Rover V8 was based at Fareham.
John Prince

148

This Alton based Volvo 244 DL was one of the few Volvos to have
received the new yellow livery.
Geoff Cadman

By 1979 the Bedford HA vans used as rural section cars were rapidly coming to the end of their useful life and a replacement was necessary. There was no similar alternative to this vehicle, which had now gone out of production. The force therefore bought several MK2 Ford Escort estate cars and they were generally a lot more comfortable and easier to drive than the old Bedford. The 1100cc vehicles could reach 85mph in relative safety and were a better quality product all round. They were fitted with a single blue light and Police signs on the front doors. In keeping with the new policy of standardisation, they were all finished in white.

One of the MK2 Ford Escort estate vehicles used on rural beats.
This one is seen leaving the yard at Alton Police Station.
Geoff Cadman

In late 1979 Hampshire went one step further with the modernisation of the traffic fleet and experimented with an American style, full width light bar. The Federal Signals unit incorporated two revolving blue lights at each end of the bar, which reflected light through a series of mirrors, thus producing the effect of more lights. In the centre of the unit was the tri-sound siren, controlled via a box mounted inside the car. The overall effect was amazing, with crews experiencing much greater public awareness of their presence whilst engaged on an emergency call. Not only could they be heard with the new sirens, but now they could be seen as well. It was fitted to a Rover 3500 SD1 based at Eastleigh, which also got the new stripe treatment and boot spoiler used on the BMW, together with an illuminated Police sign placed along the leading edge of the bonnet. The only real problem with the Federal Signals light bar was the cost. In comparison with a single blue light set up, it was hideously expensive.

This unique Rover SD1 is seen with a Federal Signals light bar, boot spoiler and new livery.
Hampshire Constabulary

This excellent photo shows the interior of the same Rover SD1 with all its associated equipment. On the far left of the dash is the force VHF radio (Pye Whitehall model), whilst in the centre of the console is the Federal Signals light and sound system. Below that is the CTG unit and just in front of that the VASCAR unit. Note also that the calibrated speedo, incorporated into a special binnacle to the left of the main instrument panel.
Hampshire Constabulary

Fareham Traffic Section circa 1979/80 showing a newer style BMW R100RT complete with BMW fairing and twin blue lights. A BMW 525 sits next to it, together with a Volvo 244 GLT and a Range Rover, all sporting the new saturn yellow livery.
John Prince

Volvo, worried by Police interest in BMWs, hit back with the introduction of an updated model, the 244 GLT. They used Hampshire as a test bed for the new car, giving the force three of the new cars, more than a year before they were released onto the public. The engine size had been increased to 2.3 litre and now came with fuel injection, a better four speed gearbox with overdrive, uprated sports suspension and low profile Pirelli tyres on smart looking, five spoke alloy wheels. It worked and the GLT gained instant cult status in Hampshire. It was quick, handled well and matched the BMW 525 in just about every department.

They were fitted with a Ferrie Plastics triangular roof box and single blue light, yellow livery and a Premier Hazard Tri-Sound siren system. Within a matter of weeks, several more GLTs were added to the traffic fleet and two more were sent to the force driving school. Using the force as a test bed for its product was a clever marketing ploy by Volvo and undoubtedly helped when it came to selling the car to the public.

One of the new GLTs then got the American treatment and was fitted with a Federal Signals light bar and tri-sound siren system, together with a boot spoiler. It has to rate as the best looking Volvo patrol car to date and the officer's at Petersfield Traffic Section would probably agree.

The Petersfield Volvo 244 GLT, call sign J-05 looks good in its new outfit.
Derek Bampton

This particular car gained local celebrity status and was pictured in the Portsmouth News as *Kojak's car*. But its sound has been captured forever on a BBC LP record called *Sound Effects No.25 The Sounds of Speed* (REC 390 or cassette ZCM 390). PC Derek Bampton was tasked with spending the day out with a BBC sound crew, driving up and down the new A3M motorway, with the cars sirens on, whilst they recorded the sound from inside and outside the car. You can clearly hear that the car is definitely a Volvo 244, especially in the sequence where the engine is started and the car roars off with its siren on! During the tracks that state the car is passing from right to left, I am reliably informed, that the Volvo was in fact flat out at 115 mph. The record includes other modes of transport considered new or innovative in the late 1970s, like Concorde, an SRN4 hovercraft, the QE2 and a Harrier jump jet. Sadly, the record sleeve doesn't show YOW 24V and only describes it on the record label as a Police car.

The BBC record 'The Sounds of Speed' featuring the Petersfield Volvo 244 GLT.
Derek Bampton

Given the fuel problems experienced in the early 1970s and further petrol shortages in 1979 during a strike by petrol tanker drivers, the force looked for alternative ideas. A Ford Escort was fitted out to test liquid propane gas and an additional tank placed in the boot of the car. Little more is known about the tests, other than at this stage in time, it didn't work out.

At the turn of the decade, the force fleet stood at 853 vehicles, covering a staggering 13 million miles a year.

CHAPTER 6

HAMPSHIRE CONSTABULARY 1980 TO 1989

Hampshire Constabulary senior officers helmet plate

Ⅰf the 1970s is to go down in history as a time of industrial strife, then the 1980s will be seen as a period of great change, increased wealth and a more productive home grown market. The country elected Margaret Thatcher as it's first woman Prime Minister in June 1979 and she took on the unions and, some would say, almost defeated them single-handed!

This in turn led to many more industrial disputes as The Government faced up to the problems of the past and this culminated in the year long miners strike of 1984/5, where Police units from all over the country were sent to police the *flying pickets* in Nottinghamshire, Yorkshire, Derbyshire, North Wales and Kent. But it wasn't just industrial action that was the problem. Rioting in our towns and cities, on a scale never seen before, affected places like Bristol, Brixton, Toxteth, Birmingham, Tottenham and Wapping. Football violence was at an all time high and there were numerous other large public disorder situations to deal with; CND marches, National Front and anti-racist demonstrations, the Poll Tax riots and just over the Hampshire border, the Greenham Common *peace women* were at war outside the American cruise missile base. Hampshire became heavily involved in this situation and the Traffic Division in particular, were used to escort these missiles out onto Salisbury Plain, in night-time manoeuvres code named *Operation Roger*. New Age Travellers, or NATs as they became known, plagued Hampshire and its neighbouring counties in the late 1980s and these to were often violent confrontations. One episode in particular became known as the *Battle of the Beanfield* where hippies and Police charged at each other in a field using derelict coaches and Police Transit vans as battering rams!

All this unrest of course had to be policed and Hampshire sent units to Nottingham,

Liverpool, Birmingham and the Thames Valley. Large convoys of Police Transit vans could be seen, almost on a weekly basis, snaking their way across the countryside, to the next trouble spot. As will become clear, vehicles had to be adapted to cater for every eventuality.

In Hampshire the best news at the turn of the decade centred on the brand new workshop facilities opened at the Wallington Industrial Estate at Fareham. This purpose built facility for the south east of the county replaced the out dated wooden garages used at Portsmouth. Staff recruitment increased and morale amongst existing staff was never better. The bad news concerned a burglary at the Bar End workshops in late 1989, where the forces latest computer hardware was stolen. With it went all the computerised vehicle records for the previous ten years and much of the authors research facts have had to come from other sources, some of which perhaps, might not be as mathematically detailed as before.

The force purchased a LWB Landrover in late 1979 to use almost exclusively to tow a Trident mobile lighting unit. This large and very heavy generator on wheels was equipped with a 20 feet high mast containing floodlights that could be used at the scene of a major incident, or more usually a fatal car accident. From around 1980 onwards this unit was kept at Headquarters in Winchester and would be taken to the scene by a member of the control room staff, in the same way that the large control unit would be utilised.

Landrover and lighting unit seen in the car park at Headquarters.
Kevin Angus.

However it did have another use in that it powered a new mobile catering unit. The old Transit chassis really wasn't up to the job and in early 1980 a Ford A Series cab and chassis was purchased. The bodywork conversion was carried out by Gowrings MVC Ltd of Westbury, Wiltshire and they built the unit around new propane gas fuelled Blodgett ovens, which were much better than the old electric ones. The unit also incorporated a constant hot water boiler, an Electrolux electric refrigerator, fluorescent strip lighting and decent ventilation fans. It could still feed up to 200 officers at a time and the unit was kept at HQ next to the mobile lighting unit. It is unclear exactly how long it was kept for but possibly by 1984 it was no longer in use.

The 'force-feeder' as it became known served up hundreds of meals at operations all over the two counties
Hampshire Constabulary

Ford launched the all-new, front wheel drive Ford Escort in 1980. Three door hatchbacks were purchased for CID use and three door estate versions were obtained as panda cars, or section vehicles as they were now officially known. These 1.1 engined cars were completely different to the old MK2 they replaced. They were quicker, had better handling and were a lot more comfortable. Each section car was fitted with a new style Wadhams roof box with blue light and Police signs on the front doors. Estate versions were chosen because of their versatility. For a couple of years, rural sections had been using the MK2 estate and they proved invaluable in the transportation of things like stolen bicycles and other large objects back to the station, so the concept was transferred to all sections.

A MK3 Ford Escort estate, call sign 'Car 10' parked outside the old Southsea Police Station.
Author

With the purchase of the new Escort came further standardisation of the vehicle fleet and the Mini was phased out in favour of the Ford. The Mini had served the force brilliantly and many mourned its passing.

The Traffic Division took delivery of something almost as politically dangerous as using foreign cars in the shape of an unmarked traffic patrol car. A MK2 Ford Granada 2.8L, finished in Sahara beige, registration number OEL 569W was passed around the various Traffic sections on a monthly basis, so that the locals didn't get to know it too well. The idea was for the car to be used only to apprehend the very worst of drivers, especially on the motorway. It was fitted with Vascar and a calibrated speedometer, two-tone horns and flashing headlamps. A single blue light on a flexible lead and with a magnetic base, would be placed on the roof by the observer in the event of stopping someone or when at the scene of an incident. But perhaps the strangest device it carried was the illuminated Police/Stop sign, which was placed face down on the rear parcel shelf. It was located in a hinged bracket and when it was required to be used, the observer would pull a piece of string on the dashboard and through a series of pulley's, set into the roof lining, the sign would be raised into position! Despite all the modern technology of the time, a system first employed by the old Southampton Mobile Patrol was still being used in the 1980s. There were those who voiced their displeasure at such 'sneaky tactics' and 'unfair methods of policing' and several vociferous letters were sent to the Chief Constable and various local newspapers, deploring the idea. But the concept proved its worth and many errant drivers were caught and successfully prosecuted for serious road traffic offences.

The first unmarked Traffic car was this MK2 Ford Granada
which had the local letter-writers up in arms
Mick Payne

Two Austin Allegro 1100 saloons were purchased at a vastly reduced rate and used as section cars at Eastleigh and Bitterne. The Allegro was already the butt of many jokes throughout the car industry, but the two cars used in Hampshire fared well against the opposition and lasted the course of their service. They were finished in white and equipped in the same way as all the other force section vehicles. No photographs exist.

Towards the end of 1980, moves were put into place to provide Hampshire with some kind of air support. This was not the first time this type of proposition had been aired, indeed we can go back to 1967, when the force trialled a Bell G4 Sioux helicopter, borrowed from the Army (see Chapter 8). Between these two periods, the force would hire military aircraft for use on special operations, but from now on Hampshire had authority from the Home Office to hire civilian fixed wing aircraft, for pre-planned operations and photographic surveillance tasks. Various aircraft were used, including Cessna 172s and 175s, which had high wings, thus making a better observation platform than most aircraft. Such was the success and demand for air support, for prisoner and high value load escorts, that a more regular service needed to be instigated and the Air Support Unit, as it became known, began to use a Cessna 175 from an airstrip at Chilbolton. The unit played an important policing role, flying frequent search tasks for serious crimes and missing persons on a call out basis. This obviously meant that a quick response facility for immediate tasks could not be provided. By 1981 a purpose-built airband radio was installed in the force control room.

It was supplied by the Home Office Directorate of Telecommunications and it cured the communications problems that had bedevilled the full use of the aircraft until now. The fixed wing option also proved to be far more economical than hiring a helicopter.

Public disorder though was starting to become a major problem and Hampshire responded by purchasing enough Ford Transit personnel carriers to boost the fleet to 45 such vehicles. A fledgling operational support unit (called the Rural Support Group or RSG) was formed, to send anywhere within the county, using the Transit minibus as its mode of transport. These officers were drawn from the force's 74 traffic motorcyclists and were chosen not because of their prowess whilst under fire, but because they were the only one's already issued with protective headgear; their crash helmets!

By 1981 Volvo was still dominating the area car sections within the force and they were about to launch something quite unique. In May 1981, Hampshire took delivery of a batch of Volvo 244s, built to Swedish Police specification and labelled as the 240 Police Special. The car's credentials were as follows; a 2.3 litre fuel injected engine, four speed manual gearbox with electric overdrive on fourth. A completely revised interior included an all vinyl rear seat, to allow for easy cleaning of blood or vomit, two-part vinyl and velour front seats and a rubber compound floor covering in replacement of the standard carpet. The exterior came with the all black body mouldings found on the GLT, but the five spoke alloys familiar to that model, were replaced by more orthodox steel units. The speedometer read mph only and wasn't a combined mph/kph unit and the badge on the boot simply read 240. The usual items like stronger alternator and wiring for emergency lighting of course were also included. These were very special cars indeed and offered for the first time ever, from any manufacturer selling to the UK market, a purpose built Police patrol car and not a modified off the shelf unit.

The car was capable of 112 mph, with a good turn of acceleration. They handled well for a big car and they remained as safe and reliable as ever. Each car was fitted with a triangular roof box and blue light, two-tone horns, flashing headlights, a calibrated speedo, VHF radio and a UHF radio booster, together with a CTG unit. A neat touch from Bar End workshops was the provision of five purple rocker switches, placed in the standard switches area, for the operation of the horns and lights. They were made to look like standard Volvo fitments and made the drilling of holes in the dash unnecessary. The 240 PS was a huge success as an area car and the crews loved them. So too did the force, with the average mileage on most topping 160,000 with excellent resale values being had at auction.

*A Volvo 240 Police Special area car. This Southsea based unit had the
call sign KS-51 and is seen parked at Eastney, overlooking Langstone Harbour.
Author*

Another unique Volvo arrived in late 1981 and appears to have been put together from the spares box! Two Volvo 264 saloons were acquired, with a 2.7 litre fuel injected V6 engine, borrowed from the Renault 25. They were fitted with a manual four-speed gearbox with overdrive, cloth seats, wind-up windows and the five spoke alloy wheels from the 240 GLT. Aficionados of the marque will quickly recognise the differences and these cars were a small attempt at seeing if the 264 could oust the BMW from its roost as the number one choice of the Traffic Division. Despite the fact that the two cars were well received, they failed to out perform the German car. The cars were striped up in the yellow livery and were fitted with a boot spoiler. On the roof came a twin blue light set up that was devised at Bar End. A new European Union directive required all emergency service vehicles to be fitted with at least two blue lights. The force had already trialled the Federal Signals unit and although it was very effective, it was incredibly expensive and the prospect of having to equip all of Hampshire's traffic and area cars with one would probably have sent the Counties rates through the roof! Public spending, under the new Conservative Government, was also being squeezed dry, so an alternative had to be found. .

The Aldershot based Volvo 264 DL with new style 'home-made' blue light system.
Mick Payne

The staff at Bar End found the answer. Standard bolt on roof racks, made by Thule in Sweden, were purchased for £10 a pair. Two Lucas LBB256K blue lights were then fixed onto one of the racks and this was then locked onto the roof rail! Problem solved and at a fraction of the cost of a purpose built unit. The 264s were posted to Aldershot and Alton Traffic Sections

Did You Know That........?
Volvo issued workshops with a special two-part spray to put onto the five spoke alloy wheels to locate any cracks in them. If there were cracks they showed up as luminous pink lines!

The old Bedford S Type Control Unit was now due replacement and a purpose built Ford 0610 A Series Custom with four-wheel drive took its place. This Headquarters based Mobile Control Unit came with a diesel engine and was fitted with a Dale stem light, similar to that used on the Range Rover. The Luton bodied vehicle was converted into a mobile control room, probably by a local firm. An awning was positioned on the nearside of the vehicle to facilitate extra cover in times of need and the white bodywork was decorated with blue and white chequers along the top edge. Police signs and the force crest completed the package. The vehicle was based at Headquarters so that in the event of a major incident occurring anywhere in the county, one of the control room staff would leave his post and drive directly to it. Although the vehicle fulfilled its role, the four-wheel drive system proved to be anything but reliable and it spent a great deal of its time at workshops being repaired.

*The Ford A Series Mobile Control Unit seen parked on the playing fields
of the old Cadet Training School at Bishops Waltham.
Hampshire Constabulary.*

*The Mobile Control Unit with awning in position.
Hampshire Constabulary.*

*The interior of the same vehicle, prior to it being fitted
with its radio communications equipment.
Hampshire Constabulary*

For some reason the Isle of Wight always seems to get different vehicles and late 1981 was no exception when they were handed another oddball car in the shape of a standard specification Volvo 240 GLT. Unlike the mainland units, which were 240 Police Specials, this model was an off the shelf GLT model, complete with five-spoke alloy wheels, electric windows and velour upholstery. It was kitted out in a different manner as well, with a return to the red and blue striping of the past. The experiment using yellow was deemed to be a failure, especially during bright conditions where it was difficult to see. One of the Thule light bars was used, but because the large black boot spoilers were quite expensive to produce it was decided to look for a cheaper alternative. Ferrie Plastics came up with a white fibreglass rectangular box to place the illuminated Police/Stop signs in. This was then positioned on the trailing edge of the boot lid and worked very well. One or two other GLT models did find their way to mainland stations including Andover.

*The Isle of Wight Volvo 240 GLT of 1981 resplendent in its new livery,
complete with boot box and alloy wheels.
Ron Flatman*

By 1982 competition for the rights to become Hampshire's number one choice traffic car was hotting up. Rover was first with a revamped Series 2 SD1, called the 3500 SE V8, it featured revised styling, with deeper rear window, big frontal air dam, power assisted steering, fuel injection, alloy wheels and a completely new interior. Build quality was at last improving, but they still had a long way to go in terms of reliability, compared with the foreign imports. Recurring problems with gearboxes and water pumps was no longer acceptable and despite the fact that the car looked terrific, it wasn't too long before it made more enemies than friends. The new Rover was given a Thule light bar, Ferrie Plastics boot spoiler, red and blue livery, with an additional blue and white chequered band underneath, tri-sound siren and all the other standard issue traffic patrol equipment. It was now a faster car at 125 mph, with better handling and a more comfortable ride and Hampshire was still getting pressure from the Home Office to buy British and to drop its foreign car policy. In return the force continued to state that it would buy the best car available to do the job at that time.

Three Rover 2600 SD1s were also purchased as Traffic Supervisory units, to replace the old MK4 Ford Cortinas. These straight-six engined cars were also borrowed from time to time by night shift area car crews, when their cars were off the road for servicing or repairs. Each car was equipped the same as any other traffic patrol car. No photos appear to have survived.

BMW of course was the other contender and it launched the new 528i in 1982. Traffic officers had grown to love the 525 model for all its virtues, even if the acceleration failed to match the big Rover, its overall performance was that much better. The new 528i was to make the choice even easier. With a top speed of 135 mph and acceleration to out do the Rover it won hands down every time. An initial batch of six were purchased and this was followed by another six later in the year. They were fitted with a Thule light bar and a Ferrie Plastics boot spoiler, together with all the necessary traffic patrol equipment. But it wasn't all sweetness and light. The all vinyl seats made working in the summer months a very uncomfortable experience compared to the luxurious velour Rover seating. The BMWs biggest problem though centred around its brakes, or rather a lack of them! Like all traffic cars it had to be driven at high speeds almost every day and when the time came for some heavy braking, the brakes would fade very quickly and the driver concerned would be left in a state of shock. After several reports of this happening to a number of the cars they were all grounded for safety checks to be carried out. Workshops were not able to ascertain the problem and BMW were called in to sort it out. It took them three months to discover that the brake fluid was evaporating in the high temperatures being created at very high speed and a new silicone fluid was used, which alleviated the problem.

A Series 2 Rover 3500 SE V8 of the Petersfield Traffic Section. PC Derek Bampton is seen posing with his car and a Chinook helicopter that had crash-landed in a nearby field.
Derek Bampton.

164

But 1982 was also a tragic year for Hampshire when two of its Traffic officers were killed in a horrific accident that was to have serious repercussions for years to come. PCs Ken Adams and Paul Salmon of Fareham Traffic, died when their Range Rover overturned near Bishops Waltham on the 17th September.

Although a replacement vehicle arrived nobody in the south of the county in particular would drive it. An internal role cage was fitted to prevent a roof collapse in the event of a similar accident, but still the officers refused to touch it. To prevent any further upset, Range Rovers were only issued to northern Traffic areas at Andover and Whitchurch. It would be many years before they were seen again in the south.

The newer Range Rover was still a 3.5 V8 unit, but now came with four doors, power assisted steering and a better interior. A Dale stem light was fitted, together with a special Ferrie Plastics rear spoiler that was positioned above the tailgate. It housed two additional blue strobe lights to match those placed in the front grille.

New four-door Range Rover seen at Fareham workshops prior to having its roll cage fitted.
Author

A BMW 528i showing its rear spoiler to good effect.
Author.

Workshops obtained the services of a new Landrover recovery vehicle to enable them to go out and pick up broken down Police vehicles. The long wheelbase, 3.5 V8 4x4 vehicles, fitted with a Harvey Frost crane on the rear bed were restricted to giving front suspended tows only. Anything else more complicated was usually put out to a private contract garage in the area. The Landrover was given orange and blue striping together with the force crest. A Thule light bar was attached with two orange and one blue light attached. No-where on the vehicle did it state that it was a Police vehicle, although it was obvious to anyone who saw it.

Landrover recovery unit at Fareham workshops

The Traffic Division was devolved in late 1982, following recommendations put forward by the Force Review Team and Traffic officers were integrated into territorial sub-divisions with effect from the 1st January 1983. This was to coincide with the new force divisional boundaries being reduced to just four on the mainland, Northern, Western, Eastern and Mid Hants.

Further monetary constraints resulted in the closure of the force driving school at Hulse Road. Advanced and Standard driving courses were now taken at Maidstone in Kent, with only Improver car courses and lightweight motorcycle courses being held on a local basis. The driving school cars were dispatched to Bar End where they were kitted out and used as operational vehicles.

Also in early 1983, the vehicle workshops at Hulse Road were closed down and the work was divided between Bar End and Fareham. This was done for two reasons; the old workshops were too cramped and new facilities could not be found and more importantly, money could be saved, by farming the work out to the other two workshops.

Because of the stringent financial situation that Hampshire found itself in, the vehicle replacement program came to a virtual standstill, with all departments having to make do with what they had got for the time being, except for one new purchase for the boys on Traffic. Still haunted by the *Buy British* brigade, the force went out and purchased 16 brand new Jaguars, 15 for Traffic and a dark green model for the Chief Constable.

The Series 3 Jaguar XJ6 4.2i Police Special was a full frontal effort by Jaguar at storming onto the now recognised lucrative Police vehicle market. The force had evaluated a Jaguar the year before (see Chapter 8) and following the recommendations of those that tested it, the 16 cars were placed on order. The test car came with an automatic gearbox, sports suspension and handling pack. The purchased cars arrived with a manual gearbox taken from the Rover 2600 SD1 and standard fit Jaguar limousine suspension! Instead of sending them straight back to Coventry, Hampshire stayed quiet and kept them.

The cars were fitted with the latest thing in blue light technology, the Federal Signals Jet Sonic light bar, tri-sound siren system and a colour coded, white boot spoiler again made by Ferrie Plastics in Blackpool. With smart red and blue graphics and the force crest applied to the doors they looked really impressive. They had what few patrol cars could ever really achieve; presence. If you got stopped by a Traffic man in a Jag, you knew you were in trouble! But sadly, it was all a bit of a façade. The average life of the gearbox was 30,000 miles, with reverse gear being the main cause of problems. Legend has it that one of the cars didn't even make it off the low loader on arrival at Bar End, because the gearbox had seized! But the biggest complaint centred on the cars handling characteristics, which were fine in a straight line on the motorway, but take it off *the strip* and onto anything resembling a bend and it was easier to steer the QE2 up Southampton Water! Unlike the test car, which could be hustled along the twisty bits with comparative ease, the 130 mph production model Police Special, had to be slowed down considerably before entering any bends. Pursuits around towns and housing estates were definitely out of the question.

The Jaguar though attained instant cult status, both inside and outside the force, you either loved them or loathed them. The Fleet Manager, Mr John Roberts wasn't impressed and at the Police Fleet Managers Conference at Devizes the following year is reputed to have marched onto the Jaguar stand and in full and uncompromising voice, told the Jaguar executives exactly what he thought of their product! He was eventually led away by colleagues, still pointing an accusing finger at them!

Did You Know That........?
The Jaguar had a strange trait in hot weather. Shortly after being parked it would dump all its fuel from its twin tanks, because a venting valve had not been fitted! Much embarrassment was caused when the Fire Service had to attend to wash the road down!

The Jaguar XJ6 4.2i Police Special seen at Fareham workshops, where many of them seemed to spend their time! You can't argue about its good looks though.
Author.

A turning point for the future of the Air Support Unit came in 1983. It was at this time that attention was focused on the Edgeley Optica, which was being built at Old Sarum airfield near Salisbury in Wiltshire. This strange looking aircraft looked like a cross between a fixed wing plane and a helicopter, but had obvious applications for Police use, given its large glass observation area. In brief, the Home Office agreed to assist in a trial of the aircraft and it was decided that Hampshire, which already had the expertise in fixed wing flying and a ready source of crews for such a venture, should be selected for evaluation trials. Hampshire worked closely with the manufacturers and took part in several flights to test the feasibility of using such an aircraft for Police duties. It would be another 18 months before a completed aircraft was ready for service though.

The year 1984 of course will be forever remembered because of the national miner's strike. Hundreds of Hampshire officers were transported north to the coalfields of Nottinghamshire, Derbyshire, Kent and North Wales. Initially they were taken there by coach and in convoys of Transit minibuses, which was a long and tedious journey, especially at the end of the week when everyone was tired. The Chief Constable Mr John Duke and his team then hit on the brilliant idea of flying everyone up to the Midlands. This was not only a novel time saving idea, but the concept actually saved the force thousands of pounds in overtime and fuel costs. Officers would arrive at Southampton's Eastleigh airport, where they would board Boeing 727s belonging to either Orion Air or Brittania Airways and take the 18 minute flight, north to the East Midlands airport in Nottingham. There they would exchange their aircraft for the Transit minibus, which had been left up there from the previous week and take the short journey to their accommodation. The whole process would take little more than one hour, in comparison to the previous four or five hours and was especially welcome on the Friday

168

afternoon. This mode of transport albeit a temporary one, made national headlines for a while and an excellent cartoon even appeared in The Standard.

Cartoon courtesy of The Standard.
Author's collection

Hampshire officers board an Orion Airways Boeing 727 at Eastleigh Airport
on route to the coalfields of Nottinghamshire.
Hampshire Constabulary

Additional personnel carrying ability was urgently required because of the miner's strike and other commitments. The force therefore purchased a second hand, 52-seat coach. It got a lot of use for the next few years, but quickly gained a reputation for being slow and somewhat unreliable. The only form of identification applied was the force crest placed on either side.

The force was desperately short of personnel carrying capability, even with the addition of the extra Transit carriers and now the Ford coach. With all the additional public disorder situations being thrust upon the Police nationwide there was actually a shortage of new Transit carriers available and trying to hire a minibus was almost impossible! However, a company in the Midlands did lease a number of green and white Volkswagen T4 minibuses to Hampshire, on a long-term contract, which did relieve the situation slightly. This allowed for the servicing and repair of the forces own vehicles, which were now covering very high mileages on a weekly basis. The VW buses were actually very well liked and were found to be easy and comfortable to drive and live with.

The Force coach, a 52-seater Ford.
Author.

Ford also updated the Transit range at this time and Hampshire purchased a number of long wheel base personnel carriers to replace existing stock, which had come to the end of their useful life. These new carriers came with a 3.0 litre V6 engine and power assisted steering, which made life a whole lot easier. Bar End then fitted a single blue roof light and twin repeater lights in the front grille. Following lessons learned by the Metropolitan Police during the bitter dispute at Wapping, where at least two officers' sustained serious injuries after spiked metal railings pierced the side of their personnel carriers, Bar End took measures to protect the occupants of Hampshire's vans. Additional inner panels made from polycarbonate were riveted into place, whilst all the side and rear glass was removed and replaced with

Perspex. The headlights got Perspex covers to. Two-tone horns were now added and the force crest applied to the front doors to aid identification amongst the hundreds of different Transits that descended on Nottinghamshire. A system called *em-bussing* and *de-bussing* was implemented to facilitate a quick and orderly method of entry and exit from the carrier. It was rehearsed time and again, until everyone could do it with their eyes shut.

One of the new style Transit carriers introduced in 1984. This photo
was taken in the West Midlands, during the 1985 riots in Birmingham.
Author.

In a continuing effort to achieve economies in running costs, a comprehensive range of specially designed lightweight equipment was issued to Traffic and area cars. The equipment included new lightweight, triangular frames made from hollow tubing, instead of the old angle iron items, for the positioning of advance warning signs, also made from a lighter material. New traffic cones, folding plastic shovels, collapsible hand brooms and reinforced towropes, all helped reduce the overall weight of the patrol cars and thus saved fuel.

A mobile communications unit was another new type of vehicle to be used by Hampshire in 1984. A short wheelbase MK2 Ford Transit van with a 2.0 litre engine and four-wheel drive, by County Conversions of Powys, carried a whole host of communications equipment, to assist at major operations. It was especially useful at Greenham Common, where difficulties in transmission meant that the unit was particularly useful. The four-wheel drive system allowed it to travel off road and this again was a bonus in that area. The vehicle was later fitted with an additional front bumper to allow it to push obstacles out of its path whilst engaged on *Operation Roger*. Protesters would quite often attempt to block the vehicles path using a variety of methods and the extra bumper came in handy.

171

Mobile Communications Unit using a MK2 Ford Transit County 4x4.
P.M. Photography

The Dog Section got slightly upgraded vehicles when Ford produced a van version of its acclaimed MK3 Escort. As with the car, the van was faster and a lot more comfortable for both man and dog. They were fitted with single blue light, two-tone horns and a Police/Stop sign similar to that used on area cars. The force crest and Police labels completed the picture. Inside the rear of the van it was fitted with a cage, sometimes twin cages and all the necessary comforts to ensure that the canine unit was comfortable whilst on duty.

A Portsmouth based Dog Section MK3 Ford Escort Van.
Author.

In early 1985 Volvo upgraded the 240 PS and area cars now got power assisted steering, central locking and electric front windows as standard. They were fitted with a Thule light bar, boot lid Police/Stop box and the usual array of emergency equipment. This new look to Hampshire's area cars was to stay for many years to come and they became a familiar Hampshire trademark. The 240 PS really was ideally suited to emergency response work and it remains a mystery why no other forces in the UK ever tried them. Maybe it was the rather unfair *tank* label given to it by factions of the motoring press that put off prospective Police customers with the thought that it wasn't up to the job on performance grounds. Or maybe it was just the politics involved that put them off.

Did You Know That........?
A packet of twenty cigarettes would snap perfectly into place on the dashboard shelf of the Volvo 240 PS and would stay there no matter what the car was doing!

A new model Volvo 240 PS showing its boot spoiler to good effect.
This Southsea based area car had the call sign KS-51
and is seen parked at Eastney.
Author.

A number of Volvo 240 PS models were also liveried as traffic patrol cars and these were to become Traffic Supervisory units, in replacement for the Rover 2.6 SD1s and were occasionally used as spare patrol cars when standard traffic cars were being serviced.

*This brand new Traffic Supervisory Volvo 240 PS was written off
in an accident only days after it went into service.
Author.*

Three more long wheel base MK2 Ford Transit vans were purchased in 1985 and these were converted into secure prisoner transportation units and were fitted with three separate cells. The vans themselves were 3.0 V6 models with power assisted steering. They would be used at all football matches and other public disorder situations, where prisoners could be placed in a secure singular cell for some considerable time, until the situation was either over or the van full up, in which case it would then travel to the nearest bridewell. It was also used to transport prisoners from the court cells to and from remand prisons, with an escorting officer sat in a special dickey seat between the cells and the cab.

*Eastern Division MK2 Ford Transit prison van parked outside
the old Southsea Police Station in Victoria Road South.*

The Range Rover was also updated at this time and now came with a 3.9 EFi V8 engine, better suspension set up and a slightly revised interior. It was fitted out exactly the same way as the previous model, including the internal role cage. Feelings in the south of the county were still running high concerning the vehicles safety and only two Range Rovers were issued to Andover and Whitchurch sections.

*Range Rover 3.9 EFi parked
outside Winchester
Headquarters.
Hampshire Constabulary*

On the 14th May 1985, the Hampshire Constabulary's Air Support Unit at last got its own aircraft. Amongst large press coverage, the Edgeley Optica was officially handed over at a ceremony at the units new home, the HMS Daedalus airfield at Lee-on-Solent. The Optica was a strange looking aircraft and when airborne produced a very high pitched whining noise, akin to a large wasp!

Within 24 hours of that ceremony, the euphoria was replaced by tragedy. Whilst engaged on a routine photographic task over Ringwood, the aircraft crashed into the woods beside the A31, killing the two crew PC Gerald Spencer and DC Malcolm Wiltshire. The subsequent investigation by the Air Accident Investigation Board failed to find a definitive explanation for the crash. Within a month of the accident, the ASU was back at Chilbolton using a borrowed Cessna 175 for routine work.

An EU ruling in 1986 made a requirement that the emergency lighting on motorway patrol vehicles had to meet certain standards including the fitment of rearward facing, flashing red lights. Hampshire looked at several different types of lighting and eventually settled on the Olympic model, made by Premier Hazard. This full width light bar came with a clear lens and contained two revolving blue lights at each end, passing through a series of mirrors. In-between the blue lights came the red rotating lights and at the front, either side of the illuminated Police sign, were two white spotlights. This lighting system could perform several different functions, including all six lights being operated through 360 degrees, the red lights only, the blue lights only at the rear or the blue lights only to the front. It was operated via two switches on the dash, a master switch and a three-way rocker switch. This system gave the Traffic patrol car a whole new look and various lighting options depending on the circumstances.

A BMW 528i complete with new style Premier Hazard light bar is photographed on Portsdown Hill, overlooking Portsmouth in 1987. The car is a Cosham based unit with the call sign CM-07. Author.

Did You Know That.........?
All the BMW 528i's suffered from dirty rear ends! The area above the exhaust pipe would turn brown and stain the paintwork as high up as the boot lid. The only way to get it off was to use an abrasive cleaner called Vim and plenty of elbow grease!

The MK3 Ford Transit was launched in 1986 and it wasn't long of course before Police forces across the land were buying them by the bucket load, Hampshire included. The MK3 Tranny was even more car like than some cars, it was reasonably quick, handled better than its predecessor and was actually good fun to drive.

In section van mode it came with a 2.0 litre engine and a five-speed gearbox. The all important rear section was caged as in previous models, with the addition of a Perspex screen between the back of the drivers head and the cage to prevent some of the nastier clients spitting at the driver! Outside, the new vans got two blue roof lights and some got twin repeater lights set into the grille. Police signs and the Hampshire crest adorned the front half of the vehicle, whilst on the rear doors a red Police sign was now attached.

The sleeker looking MK3 Ford Transit section van.
This was the new addition to Fareham station
and had the call sign HF-99.
Pete Forster.

The force crest was also modified at this time, with the Latin word *Com Southton* being dropped and the word *Hampshire* now placed inside the scroll. Most marked vehicles, except section cars, would now carry the Hampshire crest.

The new style Hampshire door crest.
Author.

In a move to cut costs and to provide a more professional service, the idea of sub-contracting Police vehicle recovery out to local garages, if anything more than a suspended tow was required was dropped and the force bought its own specialist recovery units. A Ford Cargo cab with a flat bed and electric winch enabled all recoveries to be carried out by workshops staff on a 24-hour basis. The vehicle was decorated in the force livery and had a Premier Hazard light bar containing orange lenses placed on the roof. The force crest was placed on the doors and the word *Recovery* was labelled, in reverse across the front of the cab. Given the size of Hampshire's vehicle fleet it should come as no surprise to learn that these units were utilised every day.

The Ford Cargo recovery unit based at Fareham workshops. Author.

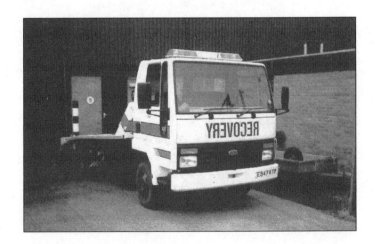

By mid 1987 there were calls from within the force that the Volvo 240 was too big a car to be used as an area car in the cities. There were those who considered that a smaller car would be more responsive, easier to manoeuvre and turn around in tight side streets. It has to be said that those who appeared to be doing all the talking had either never been an area car driver or had never driven the 240, or both. Rumours abounded of Ford Escort XR3i or Vauxhall Astra GTEs being used. What finally arrived both shocked and angered those that had to drive the new issue 'city area cars'. The Volvo 360 GLEi came with a smaller 2.0 litre engine, no power steering and handling that could best be described as vague! The package made a complete mockery of the idea that a smaller car would be easier to use in urban areas. It was, quite simply, an old mans car, with performance to match. Top speed was a measly 100 mph and MK3 Escort section cars could out-accelerate it! Stations like Southsea, Shirley, Southampton Central and Bitterne were all subjected to this change in policy and the complaints soon started rolling in. Each time the car went in for service or repair and a workshop spare 240 was issued, it would often be a long time before it was returned! Each car was equipped in the same manner as all area cars and following the experiment, no further 360s were ordered. Hampshire remains the only Police force in the world to have tried the Volvo 360 GLEi saloon. Plenty of European forces like the Dutch tried the smaller engined 340 series as a general patrol car, but no one else ever tried using it as an emergency response unit!

The Volvo 360 GLEi area car belonging to Southsea, call sign VS-50
was not a popular vehicle to drive.
Author

Public order situations, both in and out of the county continued to give cause for concern and Hampshire found itself buying more and more personnel carriers. The new long wheel base MK3 Ford Transit buses were obvious replacements for the earlier models and an opportunity was seen to give increased protection to the vehicles occupants. Having seen the multi-grilled carriers used by other forces, Hampshire followed suit and incorporated retractable windscreen grilles and front bull-bars onto three of its new Transits. These new protective shields gave the carriers a purposeful, if somewhat aggressive look. It wasn't to everyone's taste, including the Chief Constable and some members of the Police Authority, who voiced concern that perhaps the good folk of Hampshire weren't quite ready for this type of policing! After a year or so the grilles were removed, but not because of disapproval from upon high, but because of lessons learned elsewhere in the country, where the latest *game* amongst rioters, was to hang incendiary devices from the grille in front of the driver's face!

Hampshire's new units came with a 2.9 fuel injected V6 engine, twin blue lights, with twin repeater lights in the grille, two-tone horns and all the previous armour protection to the body and glass area. In addition to all this, a system was devised to extinguish fire from underneath the vehicle, in the event that a petrol bomb should explode during rioting. Twin, heavy duty fire extinguishers were placed behind the drivers seat and by releasing a single pin and pulling a trigger, the dry powder extinguishers would be sent through a series of tubes to the four corners of the van to put out the fire. It was a quick and effective method, which was thankfully never fully put to the test.

The aggressive look of the new Ford Transit carriers is clearly seen here.
Author.

In 1987 a new Optica aircraft emerged from the Brooklands Aircraft Company at Old Sarum. Renamed the Optica Scout OA7 it was an updated and refined aircraft and it soon found favour with the Air Support Unit, who combined new trials with a move back to HMS Daedalus airfield. The trial aircraft, registration number G-BMPF was rarely on the ground and it wasn't long before it became a familiar sight and sound in the skies above Hampshire. With the trial over and with the approval of the Police Authority, Hampshire went ahead and purchased its first aircraft, taking delivery of it in December 1987. The aircraft, registration number G-BMPL came in its own livery, complete with Police signs, force crest and black and white chequered band. Demand for the services of the ASU continued to grow throughout the late 1980s and it soon became an integral part of the force.

The Optica Scout seen above The Needles lighthouse on the Isle of Wight.
Hampshire Constabulary

In late 1987 an incident occurred in the Metropolitan Police area that was to have a profound effect on Hampshire's vehicle policy. The incident centred on the death of a person involved in a serious public disorder situation, when he was accidentally run over by a personnel carrier being used by the Special Patrol Group (SPG). There were dozens of carriers in the immediate area and witnesses were unable to identify the carrier responsible from the side because there were no identifying features. As a result of the subsequent public inquiry, all Met vehicles were issued with fleet numbers, which were clearly visible from the side. Hampshire was one of the few county forces which also took the *fleet number* system on board and from early 1988, all of its marked vehicles were issued with fleet numbers, placed above each wheel arch. These numbers also became an identity number used by vehicle workshops, in conjunction with a new computerised fleet management system, which gave greater control over servicing times and stock management controls. Strangely, the Met Police stopped using the system after a few years and Hampshire now remains the only UK force to have kept the idea.

181

Numbers were obviously the fashion accessory of the late 1980s, because roof numbers also started making an appearance, to help the Air Support Unit identify patrol vehicles at an incident. The black letters and numbers were at first issued to Traffic cars, then area cars, dog vans and then personnel carriers. There was no force identity number used at this time and no orange spots as used by some other forces. Hampshire tended to abbreviate the cars call sign or station designation, for example, a Traffic car with the call sign CM-07 had the roof number C7, whilst an area car from Southsea with the call sign VS-50 had the roof lettering VS.

Ford updated the MK3 Escort range in 1988 by giving it a new front end and revised interior. Commonly called the MK3 Escort facelift model, it helped modernise the image slightly. Section cars and dog vans were replaced as and when they were up on mileage and as a rule, very little was altered by the force, with the exception of the Dog Section vans. The Police/ Stop box was removed, given the fact that dog vans rarely had the need to use them.

A MK3 Ford Escort (Facelift) van of the Dog Section,
complete with the new fleet numbers above the wheels.
Christopher Taylor

Another public order situation arose in the latter part of the 1980s and that was the emergence of the hunt saboteurs. Hampshire became a target because of its high proportion of foxhunts and factions on both sides of the divide clashed on a regular basis and required a lot of policing. Sending a standard vehicle into a muddy field to collect a prisoner was obviously going to be a problem, so three specialist vehicles were obtained. A Landrover 110 4x4 with a 2.5 diesel engine was employed to follow all aspects of the hunt and to act as a control unit. It was fitted with twin blue lights on the roof and on several occasions these were damaged by overhanging branches from trees and the problem was resolved by fitting mesh grilles around them.

The second type of vehicle used was a MK3 Ford Transit County 4x4 personnel carrier, adapted with rear cage, for the transportation of officers to off road trouble spots and to convey prisoners from those areas back to the nearest road. The force purchased two such units and they were fitted with three blue lights, two at the front of the roof and one at the rear. It was a useful vehicle for the anti-hunt demonstrations, but had limited use elsewhere and became an economical millstone to maintain. The four-wheel drive system wasn't really up to the job and was the major cause of most of the repairs.

Landrover 110 used during anti-hunt demonstrations.
Author

The MK3 Ford Transit County 4x4 used for off-road prisoner transportation.
Author

Lightweight rural motorcycles became an issue again in the latter part of the decade. With the Honda CB 200 now out of production a replacement had to be found and again a Japanese manufacturer was the only viable choice. Suzuki GN 250s with a single cylinder, four-stroke engine were purchased and fitted with a full length Avon fairing and panniers, which were striped in red and blue. A single blue light was positioned above the headlight and an additional blue light was positioned on an extendible pole at the rear of the motorcycle. This Premier Hazard device was useful to help protect the scene of a road traffic accident on dark rural roads, until four wheeled units arrived to assist. It was similar in concept to the stem light used on the Range Rover.

Suzuki GN 250 rural motorcycle.
Author

In April 1988 Hampshire purchased an 18-year-old Leyland Atlantean double-decker bus, to be used as a mobile exhibition unit. Officially launched by Lord Montague of Beaulieu, the unit was painted grey, white and blue with red pin striping and toured the two counties, educating the public on all areas of crime prevention, child safety and recruitment. On the ground floor area, the bus was fitted with various displays, which could be changed, depending on the function that it was catering for. Upstairs, most of the seats were retained, except for the front portion, where a large video screen was positioned for educational videos to be used. Further display boards could be positioned outside the bus once it was in place at the hundreds of events that it attended.

184

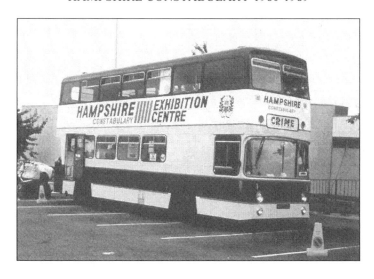

Leyland Atlantean bus, WOW 531J used as a mobile force exhibition unit.
Clifford Gray

In mid 1988 Hampshire started a feasibility study on the use of diesel powered vehicles. Four vehicles were used, a Ford Sierra with the Fraud Squad, two Ford Escorts and a Transit personnel carrier based on the Isle of Wight. Early indications showed a significant improvement in fuel economy figures, but further long term testing would need to be carried out. Another evaluation took place into the use of unleaded fuel. A high proportion of new vehicles were now arriving that were capable of using unleaded fuel, instead of four-star leaded. Again early indications showed an improvement in fuel economy, but that further analysis was required.

Radio communications equipment was updated in 1988 and new *hands free* radios were installed in all Traffic and area cars. The system, devised by Philips, was one of the most advanced in the country and was warmly welcomed by the officers using it. The unit could be operated in several different ways by the driver or by the observer. A suspended microphone was placed above the rear view mirror and this could be positioned above the driver, passenger or left in the middle. A button was then placed on the gear lever and all the driver had to do was press this and talk. Although not strictly hands free it was as close as you could get at that time. In addition to that, there was a box with a small chrome rocker switch attached. The observer could press down on the switch and then just talk via the suspended microphone, or alternatively, the switch could be placed in the *up* position and this made the whole system live by voice activation, which was especially useful during a pursuit for a single crewed unit. And on top of all that there were still two traditional, hand held receiver/transmitters for both UHF and VHF channels. It was an excellent system and revolutionised radio communications in Police vehicles.

Inside a Volvo 240 area car, showing the latest Philips radio equipment. The vox box (voice activation) can be seen above the air vents, with a Philips personal radio placed inside a booster system where the glove box should be. Note the suspended microphone and the previously mentioned row of purple switches for all the emergency lighting systems. Hampshire Constabulary.

Force communications received another boost in 1988 with the arrival of a new, purpose built mobile control unit. Built on a long wheelbase MK3 Ford Transit chassis, the custom body was specially built by Hawson Garner Ltd of Andover and was unique in its design. It housed a purpose built radio communications room, with the ability to talk to any other force in the UK. This Headquarters based unit, would be taken to the scene of any major incident by a member of the control room staff, where it would be manned as the Incident Control Vehicle and as such would become the focal point for Police and public alike. Three blue lights adorned the roof, together with a rotating spot lamp and a host of aerials. Police signs, force crest and blue and white chequered bands completed the package. The side and rear windows were blacked out to prevent prying eyes from looking inside.

The whole package was rather strange looking and more than one comment was made that it looked like a four-wheeled Optica! It replaced the Ford A Series Custom 4x4 and was eventually retired in 1998.

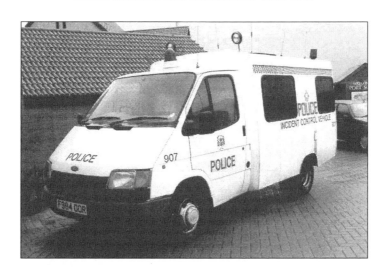

*Front and rear views of the custom built MK3 Ford Transit
based mobile Incident Control Vehicle.
Andy Bardsley*

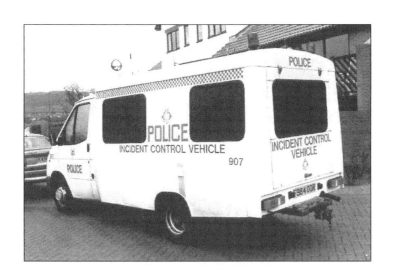

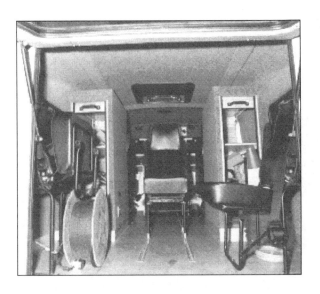

Interior view of same vehicle.
Hampshire Constabulary

Traffic got a replacement for their first unmarked car, with the new MK3 Ford Granada 2.9i with five-speed gearbox. This time the Police/Stop box was electrically powered and could be operated at the touch of a button, instead of the string and pulley system. It still meant that vehicles had to be stopped from the front and there were moves to outlaw this procedure because of a number of accidents, where the target car had run into the rear of the patrol car. Using unmarked patrol cars was still upsetting some people who considered it to be an underhand tactic, but it was nonetheless, very successful at catching the dangerous driver.

MK3 Ford Granada 2.9i
showing magnetic blue light
and Police/Stop equipment
in operation.
Christopher Taylor

188

A steady replacement program for the Ford Transit range was implemented by the end of the decade with personnel carriers and prison vans being updated with the MK3 version. Generally speaking they were equipped in the same way as previous models, except for the triple blue light system that was adopted for the roof.

MK3 Ford Transit prison van photographed at Newbury Race Course with units from Thames Valley Police during an operation at Greenham Common.
Author

MK3 Ford Transit personnel carrier based at Havant had the call sign JH-98
Author

The rather laid back, custom style of the Suzuki GN 250 motor cycles wasn't to everyone's liking and an alternative was found in the Honda CD 200 Benley. This twin- cylinder 200cc machine was in the more traditional style with flat handlebars and upright riding position. A full Avon fairing and panniers, complete with red and blue striping were attached, with a single blue light placed at the front and another on the rear rack. Reflective Police signs in red were also positioned on the rear of the panniers. The bikes themselves were capable of 90 mph and were more than adequate for the task that they had to perform. Above all they were reliable and had a good spares back-up service.

Honda CD 200 Benley lightweight, rural motorcycle.
Author

The Hampshire Constabulary celebrated its 150th anniversary in 1989 with a host of events around the two counties. A new concept in promoting public relations was the formation of the *Blue Lights Motorcycle Display Team* which had been talked about for a couple of years. After several months of planning and practising, the team performed at the force open day in June. The original team consisted of Sgt Nick Green, PCs John Steighton-Ellis, Kim Fenton, Andy Goward, Joe Morris, Tony Johnson, Martin Cripps and was managed by Chief Inspectors Ken Ellcombe and Don Bracey. It was a roaring success and gained an excellent reputation for showing off the riding skills of Hampshire's motorcyclists. They attended numerous public events and helped raise thousands of pounds for charity.

The motorcycles used were the new BMW K100RT models. These 1000cc, four-cylinder models with shaft drive were introduced in 1988, but it wasn't until 1989 that enough of them had been brought in to give the team a uniform appearance. The bikes were much quicker than the old boxer model, with a top speed of around 115 mph. The handling characteristics were completely different though and there were some who found it difficult to adapt, believing that the old BMW handled better. The new machine came equipped with BMWs own fairing, which housed a day running light above the headlight and on either side of that, two blue lights of the strobe variety were attached. Panniers and a low-line top box were attached to the rear rack, which also housed the illuminated Police/Stop box. A telescopic blue light pole was another addition, together with twin rear fog lights, that would pulse alternately with the orange hazard lights when stationary at an incident. Orange and blue livery, together with Police signs and the Hampshire crest helped complete the package. The Traffic motorcyclist now had a very well equipped, safe, fast and agile machine on which to conduct business.

The original Blue Lights Motorcycle Display Team of the Hampshire Constabulary at the Portsmouth and Southsea Show in 1989. By 1996 it was the only such unit in the UK.
Hampshire Constabulary

In 1989 BMW launched the all-new 5 Series and it wasn't too long before Hampshire obtained its first batch. The BMW 530i with its 3.0 litre, straight-six engine was billed the *ultimate driving machine* and it has to be said that it came pretty close. With a top speed of 130 mph, brilliant road holding, a quality finish and reliability second to none, it was almost the perfect Police package, straight off the shelf. The only real complaints centred around the seats, which some found gave them chronic backache. The new cars were decorated in the usual way and were fitted with a Premier Hazard light bar. Boot spoilers though were now out of fashion and the Police/Stop lights were now incorporated into a dot-matrix system located on the rear parcel shelf. In addition to the *stop* sign, the word *slow* could also be flashed up and this was found to be useful whilst monitoring traffic on the approach to a hazard.

The big new BMW was one of those rare cars, like the Jaguar, that had presence. It made a statement, it was authoritative and was to prove over the next few years to be one of the best all time patrol cars and as such deserves to be recognised as one of the landmark cars.

191

BMW 530i of the Cosham Traffic Section photographed from the top of Portsdown Hill, overlooking Portsmouth. The call sign was CM-05 and the officer standing behind it is PC Kevin Angus. You can just see the new dot-matrix box on the rear parcel shelf.
Kevin Angus

Meanwhile the revamped Rover Group had recently released its replacement for the old SD1 in the shape of the Rover 827i, a front-wheel drive car with a Honda engine! The days of Police forces and Hampshire in particular coming under pressure from Government about buying foreign, were now almost gone. Industry was becoming more multi-national and Rover had been saved from the brink of extinction by Honda, who agreed a deal with the Government to supply engines for certain cars.

Hampshire, still wary of the Rover product because of previous problems, did go ahead and purchase two variants of the new 827, a saloon and a fastback. The saloon model did the rounds of various Traffic Sections and eventually became a workshop spare vehicle, whilst the fastback spent its life at Lyndhurst. With a top speed of 130 mph from its 2.7 litre fuel injected V6 engine, they were quick and could out accelerate the BMW because it was much lighter. Its real problem concerned the front-wheel drive, which was fine when the roads were dry, but when wet, it was almost impossible to stop the front wheels from spinning. Traction control was a few years away yet! Although a far better product in terms of quality and reliability than in the past, it still wasn't up to the standard of other European products.

The Rover 827i saloon.
Author

The Rover 827i fastback.
Simon Rowley

All standard and advanced drivers have to undergo training in skid control whilst on their various driving courses and this usually meant driving an old vehicle with over inflated tyres with no tread pattern on them, on an oil soaked wet track. It was good fun and students quickly got to grips with the system needed to control such skids. The trouble was these tracks were few and far between and required a lot of maintenance. The force therefore purchased a MK3 Ford Escort fitted with a Skid Master system called Skid-One. This device meant that the

193

instructor, who would sit in the vehicle, could cause it to skid in a variety of ways by pushing a series of buttons on a control panel. With the aid of hydraulics the car could be made to simulate a loss of control and the student would have to react accordingly. The big advantage with this vehicle was that it could be used in a car park or other large piece of land. In Hampshire's case there was plenty of space at the HMS Daedalus site for Skid-One to be put through its paces.

Skid-One Ford Escort was used for many years on driving courses.
Author.

Tragedy struck the Berkshire town of Hungerford in 1989, when a lone gunman, Michael Ryan shot dead 18 people, including a Policeman in random attacks. One of the many lessons learned from his rampage was that the Police didn't have any form of armoured unit capable of getting close enough to someone armed with high velocity weapons. Hampshire, like most other UK Police forces, didn't have that capability either and a decision was taken to ensure that in the event of a similar incident, that the force was ready to deal with it. It therefore purchased a specially built armoured Landrover 110, converted by Glover Webb at Hamble, with full ballistic protection. It had a top speed of just 85 mph, weighed three and a half tonnes and stopped eventually!

Armoured Landrover 110 in 1989.
Author

By 1989 Volvo had dropped the 240 Police Special model and Hampshire now got off the peg, 240 GL versions. The only real difference now was that it came with a five speed manual gearbox, all cloth interior, carpets and wind-up windows! The steel wheels now sported smart plastic trims and slight changes had been made to the frontal area of the car. It remained the only choice for area cars within the force; it had a proven track record second to none and was still capable of mixing it with more modern vehicles.

The Isle of Wight continued to use them as joint Traffic and area cars of course. As such they obtained all the necessary up to date Traffic patrol equipment, including the Premier Hazard light bar and tri-sound siren. They retained the old boot mounted Police/Stop box and were decorated in the standard Hampshire Traffic livery. They were quite unique in their appearance and of all the variants that Hampshire ever used this was probably one of the best looking.

The Volvo 240 GL traffic/area car from Ryde on the Isle of Wight.
Simon Rowley

Southampton Police had a major problem with prostitution in the St. Mary's area of the city and used a MK3 Ford Transit personnel carrier to help reduce the problem of kerb crawling motorists. The vehicle had the words *Vice Squad* emblazoned across the bonnet and *Anti Kerb Crawler Unit* in bright red lettering along the sides. The idea was to let the residents of the area know that the Police were taking the problem seriously and to embarrass the kerb crawlers into thinking twice about entering the area.

This unit told you in no uncertain terms what its role was!
Hampshire Constabulary

196

By the end of the decade Hampshire entered new territory, by equipping three, unmarked BMW 530i's with video cameras. Technology now allowed the fitment of a fixed video camera, linked to the Vascar unit, from a bracket placed on top of the dashboard, with the video recorder and viewing screen being positioned inside the area previously used as the glove box. An extended remote control unit, allowed the operator to zoom in or out on the target. The whole outfit was a bit cumbersome, but it worked and for the first time ever, video evidence of bad driving could be shown to the courts. There were of course the usual cries of foul play, but no one could really argue with the results and the protests soon died down. The three cars came in different colours of red, blue and green and were moved around the different Traffic areas on a three-monthly basis, to prevent anybody becoming too familiar with them. Other forces of course were experimenting with similar units and between them spawned an entirely new form of public entertainment, with the *Police, Camera, Action* television shows.

BMW 530i unmarked video unit.
Hampshire Constabulary via John Prince

Interior shot of video unit and viewing screen.
Hampshire Constabulary via John Prince

CHAPTER 7

HAMPSHIRE CONSTABULARY
1990 TO 1999

Hampshire Constabulary revised style helmet plate

By the start of the 1990s large scale disturbances were thankfully becoming fewer and fewer, although Hampshire was to experience several problems with protesters at the M3 extension and had to assist neighbouring Thames Valley with a similar situation at the proposed A34 Newbury by-pass.

Following the boom of the late 1980s, the early 1990s saw bust and the country was plunged into a deep economic recession. As a result, the Hampshire Constabulary was forced to tighten its monetary belt still further and found itself buying vehicles not in keeping with its usual policy of purchasing the best vehicle for the job. As will become clear, some were purchased because they were the cheapest available at that time.

Technology, the personal computer, mobile phones and massive road congestion were to become the hallmarks of the 1990s, all of which directly affected the Police service.

And it all got off to a terrifying start. On the 11th March 1990 the Air Support Unit's Optica Scout, suffered a propeller failure during take off from Lee-on-Solent, but was somehow kept under control and brought back down safely onto the runway. An investigation by the Air Accident Investigation Board revealed major fatigue failure in the fan hub, which resulted in all Optica Scout aircraft being grounded. The fault proved to be of huge importance and resulted in the long term grounding of the range, which in turn conspired to bring about the near collapse of the company.

The ASU was now forced to look elsewhere for a replacement and in May 1990, took delivery of a Pilatus Brittan Norman Islander, registration number G-TWOB made at Bembridge on the Isle of Wight. The aircraft was leased to the force and the crews commenced a period of conversion to an aircraft with not only the ability to perform identical tasks to the Optica, but with the additional capability of providing transportation and sea search facilities. The evaluation was extremely successful and due to the problems with the Optica fan hub and serious doubts as to its life span, a decision was made to purchase a purpose built Islander. An order was placed with the manufacturers on the island, whilst operations continued with G-TWOB. Meanwhile the Optica was sold back to Lovaux at Bournemouth, who had taken over the Optica operation from the now defunct Brooklands.

The temporary replacement for the Optica, a Pilatus Brittan Norman Islander G-TWOB, built at Bembridge on the Isle of Wight.
Hampshire Constabulary.

Another departure in 1990 was the Volvo 240 area car. Production of the saloon ceased, although Volvo did continue with the estate for another 18 months or so, it left a void that was to prove difficult to fill. The 240 was essentially a 1960s product and as such was really starting to show its age, although as an area car it was truly outstanding. When you consider that the first 144 saloons used by the force were obtained in 1969 and the basic concept was still going strong in 1990, it speaks volumes for the overall quality of the car. These latter versions only differed in that they were fitted with catalytic converters and ran on unleaded fuel, which because they were not originally designed to do so, did create one or two reliability problems. The final batch of ten 240 GLs took the total number of 244s and 240s in all its variants, purchased by Hampshire, to a staggering 270 units.

Last of the breed, this Volvo 240 GL was based at Ringwood.
Simon Rowley

A new concept in obtaining vehicles for the fleet was brought into being in early 1990 with the introduction of lease hire instead of purchase. Following European Commission policy on tendering and contractual procedures, the force was obliged to put out to tender new vehicles for its fleet. This would ensure that vehicles would be obtained by the cheapest means possible and would be replaced after a set period of time and not on mileage. It also meant that if a vehicle never used before met all the Home Office criteria for that particular type of vehicle, then the force was obliged to take it. The scheme was short lived though, following many contractual difficulties it was discontinued by the Home Office.

Meanwhile BMW had made alterations to its brilliant 5 Series by ceasing production of the 530i and re-issuing it as the 525i with multi-valved engine. The difference was quite staggering; it was slightly faster, had far greater acceleration and the whole package felt so much lighter and more agile. Hampshire obtained its first few via the lease hire scheme and these came with subtle differences over the standard Police units, with electric windows and a better-finished interior. After two years, the cars were taken back under the agreement, even though they had travelled less than 90,000 miles.

*A BMW 525i of the Cosham Traffic Section, call sign CM-04 photographed
on Southsea Common. This was one of the lease hire vehicles.
P.M. Photography*

As the force moved into 1991, so the Traffic Division was re-established as a separate division once again.

The effect of European Community regulations meant considerable change to existing tendering procedures relative to vehicle brands and in consequence meant that different types of vehicles from a range of manufacturers were introduced onto the fleet. There was none stranger than the Fiat Ducato van. Purchased because it was the cheapest thing available at the time, it was quite simply a disaster, with driver comfort, or rather a complete lack of it, being its worst feature. The driver's seat did not adjust in any way, the ignition was on the left and turned towards the driver and the pedals were positioned too high from the floor and were so far offset that they were difficult to use. The 1.9 litre engine was slow in comparison to the Ford Transit unit and they weren't terribly reliable. Each van was fitted out the same as any other section van of the time, with twin blue roof lights, front repeater lights and a grilled rear area, for the transportation of prisoners. Only one batch of Fiats were purchased, numbering 20 in total.

The Fiat Ducato personnel carriers were not a popular choice
because they were uncomfortable to drive.
Author

Another new car to arrive on the scene, although no-where near as controversial, was the replacement for the Volvo 240, in the shape of the Ford Sierra Sapphire 2.0i LX. Ford's *jelly mould* car had been around since 1984 and had recently gone from hatchback only to saloon model. It looked all the better for it and at that time appeared to be the only viable successor to the Volvo, who had no natural replacement for their old model. The Ford had a top speed of about 108 mph with reasonable handling characteristics. For those who had been driving the Volvo for a while, the Ford felt very light in comparison and there were those who thought it wouldn't be up to the job in terms of reliability and longevity.

The obvious changes in equipment included the fitment of a full width bar light, made by Premier Hazard. In essence this was merely two single spinners placed inside a fancy blue box, with an illuminated Police/Stop light centred in between. The previous Thule light bar units weren't scrapped though. In the interests of saving yet more money they were actually sold to another force and in essence cost Hampshire next to nothing! Two-tone horns were fitted of course and the new area cars also sported what some glibly called 'go faster stripes' along the sides in the form of a blue and white chequered band. This reflective tape helped aid visual safety at night and helped give the cars a distinctive appearance all of their own. All in all, the Ford Sierra Sapphire was a successful area car, but its days were numbered almost immediately by Ford's replacement for it, the Mondeo.

The Ford Sierra Sapphire 2.0i LX was a good replacement for the Volvo.
This area car was stationed at the old Cowplain Police Station
and had the call sign CW-52.
Author.

Did You Know That.........?
Some of the 'boy racer' element were quite convinced that the Sierra Sapphires were actually Cosworth Sierras because of the rear spoilers, wheel trims and grille attachments that had been fitted and wouldn't dare attempt to get away from them! Of course it goes without saying that area car drivers never attempted to put them straight!

Ford now saw its chance to get back into the Police fleet market in Hampshire on a larger scale and offered the force two new Traffic cars at a vastly reduced rate. Two MK3 Ford Granada 4x4 saloons, fitted with a 2.9i V6 Cosworth engine were delivered; one to Cosham and the other to Winchester. Each car was fitted with a Premier Hazard Maxim light bar, a tri-sound siren system and was fully fitted out as per any other Hampshire Traffic car. The Fords were pitted against the BMW 5 series and most considered it a none contest. Despite the Fords four-wheel drive system, it felt somewhat ungainly if pushed too hard and its V6 engine, now some 20 years old, was a dog. With a top speed of no more than 110 mph it simply couldn't cope and it wasn't long before both cars were removed from the Traffic Sections and put out to graze as workshop spares.

The MK3 Ford Granada 2.9i Cosworth 4x4 saloons just weren't advanced enough to cope with the likes of the BMW as a mainstream traffic car. This former Cosham based car got the call sign HK-02 when it went to Fareham workshops as a spare.
Author.

Ford also revamped the Escort range in 1991 and brought out the MK4, following much criticism of its MK3 model from some factions of the motoring press. The result though was a disaster for Ford with the level of adverse comments rising even further, due mainly to its lack of style and technical innovation.

Hampshire wasn't in the market for a large-scale purchase of replacement section cars and vans and only bought a handful of the newer model, including estate variants for section cars and the van for use by the Dog Section. The section cars were fitted out in the same way as before, but the dog vans took on a whole new look.

Dog Section vehicles are expected to travel long distances at high speed during the course of their work. If a dog is required at an incident, it is usually needed in a hurry. To help facilitate this, the new vans were ordered with Fords 1.6i engine, giving it a top speed of around 110 mph. Two-tone horns and a new twin blue light system made by Britax, was fitted. As these units were generally described as emergency response, they were now fitted with a full traffic car livery of red and blue reflective stripes with the addition of the blue and white chequers placed above the striping, instead of below it. The words Police Dog Section were placed along the side panels of the van, together with the force crest, roof numbers and fleet numbers. The new vans looked like a purposeful package and were very well received by those handlers that got them.

The MK4 Ford Escort 1.6i van of the Hampshire Police Dog Section. Note the new style Britax light bar.
Author.

A new initiative arrived in 1991 with the introduction of the Southern Crime Stoppers direct phone line system and to help promote this, almost every marked vehicle in the Hampshire Constabulary was adorned with its logo. It incorporated the Hampshire crest together with the Crime Stoppers unique telephone number and each sticker was positioned in a prominent area on the vehicle.

The Southern Crime Stoppers logo.
Author.

206

BMW altered the K100 motorcycle slightly, by giving it a more upright touring screen and slightly increased power plus a revised name, the K100LT. It was essentially the same machine as the RT and was equipped in the same manner.

A BMW K100LT at rest in the New Forest.
Simon Rowley.

1991 will be remembered for two major additions to the fleet, a purpose built mobile control unit and an aircraft. The new Mobile Control Unit was a Ford Iveco Cargo with bodywork by Hawson Garner Ltd of Andover, fully fitted out with all the latest in mobile communications equipment. This was the largest mobile communications unit the force had ever employed and was utilised at everything from murder scenes to large-scale public events. Inside the rear of the vehicle it was fitted with a range of purpose built consoles with room for at least three controllers to sit in comfort. Side windows gave them excellent viewing positions and the whole unit could be made self-sufficient with its own on board power generator. On the outside a double width Premier Hazard Maxim light bar was fitted, together with twin repeaters set into the grille.

Ford Iveco Cargo Mobile Control Unit, photographed beneath
the statue of King Alfred in Winchester.
Hampshire Constabulary

On the 22nd December the Air Support Unit finally took delivery of its new Islander aircraft from the Pilatus Britten Norman factory on the Isle of Wight. Based at the HMS Daedalus airfield at Lee-on-Solent the unit soon gained recognition amongst officers on the ground that it could assist them greatly during searches for persons responsible for serious crimes or for missing persons. It rapidly became an integral part of the force resources and flew a total of 518 hours in its first year alone.

Other equipment fitted included a communications system giving access to all Police VHF

AM/FM and UHF frequencies as well as HM Coastguard and other agencies frequencies. A Global Positioning System (GPS) was fitted, giving it instant position information from satellites. The position of the majority of villages and hamlets in Hampshire and the Isle of Wight were programmed into the system giving immediate navigational information on bearing and distance to ground speed and actual track of the aircraft, together with estimated time of arrival at a selected point. Full Instrument Flying Rules (IFR) equipment was fitted together with full anti-ice fit, allowing it to operate in most weather conditions. However if the cloud base is too low and the crew are unable to see the ground there is little point in flying! The aircraft would usually carry six seats, allowing plenty of room for the crew to operate, although if necessary it could seat ten. Most tasks were flown at altitudes between 500 feet and 4000 feet, although that varied as to the particular task. The cruising air speed was 120 Knots with an on task speed of about 65 Knots. Its minimum speed could be as slow as 40 Knots and if fully loaded with fuel had an endurance time of five hours.

Despite its obvious policing advantages there were those that would phone or write in to complain bitterly that their sleep had been disturbed by the circling aircraft. Some of the residents of Lee-on –Solent were particularly unhappy at the number of night-time take offs that the aircraft undertook.

Hampshire's all new Islander aircraft, call sign Boxer-One-Zero. This is a later photograph showing the nightscan device fitted to the underside of the nose allowing thermal images to be seen on board. Later in its career, live video footage could be downloaded direct to control rooms to assist with searches. Hampshire Constabulary.

The Air Support Unit also got a Landrover 110 Defender 2.5Tdi 4x4 to utilise as its ground support unit. This vehicle would accompany the aircraft to and from the runway and would carry a range of fire fighting and first aid equipment to facilitate a first response if there was an accident. The vehicle came in Landrovers standard blue and white colour scheme and was adorned with a single blue light and twin amber beacons, befitting all airfield vehicles. Three roof mounted halogen spotlights were also fitted to assist at night.

The ASU's Landrover 110 Defender carried fire-fighting equipment.
Author.

By 1992 the strength of Sterling against the Deutsch Mark had weakened significantly and the purchase of German vehicles suddenly became very expensive. Despite the fact that the force favoured buying BMWs for its fleet, the German manufacturers refused to lower their prices and Hampshire simply couldn't afford the luxury of buying the *ultimate driving machine* anymore. The last batch of BMW 525i's arrived in early 1992 and were equipped in the same manner as all previous Traffic patrol cars. As a driver's car there have been few, if any, to match its overall package of power, handling and sheer quality. The car pictured here became quite famous. It was the last one to be issued and covered an incredible 201,116 miles before being retired and was almost as good then as it was when new. The Cosham based car was also the subject that was modelled by Corgi as a diecast model (see Chapter 9) and was also used as the base for a collectors tie tac (see Chapter 9) and became the subject of one or two local newspaper articles.

*Last of the breed, this is CM-06, a Cosham based traffic patrol car
made famous by the Corgi model.
Hampshire Constabulary.*

*Interior of the same car, showing the Tracker stolen vehicle device on top of the dash, the
Philips radio system, the UHF personal radio and VHF 'yellow top' radio in its booster pack, vox
box and the Vascar, mounted in a specially made centre console incorporating the various light
and siren switches.
Author.*

Hampshire had to find an alternative and quickly. It opted for the MK2 Vauxhall Senator 3.0i, with its straight-six 24-valve engine and five-speed manual gearbox. The Senator was a smooth looking, aerodynamic car, which had found favour with just about every other Police force in the UK at that time. In comparison with the BMW though it was light years behind in terms of quality and many complained about its lack of grip in the wet. The really ironic thing about the Senator though concerned the fact that it was built in Germany! There were many who just couldn't work out the logic of that at all.

It was a quick car though with speeds of 135 mph easily attained and it got there quicker than the BMW as well. Its engine was smooth and quiet, but the gearbox was a notchy affair and clutch judder was a common problem. Quality control was its biggest problem though and for the first time in several years the force had a car that tended to have bits fall off it and with a spares back up that could best be described as slow, it wasn't economically friendly either.

Standard traffic livery was applied and it carried all the usual amounts of emergency signs and kit in the boot. Most had the Premier Hazard Olympic light bar fitted, but one or two, including the Cosham based unit seen here came with a Premier Hazard Maxim light bar incorporating a dot matrix information system at the rear. This unit had pre-programmed messages built in and these could be activated from a small control panel inside the car. Messages included the usual Police/Stop, Slow, Accident, Fog Lights On/Off, a series of arrows pointing left or right and the words *Follow Me* in English, French, Spanish and German. This was particularly useful when used at multi checks where foreign goods vehicle drivers got the message immediately. For some reason the system never really caught on and the standard Olympic light bar was used instead.

Rear view shot of CM-05, a Cosham based Vauxhall Senator with the Premier Hazard Maxim light bar incorporating a dot matrix information system. This car was totally destroyed by fire after it hit a gas main on Hayling Island in 1995!
Author.

The Senator also found favour as the new unmarked video car and the force purchased three altogether, including the red model shown here. They were identical in every respect to the marked cars and were fitted with twin blue repeater lights set into the front fog lamps, a second set of blue lights were positioned on the passenger side sun visor and red and blue strobe lights were also placed on the rear parcel shelf. A dot matrix Police/Stop box was also positioned on the parcel shelf and the video camera located just beneath the rear view mirror. The actual recorder was now located in a specially made frame, inside the boot. This allowed more room inside the car for the display monitor, which with the advances in technology now provided a better quality picture than on the previous system employed on the BMW.

One of Hampshire's unmarked video traffic cars, the MK2 Vauxhall Senator.
Author.

The Northern Traffic Area got a new Range Rover in 1992 and it would prove to be the last of its type issued to the force. The 3.9 EFi 4x4 was stationed at Whitchurch to cover the busy A34 and surrounding areas, where adverse weather conditions in winter meant it could be utilised to its full potential. The upgraded engine and adjustable air suspension gave much better performance, although reliability became a sore point with everyone. It was a great car, made badly.

All previous Range Rovers of course were fitted with a stem light and rear spoiler, incorporating the Police/Stop signs. This new model was fitted with the Premier Hazard unit used on the aforementioned Vauxhall Senator, complete with on board dot matrix system. Fitted separately and positioned just in front of the bar light was a Woodway Speed Lite. This hydraulic stem light system was basically the same as all previous flood lighting options, but wasn't as heavy or as ungainly.

Across the lower half of the tailgate the orange side striping was continued to give a degree of reflective material to the rear of the vehicle. To aid safety further a rigid tubular roll cage was fitted to the interior of the car.

Last of the line for the old Range Rover V8. This unit was based at
Whitchurch and had the call sign MN-01.
Andy Bardsley

The Range Rover of course drank lots of fuel and in a fleet of 500 or so vehicles Hampshire's annual fuel bill was getting bigger every year. In an effort to reduce costs further, a working party was set up to look at alternatives and by mid 1992 the Diesel Fuel Project set about some research into the possibility of using diesel powered cars for the first time. It would be some months before any firm proposals were laid down.

Meanwhile there were still some oddity vehicles to be found. A Mercedes Benz 1010D with bodywork by Bedwas, was a mobile detention unit, containing ten single unit cells, in a secure body. This rather large vehicle had a limited but useful role in large-scale public order situations or during category A prisoner transfers. It had twin blue repeater lights set into the grille, the Hampshire crest and a Police sign above the cab. Two officers could sit in relative comfort in the rear of the vehicle, which also had escape hatches placed in the roof, to be used in the event that the vehicle overturned. Its role was relatively short lived and by the end of 1999 the vehicle was refitted and given a new lease of life for an entirely different status (see end of this chapter).

This rather poor quality photo shows the Mobile Detention Unit
based on a Mercedes Benz chassis.
Author.

Vehicle examinations were traditionally carried out by Traffic officers as part of their duties. A basic City in Guilds Vehicle Examiners course was deemed to be sufficient enough until it became obvious that given the technical advances of the car over the last few years, that most, if not all of them, were now way out of their depth. Civilian vehicle examiners, with more qualifications than the average brain surgeon were then employed and given their own marked vehicles to go about their business in. The MK4 Ford Escort van with a 1.4i engine was enough to keep all their necessary tools and equipment in. The vehicle was given orange and blue striping, because on occasions it might be necessary for them to attend the scenes of fatal road traffic accidents, to assist the Traffic officers with the investigation, in times when a mechanical defect might be responsible for the crash. The words 'Vehicle Examination Unit' were placed on the vans side panels, together with the Hampshire crest.

MK4 Ford Escort 1.4i of the Vehicle Examination Unit seen here at Fareham.
Author.

The Isle of Wight of course was still doing things slightly different to the mainland as far as Traffic and area car duties were concerned. As was the tradition the joint unit vehicles would be decorated the same way as all Traffic cars and thus, the islands Ford Sierra Sapphires were adorned with stripes.

This Isle of Wight Sierra Sapphire is on a day trip to Lyndhurst Police Station and the strong
shadows make it look as if someone has stolen the wheels!
Author.

By December 1992 the Diesel Fleet Experiment was ready and waiting. Inspector John Jackman from Cowplain and Inspector Zen Stopinski from Bitterne would oversee the experiment. Cosham and Bitterne stations were selected to take part. Each stations vehicles would be replaced immediately by all new diesel powered MK5 Ford Escorts for section cars, MK3 Ford Transit 2.5 Tdi Multi Role section vans and some Scenes of Crime and Photographic Units, together with the Process Unit vehicles would also be replaced. Unfortunately not all the vehicles were ready in time and most were not operational until February 1993.

A MK5 Ford Escort 1.8D Section Vehicle seen outside Cowplain during the Diesel Fleet Experiment.
Author.

As well as the new engines, the force was also trying out a new concept in section vans. By combining the section van with the capacity to carry six officers in the rear, as per new national guidelines on public order deployments, it did away with the necessity of using two different types of vehicle. By using Ford's long wheelbase MK3 Transit, Hampshire designed its new *multi-role* vehicle by encompassing a cage at the rear of the unit, capable of housing four adult prisoners on a temporary basis. In the centre section of the van would be two rows of seats, capable of seating six officers, with a small table positioned in-between. Above them there was sufficient room for shelving to locate helmets and other items. Between those seats and the cab was a racked area capable of housing enough round shields for the entire crew. A self-contained electric heater was also incorporated and this could be run even when the engine was switched off. With laminated body protection and Perspex windows, the new multi-role units could be used anywhere and for any purpose, from everyday prisoner transportation duties to full blown public order situations. Each unit was fitted with twin blue repeater lights in the front grille and six more repeater lights, placed in pairs along both sides and the rear. These would all flash alternately to let everyone around know that this vehicle was in a hurry. To aid that process a decision was made to re-fit these vehicles with an emergency audible warning device and a system similar to the Traffic cars was used, giving a wail and yelp siren. This was long overdue and was a welcome addition. Most were built under licence by either Bedwas, Kinectic Engineering or by Hawson Garner. These vehicles were a clever design by all concerned and are unique to the Hampshire Constabulary and as such deserve to be recognised as one of the landmark vehicles.

The Cosham based MK3 Ford Transit multi-role unit, powered by a 2.5 Tdi engine as part of the Diesel Fleet Experiment. NB; that this unit is fitted with 'bull bars' to the front. These were later removed following concerns over road safety, should the van collide with a pedestrian. The vans call sign was CC-99.
Author.

Another part of the diesel experiment was the inclusion of a diesel powered area car. There were those who voiced an opinion that such a car wasn't suitable as an emergency response unit, because it wouldn't be quick enough. In February 1993 the force borrowed on long term test a Peugeot 405 Turbo Diesel saloon. The car was initially used by the Crime Squad, but was later fully fitted out as a sub-divisional area car and was based first at Bitterne and then at Cowplain. In total it completed some 10,000 miles as an area car, so it got a full and thorough testing. Most of the drivers were pleasantly surprised by its performance with the gearbox coming in for particular praise. But overall it failed the performance test. When it came to outright speed, or acceleration required for overtaking, it just wasn't up to the job and in July it went back to Peugeot. The car was fitted out in the same way as any other area car, except for the roof lights, which were a new concept from Britax.

218

Peugeot 405 TD experimental area car although reasonably successful didn't quite make the grade. It is seen here parked outside Woolston fire station in Southampton.
Geraint Roberts

Overall though the Diesel Fuel Project proved to be a huge success. There was little or no complaint from officers required to drive the diesel powered section cars and vans, because there was little difference in performance, save for the noise and the extra fumes! As a means of saving money, the arguments for using diesel fuel on a fleet the size of Hampshire's for all but the emergency response units, was overwhelming. On the Ford Escort 1.8D the saving was 11.33%, on a Ford Escort 1.8D van, the saving was 18.35% and on a Ford Transit 2.5 Tdi the saving was an impressive 35.9%. It was estimated that the force would therefore save almost £106,000 per year. It was therefore decided at the highest level that the experiment be extended by another 12 months, with the addition of further vehicles. Only then would the move be made to transform station fuel pumps from petrol to diesel.

One of the first vehicles outside of the experiment to be obtained was a MK3 Ford Transit 2.5 Tdi for use as a Mobile Workshop for use by the mechanics at Bar End. This vehicle was fully equipped with all the necessary tools and accessories to undertake minor servicing and repairs to rural section vehicles and motorcycles in situ. This again helped save fuel and time for all concerned. The vehicle was striped up and had twin amber beacons fitted to the roof.

MK3 Ford Transit 2.5 Tdi Mobile Police Workshop unit based at Bar End workshops, Winchester

Towards the end of 1992 and the beginning of 1993 the Traffic Division formed a new department within its ranks. The Accident Investigation Unit took those Traffic officers already specially trained in the science of fatal accident investigation and posted them full time into the new unit. Their expertise was to prove invaluable in many court cases and to assist them getting about to the various serious accidents they were to attend, the force purchased several Ford Courier 1.7D Popular vans. These Ford Fiesta based vehicles weren't exactly fast when fully laden with all the necessary equipment and the complaints rolled on for years! It was often said that when they were flat out on the motorway, with blue lights flashing and sirens wailing, that the local *reps* in their Sierras and Cavaliers would flash at them from behind to get them to move over! But they were here to stay and were equipped with a Britax light unit with twin blue repeaters placed either side of the Police sign above the cab roof. The standard Traffic livery adorned the sides and the words *Accident Investigation Unit* were placed along the vans side panels. The units were initially based at Fareham, Lyndhurst and Overton, but later combined to form one central unit at Ember House on the Winnall Trading Estate, Winchester.

*One of the Lyndhurst based Ford Courier 1.7D vans used
by the new Accident Investigation Unit.
Simon Rowley*

Several more Ford Courier 1.7D vans were purchased by Hampshire and these were used by the forces Civilian Driver's as admin support units. On a day to day basis the force moves an incredible amount of paperwork and packages from station to station, to and from the courts, to prisons and to other outside agencies. Previously the *civvy* drivers would have to use a section van or car, usually to the detriment of the station concerned, but now they had their own units, life was made somewhat easier for all concerned. Each was decorated as a Police section vehicle, but did not need any form of blue light or siren of course.

*An Admin Support Unit Ford
Courier 1.7D Popular seen at
Fareham Police Station.
Author*

The force continued to look for an alternative area car and tested diesel options from Rover, Ford and Volvo. Eventually BMW came back onto the scene with its all new 325 TDS saloon. This six-cylinder, 2.5 turbo charged diesel was said to be unlike any other diesel motor ever put into a car. It was smooth, uncannily quiet and very quick, almost 130 mph quick! It was small and agile and scored top marks from all who drove it. At first, two were purchased for use at Bitterne and Cowplain who had obvious experience with the Peugeot 405 and they loved it. The car had a quality feel to it and had obvious street credibility, even if it was a diesel.

All new area cars were striped up as per the Traffic cars, owing to yet another European Commission ruling that all emergency response vehicles should be highly visible in all light and weather conditions. This meant that the area cars lost some of their identity and the ruling sometimes confused the public to. Apart from the side striping, it was pretty much the same standard of equipment as on previous area cars, but with the addition of a tri-sound style siren system devised by Premier Hazard, who also provided a revised Maxim 90 light bar. The old two-tone horns were now almost a thing of the past, confined to the history books and the dustbin!

First of the new BMW 325 TDS saloons is perched on top of Portsdown Hill overlooking Portsmouth. This was Cowplain's all new area car, call sign CW-52.
Hampshire Constabulary

But it wasn't all diesel fumes in the county! The force still required the occasional petrol driven motor and none more so than the Traffic Division, who, following a very successful trial (see Chapter 8) purchased a VW Vento VR6 as an unmarked video equipped patrol car. This hooligan-on-wheels came with a brilliant 2.8i V6 engine and handling that was more akin to that on a racetrack. This was a real driver's car, the sort of vehicle you drive with a smug grin on your face. Better than that though, was that the public had no idea that the Police would stoop so low as to buy a VW and thus treated it with disdain, until its secreted blue strobe lights were operated and the red faced motorist was caught with his pants firmly down!

The Vento just didn't look the part and it worked all the better for it. It came in a dark maroon colour, complete with sunroof and smart alloy wheels. It was fitted with the latest in video cameras with a superior picture over previous models. Blue strobe lights were placed inside the front fog lamps with additional ones available on the nearside sun visor. Red and blue repeater lights were also placed on the rear parcel shelf together with an electrically hinged Police/Stop sign in the dot matrix format. In front of this, facing forward, was an illuminated Police/Stop sign in yellow and with the words reversed. This could be operated when stopping a vehicle from behind and the driver could clearly see the words, the correct way around in his rear view mirror. The Vento was a huge success, not just with the officers lucky enough to drive it but also with the force mechanics and those that controlled the purse strings. In over 180,000 miles of service it didn't break down once and still holds the record for the lowest *down- time* of any car ever owned by the Hampshire Constabulary.

The VW Vento VR6. One of Hampshire's most successful
patrol cars for many reasons. Its call sign was MM-02.
Author.

Whilst the diesel experiment necessitated the need to examine new products over a period of time, the rest of the fleet needed to be replaced now. In truth there wasn't that much to choose from and the force eventually settled on the MK2 Rover 820 Si saloon. This second generation 800 series Rover had recently undergone a major revamp and was a much-improved vehicle. Its 2.0 fuel-injected engine and five-speed manual gearbox gave reasonably reliable service, but like many of its predecessors it wasn't entirely *Policeman proof* and bits of interior trim tended to break or fall off, with door handles, both inside and out being the main weak point. There were also recurring problems with the electric windows and failing alarm systems. These were annoying, niggling little problems, which nonetheless caused the vehicle to be off

223

the road for considerable periods of time. But it would be another 18 months or so before its real problem came to the surface.

As per the new BMWs, these cars were fully striped and now sported the new Premier Hazard light bar and siren system. They were also fitted with a new item of equipment similar to the Vascar speed detection unit fitted in Traffic cars. The SPDM now allowed area car crews to measure and record the speed of vehicles, without having to use the time honoured system of using a calibrated speedometer, tested each week with a stop watch. Area cars at Havant and Cosham were also tasked with testing out a new device from IBM in the shape of an encrypted message sender. This unit was placed on top of the dash and received messages on a screen from the control room, deploying the crew to certain sensitive jobs, like alarm calls. The system was designed in order to prevent those from carrying out crimes such as burglary, using scanners to listen in on Police frequencies, being able to detect when a Police unit had been sent to their location. The trial lasted several months but the system proved unreliable and was removed.

MK2 Rover 820 Si area car from Fareham, call sign HF-51.
Andy Bardsley.

The Dog Section also got new vehicles in 1993 and in keeping with their upgraded role of emergency response, got vehicles to help cope with that, in the shape of the MK3 Vauxhall Astra van. Most civilian Astra vans of course were fitted with the basic 1.4 petrol engine or more likely a diesel. These units however came with Vauxhalls acclaimed 1.6 fuel-injected motor, making it the quickest canine unit ever! With a top speed of around 110 mph, depending on the load, it was now easier to obtain a dog unit when you needed one.

Most of these vans were striped up as before and were now fitted with the Premier Hazard light unit and sirens. Twin blue repeater lights were fitted into the grille of some vehicles. Although most received the new livery and equipment there were a few that for some reason got the old style graphics. Overall these vehicles proved to be reliable and popular with the crews that used them, although there were those that complained of a lack of room to store items like ballistic helmets, body armour and other equipment necessary in the 1990s. Most of it tended to get dumped on the front passenger seat or the floor.

MK3 Vauxhall Astra 1.6i van of the Dog Section.
Author.

A couple of new Astra dog vans but with the older style livery
are seen here outside the force's Dog Section base at Netley.
Steve Greenaway

Hampshire was still buying lightweight motorcycles for its rural beats, albeit in slightly fewer numbers than in previous years. The next generation Honda CB 200, with a single-cylinder 200cc engine found favour, due mainly to its proven reliability record. Although only a single pot motor, it could top 90 mph, which was plenty fast enough for what it was required to do. Each bike was fitted with a full Rickman fairing, panniers and top box, fully decorated in red and blue stripes. A large blue light was positioned at the rear to warn oncoming motorists, whilst engaged at the scene of an accident and a smaller one was placed on the front of the fairing. These small motorcycles were still in use in many of Hampshire's rural beats, but their days were numbered.

Honda CB 200 rural beat motorcycle.
Author.

BMW meanwhile, updated their K series bike to the K1100LT, increasing the engine capacity by 100 cc and giving it, amongst many minor modifications, an electrically adjustable screen. This allowed the rider to adjust the height of the screen to suit his own size. Gone were the days when motorcycles were allocated on a personal basis for the duration of its service, Traffic motorcyclists now had to share machines. Top speed was around 125 mph and there were improvements to the handling. Livery and equipment were the same as on the previous issue K100s, except for the addition of the SPDM speed detection unit.

The new BMW K1100LT complete with
electrically adjustable screen.
Author.

Towards the end of 1993 the force purchased several four-wheel drive vehicles to add to its still growing fleet. A one off vehicle was acquired for the New Forest area in the shape of a Landrover 90 Defender 2.5 Tdi. Based at Lyndhurst this unit was deemed necessary because of the obvious amounts of forest and heath land that required policing. In essence the vehicle was a rural beat unit, covering several areas and could be called upon from anywhere within the Forest Division to assist as and when necessary.

Fitted with a Britax light bar, an old set of two-tone horns and the livery formally used by area cars, it was fairly unremarkable. To aid the recovery of other vehicles or to remove fallen trees or other obstacles, a powerful electric winch was fitted to the front of the vehicle. Like all Landrovers of this type, it proved to be a reliable and robust workhorse.

Landrover 90 Defender 2.5 Tdi based at Lyndhurst.
Andy Bardsley

The other four-wheel drive vehicles purchased were a batch of series 1 Landrover Discovery 2.5 Tdi's. Two were given to the Traffic Division, following a Home Office directive that every Traffic area within the force should have a four-wheel drive capability. As the Northern Traffic area already had the services of a Range Rover that just left South Western and South Eastern Traffic without. The time had come for them to move on from the tragedy of the past and look forward.

Both the Traffic Discoverys were identically equipped and marked and it is here that the force took another step forward, by applying rearward facing, diamond grade reflective striping. The rear of the vehicles were decorated with red and yellow diagonal stripes and this was also carried forward along the sides of the stepped roof. This addition did look slightly odd as it clashed with the standard livery applied to the sides of the car. The idea was to extend the reflective area seen by approaching motorists when the Discovery was parked echelon fashion. Equipment included a full width light bar made by Woodway Engineering of Coventry. This unit incorporated a pneumatic flood light system, with 1000w of power, operated from inside the vehicle. The mast would extend upwards by about ten feet (approx. 3m) and would illuminate a darkened scene using four halogen lamps. The actual light bar incorporated blue strobe lights instead of the mechanical spinners used on Premier Hazard systems and were a considerable improvement, especially in bright weather conditions. At the rear of the bar were two red flashers and illuminated Police/Stop signs. At either end of the bar were side alley lights in white. These were a novel and very useful addition and helped pick out house numbers in a darkened street or search a motorway embankment with. A pair of twin blue repeater lights were also set into the front grille.

Inside the vehicle a fully padded tubular steel roll cage was installed in the passenger compartment to help protect the occupants in the event of the vehicle overturning. In the rear load compartment of the Discos (as they were commonly called) the workshops staff had excelled themselves in building a purpose made racking system to house the large amount of extra emergency kit that it was expected to carry. Now everything had its place instead of the hit and miss situation you had with equipment being stored in the boot of a saloon car.

The Discoverys were to be used as motorway back-up units to the standard motorway cars and were there to provide additional kit should it be required. However, with a full load of equipment, a heavy stem light system, steel roll cage and two overweight policemen on board, the turbo diesel engine really struggled to get going, especially up hill. Its top speed down hill, with a strong tail wind would only be 95 mph at best and it took a long while to get it to that speed! Needless to say there were those who became increasingly reluctant to use the vehicle.

The two vehicles were stationed at Lyndhurst and Fareham, although the Fareham car was eventually shared between there and Cosham on a monthly basis. Both returned around 145,000 miles service and were retired in 1999.

The Fareham/Cosham based Landrover Discovery 2.5 Tdi 4x4 showing off its new rear 'tiger stripes'. The call sign was HM-01.
Author.

Did You Know That.......?
The Discovery's used on Traffic got the name 'the tractor' because they were noisy and just as slow!

The other Discoverys were used as rural area cars. This was a completely new concept and combined the need for an emergency response unit with the ability to go off road, should the need arise. They were fitted with a Premier Hazard light bar, placed on the upper part of the roof, sirens and all the usual area car equipment. The only anomaly here concerns the livery, which didn't exactly comply with the directive that all emergency response units should be conspicuous and reverted back to the graphics used on previous area cars. These Discoverys were also fitted with the internal roll cage, but not the heavy racking system or stem light unit fitted to the Traffic units and were all the better for it. Because they weren't required to perform the outright speeds like their motorway counterparts were, they were considered perfectly adequate for the task they were brought in for. Generally speaking they got an easier life and were that much more reliable than the Traffic units.

A later model Landrover Discovery 2.5 Tdi 4x4 rural area car.
Author.

The Diesel Fleet Experiment was now fully implemented, with more and more non-response units being purchased with diesel engines. Those stations that supplied fuel had their tanks and systems transferred to accept diesel fuel only, whilst those petrol driven units were now supplied with agency cards and refuelled at regular petrol stations. Unfortunately, there were those who couldn't tell the difference when it came to refuelling time and on several occasions, diesel cars were filled with petrol and visa versa!

As has been discovered on several occasions whilst researching this book, the Hampshire Constabulary has acquired an oddity vehicle from time to time, not in the usual fleet line up, the Austin Allegros and Volvo 264s springing to mind. At Basingstoke in late 1993 or early 1994, they obtained the services of a MK1 Vauxhall Corsa 1.7D Merit, five-door hatchback. This was offered on the cheap by Vauxhall in an attempt to break Ford's stranglehold on the section vehicle market. Fitted with a Britax light unit and blue and white chequered side stripe, Police signs and Hampshire crest, it was used as a section vehicle in the Basingstoke area. Although generally well received, it wasn't as popular as the Escort. It was cramped inside and had slightly offset driving pedals, making life somewhat uncomfortable for the driver over long periods of time. It was also marginally slower than the Ford and because it wasn't a regular car would take longer to service than most.

MK1 Vauxhall Corsa 1.7D Merit used as a Basingstoke section vehicle.
Andy Bardsley

In early 1994 Hampshire's Fleet Manager Mr John Roberts retired, after many years in the motor trade. He had overseen many changes in his career, some of them controversial, some of them quite radical, but always with the best interests of the Constabulary at heart. His replacement was Mr John Bradley, who had already served the force since the mid 1960s, starting life at the old Winchester HQ workshops as a stores man, gradually working his way up through the ranks. He had previously worked in the private sector as a vehicle mechanic and his father had owned the local Renault dealership in Winchester.

The year 1994 was rife with rumours that the Government were about to privatise a large part of the Police vehicle maintenance operation throughout the country by making about 40% of the operation the subject of Compulsory Competitive Tendering (CCT). The Hampshire Constabulary spearheaded a national campaign to lobby MP's in an effort to reverse the proposal. The campaign's main objections were the safety and security of Police vehicles, the possible loss of jobs, more expense to the ratepayer and less flexibility. A united front was shown to the Government, with members of the Police Federation, ACPO, Unison and members of the Police Authority all joining forces to stave off the threat. After months of lobbying the Home Secretary, Michael Howard, finally scrapped the idea in February 1995.

The Marine Unit's long-term love affair with the launch Ashburton came to an end in 1994, when it was decided that she was no longer economical to run and she was decommissioned. In her place came three smaller 25-foot Seaward motor launches from T.T. Boat Designs at Seaview on the Isle of Wight. One of these replacements was named Ashburton, with the others called Scott and Mountbatten.

One of the three new Hampshire Police launches
on patrol in the seas off the south coast.
Hampshire Constabulary

By mid 1994 an increasing number of special programmes were being implemented to keep kids off drugs and away from a life of crime. One of the bigger Hampshire projects was the *Getting It Right* program, which involved the Police, schools, social workers and other professionals, with the added backing of local commercial companies. As part of that package, these companies were persuaded to sponsor a vehicle that could be used by the Police whilst attending various *Getting It Right* activities. One of the first such vehicles was a Volvo 460 GLEi sponsored by the Volvo dealership of Cambridge Garage at Havant. The white bodied saloon car was decorated with various logos, including the Hampshire crest, the *Getting It Right* graphics and the name of the sponsors. This was the first time ever that a Hampshire Police vehicle, albeit a loaned vehicle, was allowed to bear a commercial name on its sides. There would be more to follow.

First of the sponsored cars, a Volvo 460 GLEi for the Getting It Right program.
Author.

The fleet of diesel section vehicles continued to expand and as older petrol engined cars came in for replacement, so a diesel would be sent back in its place. The earlier experimental cars were three door hatchbacks of course. Some of the later cars were five door estates and were a lot more versatile. All the livery and equipment remained the same.

MK5 Ford Escort 1.8D estate section car.
Author.

233

A problem arose in many rural areas and in some urban districts, where youths on stolen mopeds and motorcycles would ride off into areas where either a car or road going motorcycle just wasn't able to. The force therefore bought several Kawasaki KLR 250s, an off-road trail bike, capable of going just about anywhere. Decorated with a couple of Police signs on the side panels and on the area above the front headlight, they were very successful and were directly responsible for the apprehension of many a bike thief.

Go anywhere Kawasaki KLR 250.
Author.

Ford made another attempt on the upper end of the fleet market with the introduction of the MK1 Ford Mondeo 24v 2.5i V6 saloon. Hampshire was offered two, first on long term test, then at a vastly reduced rate. The cars were sent to Winchester and Fareham Traffic sections, where they were considered to be underpowered for use as a motorway car, but good enough as an urban Traffic car or perhaps as an area car. In comparison with the BMW 5 series and the Vauxhall Senator they were rather cramped inside with a smallish boot. Performance was brisk up to around 100 mph, but thereafter it struggled to reach its top end of 115 mph. Needless to say they didn't catch on and after 120,000 miles or so they were retired.

The Fareham based MK1 Ford Mondeo saloon, call sign HM-04.
Christopher Taylor.

A second sponsored car arrived in the county towards the end of the year, in a deal between Gosport Police and one of their local garages, Wadham Kennings of Fareham. A MK1 Vauxhall Omega saloon was used to help educate the public of Gosport about rising vehicle crime, in conjunction with the Governments *Crime-Together We'll Crack It* advertising campaign and a local car alarm business *The Alarming Company* they helped distribute leaflets and advice concerning vehicle security.

MK1 Vauxhall Omega sponsored unit used in Gosport.
Hampshire Constabulary.

235

As the force moved into 1995 it was unlikely that anyone could have predicted the amount of change that was about to take place.

On the 13th March the Hampshire Constabulary held a press conference to announce that it was about to commence a 30-month trial with Britain's first ever electric Police vehicle. The Ford Ecostar van was to be used as a section vehicle at Fleet, where it would be directly compared against a Ford Escort 1.6 petrol van based at Hartley Wintney and a Ford Escort 1.8D van at Odiham. Comparisons would be made on the basis of performance and environmental impact. The idea of using a silent vehicle to approach a crime in progress in the middle of the night captured the media's imagination and the vehicle made national headlines as well as local, featuring in several TV programs and car magazines.

The vehicle was built around a MK4 Escort van shell. It incorporated unique battery technology and some of the most sophisticated electronics ever installed in a vehicle designed for normal day-to-day use. Some of the Ecostars key features included a sodium/sulphur battery, providing up to three times the power of a conventional lead/acid automotive battery. It gave a driving range of 120 miles between charges. A high-speed, three-phase, AC drive motor delivered the power to a single-speed, direct-coupled transaxle. A system called regenerative braking recharged the battery whilst the vehicle was decelerating.

Its top speed was restricted to 70 mph, with a 0 to 50 mph time of 12 seconds. Acceleration from a standing start to 30 mph was quicker than the comparable petrol and diesel vehicles, due to the high torque at low speed. At the end of each day, the car would quite simply be plugged into a special socket located in the rear yard at Fleet and recharged.

Other differences included a unique front grille with a series of different sized holes in it, unique wheel trims and colour-coded bumpers. A Britax light bar, together with blue and white chequered side stripes and all the necessary Police signs and force crest were also fitted.

Generally speaking the trial was a success. Those officers that drove the Ecostar were impressed with its performance, even if driving a silent vehicle took some getting used to! There are no records to state how many criminals it surprised by creeping up on them! At the end of the day it was just a trial, for the force and for Ford and has only found itself in this chapter instead of chapter 8, because it was more than the standard demonstrator model. It was used on a daily basis for two and a half years and is now a force museum piece, in fact the only vehicle the Hampshire Constabulary has ever kept. John Bradley managed to purchase the vehicle from Ford for a mere £100, not bad when you consider that the estimated value of the car when it was first built was a cool £250,000!

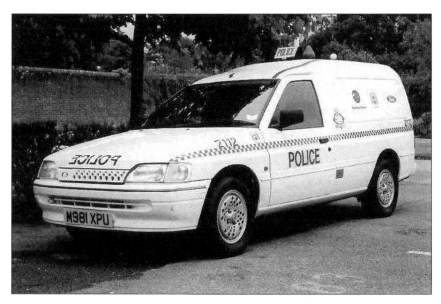

Front and rear views of the unique Ford Ecostar van,
Britain's first electric Police vehicle.
Author

By mid 1995 a rather public row blew up between the Hampshire Constabulary and Rover Cars Ltd. An area car crew complained to workshops that their Rover 820i wasn't handling very well and despite all the usual checks they couldn't work out why. It was eventually discovered that a large crack had developed around both the rear suspension turrets, causing some slight flexing in the body shell to occur. This was thought to be a one-off, until workshops starting checking all the others and found that the majority of them had suffered the same fate. All Rover 800 series cars on the fleet were immediately grounded and as is usual in such circumstances an urgent safety message was dispatched to every Police force in the UK advising them of the fault. Rover by all accounts were none too pleased when this hit the headlines and blamed Hampshire for over loading the boot with heavy emergency equipment! However, a deal was struck between the two and Rover took back the entire fleet to commence repairs and leant the force enough vehicles to replace them whilst they were gone. A fleet of Rover 620 SLi's arrived, with a magnetic single blue light attached to the roof and enough Police signs to enable the public to know what it was. The cars were a huge success and most of the area car drivers actually preferred driving them to the 820! Despite their protestations they had to hand them back after a couple of weeks, when their own vehicles were returned.

The Rover 620 SLi temporary area car stationed at Havant.
Author

Meanwhile two other car companies were about to start a fight over who could make the better Police patrol car. Vauxhall started it all, with the introduction of the Police specification MK1 Omega 3.0i V6 saloon, to replace it's ageing Senator. Billed as the *definitive Police saloon* the sales brochures made much of the fact that the Thames Valley Police were now almost exclusively a Vauxhall fleet and went on to suggest that they supplied more cars to the

Metropolitan Police than any other manufacturer, which was open to debate! Nonetheless, Vauxhall pulled off a masterstroke of sales bribery and delivered a Police spec Omega to every force in the country free of charge! Never one to look a gift horse in the mouth, Hampshire said 'thank you very much' duly striped it up, kitted it out and posted it to Lyndhurst.

With a top speed of around 130 mph, competent handling and a good level of comfort, the rear wheel drive Vauxhall found favour with most Traffic officers who drove it. In truth it wasn't that much different from the old Senator, which is partly why it wasn't that popular with the Finance Department at Headquarters or with the mechanics at Bar End.

The Lyndhurst based MK1 Vauxhall Omega 3.0i.
Andy Bardsley

There was another reason why the Vauxhall was put on hold, because following in its wake was a brand new car, something completely different. Volvo was back and brought with it a car that had gained almost legendary status overnight; the 850 T5. It was, quite simply a sensation to drive, with a top speed of 145 mph and neck breaking acceleration, it outclassed everything else. Like Vauxhall, Volvo sent a test car to every Police force in the UK in an effort to steal sales away from its rivals. Hampshire's test car, a manual saloon went to Cosham for a two-week trial (see Chapter 8). That trial was extended to four weeks, then three months, during which time officers from other areas had heard about the car and came over for a test drive. The verdict was almost unanimous in favour of the T5. Here was a car that was incredibly fast, had truly excellent road holding, was big enough and very comfortable to live with. The only reservation expressed by some was that it was front wheel drive and that the speeds it was often required to drive at, would need some serious re-thinking in terms of driver control.

Hampshire purchased the test saloon and Cosham got to keep it. Following a two-week trial with the force driving school the car went back to Bar End where Volvos own livery was removed and Hampshire's applied. The standard Woodway light bar was retained, as was the slightly different sounding siren system.

Volvo won the contest and following further testing with an estate version (see Chapter 8) an order was placed with them for an initial batch of ten 850 T5 estates instead of the saloon. This was followed shortly thereafter by an order for another six and in 1996 by another eleven. These cars replaced the out going BMW 5 series and eventually the Vauxhall Senator.

A legend is born the Volvo 850 T5 2.3i Turbo. This was the original test car,
now dressed up in Hampshire colours. Its call sign was CM-07.
Author.

Did You Know That.......?
The original trial T5 wasn't fitted with traction control and the front wheels would spin a lot. It was driven so hard by those that tested it that the front tyres needed replacing after just 4000 miles! At over £200 a tyre, one or two questions were asked in some very high places!

All this activity got Ford seriously worried and they jumped in with both feet and offered Hampshire two more cars on the cheap. It had just released the Scorpio 24v 2.9i V6 as the replacement for the old MK3 Granada. The new Scorpio had curious styling, which received some words of wisdom from the BBC's Jeremy Clarkson, on its Top Gear programme, when he described the front end as looking like a "wide mouthed frog". Unfortunately for Ford this touch of Clarkson prose stuck like a limpet and he undoubtedly cost them some serious money in lost profits!

The two cars found themselves at Lyndhurst and Eastleigh Traffic and in comparison with the Volvo and even the Vauxhall, just didn't stand a chance. With a top end of just 120 mph, outdated handling characteristics and looks that made school children giggle as you drove past, it wasn't too long before officers found a variety of excuses not to drive them.

Ford's wide mouthed frog, suffered from an identity crisis as well as a shortfall in performance. This Lyndhurst based car had the call sign DM-05.
Christopher Taylor

In June 1995 the Air Support Unit's aircraft was fitted with up-rated engines, with the old 260 hp engines having served their time. New 300 hp Lycoming engines, which gave improved performance and payload were fitted, together with all new video and thermal imaging equipment during a major refit. Boxer One Zero continued to give the ground troops a very good daily service with some excellent results.

But the biggest news of the year still centred on the new Volvo estate Traffic cars. Following Volvo's outstanding success with the 850 T5 estates in the British Touring Car Championships, it should have come as no surprise really that it was the estate, rather than the saloon that was to become the number one choice for the Traffic Division. But the biggest surprise of all was that they were to be automatics and not manual's, that got the tongue's wagging. There were some Traffic officers that had little or no experience at all of using an automatic gearbox and most of course had certainly never used one at the speeds that were used in Traffic patrol. To add to the confusion, the gearbox was a switchable unit, encompassing three modes of gearing via an electric switch, from *winter* to *cruise* to *sport* mode. The force driving school quickly set up one-day tutorials giving invaluable advice on the new front-wheel drive automatics. During these lessons, Traffic drivers were also shown a unique facility available to this car and that was a *lock-down* system on the gearbox, which enabled the car to travel from 8 mph to 85 mph in second gear without it changing up or down automatically. This system was especially useful during pursuits in built up areas like housing estates, where the car could be kept in second gear throughout.

241

There were other new innovations to get used to on the Volvo, including a new radio system made by Cleartone, which incorporated both UHF and VHF radio's in one neat unit. This did away with the need for two separate radio's and meant that on arrival at an incident the personal radio didn't have to be removed from it's booster pack and could be retained by the officer on his belt at all times. The hands free button, previously placed on the gear lever, was now moved to the floor, in the area where the clutch pedal would have been. This meant that the system really was now hands free.

The new traffic car of the late 1990s the automatic Volvo 850 T5 estate. This wonderful photo was used for several publicity and 'in-force' publications.
Nick Scott for Hampshire Constabulary

The Whelan light bar was a full strobe light unit, with the ability to have blue lights showing to the front only, rear only or at 360 degrees. It also had red rear lights, twin spotlights to the front and side alley lights. It was an effective unit in bright day light conditions as well as in night time use. Twin blue repeater lights were also incorporated behind the grille to add to the effectiveness of the roof lights. The whole system was operated via a neat control panel with illuminated touch sensitive buttons.

In the rear of the estates, workshops staff had built a tough, carpet lined, wooden racking system to house all the cones, signs, frames, tools and other emergency equipment necessary in a modern day patrol car. To prevent the whole lot being catapulted into the passenger compartment in a collision, a Volvo dog-guard was also fitted. Other equipment included the Police/Stop dot matrix box attached to the inside of the rear window, a mobile phone hands-free set, new style map reading lights, complete with red lens and a set of blue repeater lights placed on the inside top edge of the tailgate. These were necessary because when the tailgate was fully opened it wasn't possible to see the roof lights from the rear. Standard Traffic livery was applied to the vehicle, including the orange and yellow tiger stripes first seen on the Discovery.

Interior view of the Volvo 850 T5 showing the automatic gearbox lever and new Cleartone radio system.
Author.

This photo shows the excellent racking system devised and built by Hampshire's workshop staff.
Author.

But it wasn't a complete bed of roses. There were two grounds of complaint when the new cars starting arriving on division. The Volvo was undoubtedly quick, but it didn't seem to be as quick as the original test car and there were those who accused Volvo of re-chipping the test car, in order to make it that much quicker than the opposition. This of course was always denied and the difference in speed was put down to two area's; the fact that the new cars were automatics and therefore marginally slower and that the estates were somewhat heavier than the saloon and carried a lot more equipment, like the racking system, dog guards etc. It still had a top speed of 140 mph, but acceleration, although fast was definitely not as quick as the original test car. Eyebrows were further raised, when M493 SUD started to develop engine problems with only 70,000 miles on the clock. A new engine was fitted by Volvo and this was much slower than the old unit! The second and potentially much more serious problem centred on the brakes. In a nutshell they were inadequate. Unlike previous patrol cars, the Volvo had very little in the way of engine braking and consequently driver's were arriving at a hazard that much quicker than before and found that the brakes weren't up to the job of hauling the car down to a safe speed. Volvo eventually conceded that Police Traffic cars were required to perform over and above that of a normal car and fitted larger discs and high performance brake pads, which eventually did the trick. A total of 28 T5's were purchased by Hampshire over the next couple of years and they became the standard Traffic patrol car for the force. But unlike previous Volvos it wasn't just Hampshire that had taken the plunge. The T5s started to take over in many other forces across the UK, from the south of England to the tip of Scotland; it became the number one choice.

The last 850 T5 issued to Hampshire was this car. It was originally based at Cosham where it had the call sign ME-06, before later going to Fareham where its call sign became MH-06.
Andy Bardsley

The motorcycle fleet was also about to see radical change, with the purchase of Honda ST1100 Pan Europeans as the next generation Traffic bike. BMW basically shot itself in the foot over this. Police forces across the UK were being offered the new Honda as a complete Police package, with full wiring, lights, panniers and all the other necessary items already in place and at a very competitive price. BMW on the other hand refused to include said items as part of the package, because they believed, quite wrongly, that no Police force would buy the big Honda in bulk, because of political pressures brought about by the UK's involvement with Europe. By the time BMW realised its mistake it was too late. Hampshire and many other forces besides had fallen for the Japanese V4 motorcycle, albeit there were some Traffic motorcyclists who preferred the performance and handling of the big BM.

The Honda was an 1100cc V4 with shaft drive, a fully enclosed fairing and stunning good looks. It was marginally slower than the BMW at 122 mph and the arguments over its handling would depend on which officer you spoke to! Some liked it, some didn't. Above all though it was incredibly reliable and because most of the accessories were already in place on arrival, all the force had to do was dress it up in the standard Traffic livery and send it out to work.

The Honda ST1100 Pan European, the new standard in traffic motorcycles.
Hampshire Constabulary

As the force moved into 1996, there were several exciting new ideas on the horizon that would transform both the economic and visual look of the vehicle fleet.

But first, it was business as usual with the gradual replacement program of new for old. Ford made subtle but important changes to its range, including the MK6 Ford Escort and Hampshire bought both hatchback and estate variants in petrol and diesel.

The new MK6 Ford Escort estate section vehicle.
Author

The new section cars were equipped in much the same way as before, with a Britax blue light system, which incorporated a Police/Stop light to the rear, but no siren of course. Strict new guidelines were issued at this time, reminding section vehicle drivers that they were not permitted to break speed limits or use their vehicles as emergency response units as they were not trained to do so. This, quite naturally, caused some difficulties at times and a degree of resentment that officers were being restricted from doing their job effectively.

The new Escorts, which were the last of the line from Ford, came with either a 1.8 diesel or 1.4 petrol engine, depending on the area they were to be used in. They were a significant improvement over the previous two models, which had been slated by the motoring press for being out of date before they were even produced!

The MK6 Ford Escort hatchback section vehicle. This unit was based at the old Cowplain Police Station. Author

247

Ford also updated the Transit range in 1996 with the introduction of the MK4. Although basically the same vehicle as the MK3, it did get an all-new interior, a smiling face grille and other more subtle styling changes. Hampshire of course bought the new Transit for a variety of jobs, including two to be used as Administration units. These vehicles would be driven by civilian drivers, who would be responsible for moving large bulky items around the county. Each van, which was a diesel variant, was decorated with Police signs, the Hampshire crest and Southern Crime Stoppers logo, but no lights or sirens of course. Inside, a removable racking system was built in, to keep smaller items in place.

MK4 Ford Transit Administration Unit.
Author

Sponsored Police units were beginning to catch on in a big way across the country and there were several used in Hampshire, including a Citroen Saxo sponsored by Solent Citroen of Hilsea, Portsmouth for the new *Get Real* project. In the north of the county a Honda Civic, sponsored by Webbers Honda was used for the same project. But the most successful station in the county at acquiring sponsored cars has to be Gosport who built up an excellent relationship with Pooles Peugeot and used a variety of Peugeot cars, brilliantly liveried to carry certain messages to the local population. In many ways these cars can be compared to the American D.A.R.E cars (Drug Abuse Resistance Education) which were also highly decorated vehicles, used to send a message by dedicated officers. Gosport Police also made a point of having the vehicles photographed in prominent local areas and then using those photos as part of the publicity machine to promote the project. The whole concept of using sponsored vehicles to push home important messages to the public is clearly a good idea and will no doubt develop further over a period of time.

*Peugeot 406 sponsored by Pooles Peugeot to help Gosport Police
promote its anti car crime initiative, seen parked outside
the Air Support Units control tower at HMS Daedalus.
Hampshire Constabulary*

*Peugeot 106 used to promote the 'Enforcing The Peace'
Initiative seen outside the gates to Fort Brockhurst.
Hampshire Constabulary.*

Meanwhile area cars were getting slightly revised graphics, with the addition of tiger stripes across the rear end. This added safety feature was considered necessary because of area cars responsibility as motorway back-up units, in the event of a major accident. Also because a Traffic unit might not be available to attend other accidents, the area car would be the main source of protection at a darkened scene. Another addition to every area car was a mobile phone. Used as a covert method to deploy units from the control room, it was a similar idea to the aforementioned IBM system, to prevent those engaged in criminal activity from listening in. A fully hands free system was used and eventually this was also fitted to all traffic cars, although they were not afforded the luxury of a dedicated phone for each unit.

BMW 325 TDS area car showing off its new rear end striping.
This is Cosham's area car, call sign CC-50.
Author

The force's armoured Landrover received a new look in 1996 as well. A more subtle colour was called for, to make it look less like a Police vehicle. Out went the white paintwork and orange stripes. Off came the blue lights and windscreen grille. In came additional plating to the bonnet, wings and bumpers, grab rails for the roof and all green paint. This was to make the vehicle less conspicuous when in the process of evacuating casualties or providing hard cover during a firearms incident.

New look for the force's armoured Landrover.
Author

The Hampshire Exhibition Unit also got a new look for 1996. The old Leyland Atlantean double-decker bus was spruced up with new paint job in light blue and green with smart Police graphics. It gave the unit a much more modern look and helped promote the various new initiatives that Hampshire would take on the road to various public events throughout the year, including the *PC Wise* scheme, which the kids loved.

Old bus, new style. The force exhibition unit is seen
here at the Portsmouth and Southsea Show in 1996.
Author.

Hampshire started to look at the competition to the Ford Escort in 1996. For the first time in many years there were actually a couple of viable alternatives. Following a successful trial period, a batch of 12 Rover 220Ds arrived in the north of the county. This lovely looking five-door hatchback was a better quality car than the Ford, but lacked interior space. Its diesel engine was quieter and marginally faster than the Escort and it was difficult to separate the two overall. Despite the difficulties of the past, this Rover didn't suffer from repetitive reliability problems. The Rovers were equipped in the same way as all other section vehicles. Although the first batch of cars were confined to the northern area of the force, they were eventually dispersed to various other areas and eventually most stations had at least one of the Rovers.

The Rover 220D section vehicle.
Author.

The other new car to arrive was the MK1 Peugeot 306 GRD, another five-door hatchback with a diesel engine. The first of these new cars went to Gosport, who already had experience with using Peugeots of course, with their sponsored units. The *Pug* was a great success, being quicker than the Ford Escort, with just as much room and good reliability. Its diesel engine was rather loud though and this would put off some officers from driving it. Overall though it scored highly and Ford's dominance in the small scale Police vehicle market was losing some of its grip.

Gosport's first marked Peugeot 306 GRD section vehicle.
Author.

The Chief Constable, Mr John Hoddinot got a new car in 1996 in the shape of the new Jaguar XJ6 4.2i. This fabulous looking vehicle, finished in burgundy would be chauffeur driven by a dedicated class-one Traffic driver, to convey the Chief Constable to and from the many and varied public functions and official engagements he had to attend. It was also fitted with all the necessary radio and telecommunications equipment necessary, to keep him in touch with the force whilst on the move.

The Chief's Jaguar XJ6.
Author.

The biggest change of all though came in late 1996 when Hampshire took the decision to update its image and give itself a *corporate identity*. This would involve a whole degree of new ideas and changes and where best to push that idea than on the forces fleet of over 600 vehicles.

Part of that new image centred on the idea that the graphics used on the force Traffic and area cars needed modernising. Hampshire's Fleet Manager John Bradley was given a clean sheet of paper and tasked with coming up with something new. At the same time the force was starting to get pressure placed upon it from the Home Office concerning its idea for a national Police motorway livery, in the form of the yellow and blue battenburg style blocks. Fearing it would lose its identity completely and faced with the fact that the battenburg livery was incredibly expensive, Hampshire decided not to take this idea on board and opted instead to design its own.

John Bradley sat down with the designers from 3M, the manufacturers of the reflective material used on emergency service vehicle graphics. John asked the simplest of questions; "What colour reflects the most light?" The obvious answer was "white". Between them, they decided to base the new scheme around a white reflective material and eventually arrived at red and white diagonal striping for the sides of the vehicle. It certainly looked different and in Police vehicle graphics, was totally unique. A Volvo 850 T5 estate was used as the test model and the livery applied. The standard tiger striping was left on the rear, as this was considered to be sufficient and contrasted well with the new side stripes.

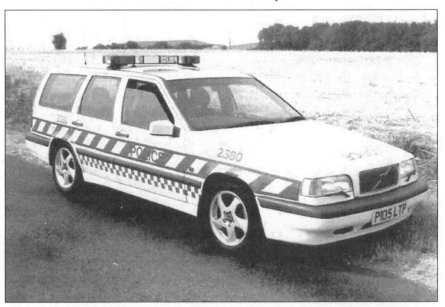

The new graphics are seen here for the first time on P105 LTP,
the only Volvo 850 model that was liveried in this way.
Author

At first the new graphics received a mixed reaction, some liked it, some didn't. But its real test came when it was placed in the position for which it was designed for, to maximise the car at the scene of an incident and to protect the officers going about their duties, especially in the dark. The difference between the old style and the new, diamond grade white material was staggering. In the dark, when picked up in the headlights of an approaching vehicle, the white material positively glowed and could be seen from a far greater distance than before. This had obvious safety advantages. In daylight, the idea was just as effective and really caught the eye. The only real concern was that the Police sign attached to the front doors couldn't be seen properly and on all later models this was enlarged and the striping stopped at either end. The experiment lasted through the rest of 1996 and it wouldn't be until 1997 that the fleet would start seeing the change and even then it was only to be fitted to new cars.

The new design earned the Hampshire Constabulary a special award in the over-seas category of the competition run by America's *Law and Order* magazine. The judges evaluate the vehicle graphics and the contest aims to raise Police and public awareness of the value of easily recognised, professional looking Police vehicles.

There were two other new ideas placed on the bonnet of this vehicle and these were more to do with the corporate identity. The first concerns a new look to the Hampshire Constabulary crest, which now had the wording placed in a circle around the actual badge. The second and more controversial idea was the application of the wording *Working Together For A Safer Community*. This really did stir things up with many people, both within the force and from the public, slating the idea as being *'too American'*.

The new bonnet graphics seen on the same Volvo.
Author.

Apart from those that simply didn't like the new slogan, there were more constructive criticisms levelled at the fact that it was simply too small to be seen by the public and a decision was made to increase it in size, to occupy the full width of the bonnet and to make the font a bit bolder. In doing so, the force created a bit of stir when it was discovered that the style of the lettering used in the word *working,* if viewed from a certain direction, could look like something rather obscene! The letters o and r being the culprits. Unfortunately, this wasn't discovered until several months after the logos had started being applied to the fleet. The idea was briefly suspended whilst a revised slogan and new font style were introduced. This time it read *Working For Safer Communities* and the separated lettering helped alleviate any misconceptions about the slogan!

Viewed from a certain angle, this slogan didn't say what it was supposed to!
Author

Did You Know That........?
When the new striping was first applied by workshops that some of the stripes sloped forwards and sometimes it sloped backwards, depending on who had done it!

256

The revised style and wording was eventually accepted by all.
Author

Meanwhile Gosport Police took delivery of another sponsored car, again from Pooles Peugeot.

This time a 306D in dark green got some very eye catching graphics and was used by the Community Beat Office to patrol known juvenile trouble spots. And in the north of the county, PC. Williams a local beat man, got the keys to another Honda Civic to promote the *Getting It Right* scheme from Webbers Honda in Andover.

The Peugeot 306 sponsored by Poole's Peugeot sits beside one of the exhibits at Gosport's Submarine Museum.
Hampshire Constabulary.

257

This Honda Civic from Andover carries the Getting It Right logo.
Andy Williams

At the beginning of 1997 types of fuel came to the fore once again. Advances in the use of Liquid Petroleum Gas or LPG over the last few years had prompted the force to look at this as a cheaper alternative to diesel fuel. It was not only cheaper to buy, but was environmentally much cleaner. In the late 1990s environment issues were a very political topic and it was considered expedient to at least have a good look at the practical use of LPG. Several leading car manufacturers were also giving this idea a long hard look and Hampshire acquired a MK4 Ford Transit and a MK3 Vauxhall Astra, already converted to accept LPG by leading experts in the field Powershift, to conduct the experiment with.

The only MK3 Vauxhall Astra on the Hampshire fleet was this LPG powered car. The 1.4 unit was used as a section car at Shirley for 18 months.
Author.

258

The MK4 Ford Transit LPG van was used as an admin and postal unit.
Author

The new experimental LPG vehicles
carried this additional logo on the sides.
Author.

As has been seen, every now and then Hampshire acquires an oddity vehicle for its fleet and what could be stranger than the following, which for the first time saw the force using a car from Japan! The MK2 Nissan Primera 2.0 Si was seen as a possible candidate as an area car and although it was primarily a Japanese car, it was built in the UK at its Sunderland plant. The sceptics gave it six months to live, with most believing that it just wasn't policeman proof and would fall to pieces a long time before that!

How wrong they were. The Nissan proved itself time after time, with an impressive performance record, a top speed of 120 mph, good handling and acceleration, comfort, space and above all, incredible reliability. The car came ready fitted with a Whelan light bar and all the necessary electric's and extra Police specification modifications. As this was the first time Nissan had been able to move in on the lucrative Police market, it didn't have a full Police spec vehicle available and this one therefore came with a glass sunroof, which the officers probably made good use of! This car then became the first full time area car to receive the new force graphics, with the revised Police sign on the doors and the whole package really did look very good indeed. The car certainly made the critics eat its words, because it more than lasted the course, covering 140,000 miles in three years.

It was posted to New Milton station in the New Forest and the combination of Japanese car and new graphics had an immediate impact on the public.

The Nissan Primera 2.0 Si area car used at New Milton.
Andy Bardsley

Another one-off car came in the shape of a new unmarked video Traffic car, the BMW 328i. This third generation, three-series car came with a 2.8i, straight-six engine, automatic gearbox and a top speed of 145 mph. It was an excellent driver's car with superb handling and a build quality second to none. Its only real down point was the lack of legroom for all concerned. Even the driver found it cramped and was unable to push the seat as far back as might have been desired.

The equipment fitted was much the same as on previous unmarked Traffic cars, with blue repeater lights set into the grille, a second set placed on the nearside sun visor, red and blue repeater lights on the rear parcel shelf, together with Police/Stop matrix lights. For the first six months or so of this cars service it went out on patrol without a video camera fitted, because of problems concerning the fitment in relation to the passenger air bag. This had not been a problem in the past because such items were not fitted to cars, but in the late 1990s most cars were being fitted with an increasing number of air bags.

The unmarked video traffic BMW 328i had the call sign MM-02.
Author

The force exhibition bus got yet another change of livery in 1997, its third since it was purchased. The restyled bus was now painted in navy blue with a light blue outline of Hampshire and the Isle of Wight depicted on the sides. The new corporate logo was placed on all four sides of the bus and inside it received all the latest force project news and details to keep the public up to date with Hampshire's initiatives. The bus would be taken out to various public events around the two counties all year round and was very popular with the kids. It was eventually replaced in 1999, with a purpose built exhibition and recruitment unit.

The old Leyland Atlantean exhibition bus, now on its third livery.
Christopher Taylor

Volvo underwent a major redefinition of its range in 1997 and in doing so badged its cars in a different way. All saloon cars were to be prefixed with the letter S whilst estates would get the prefix of V, which stood for versatile. The hugely successful and award winning 850 T5 estate therefore became the V70 T5. The car itself also came in for a major revamp, with the most notable changes being a completely new front end, new wheels and a much better interior. The car was even nicer to drive, it was much smoother and made the previous model feel positively agricultural. Together with the new graphics, the car was to become the symbol of Traffic policing in Hampshire for the latter part of the 20th Century and into the 21st. Because the car was so good, Hampshire put all its eggs in one basket and for the first time since the 1950s when the entire fleet consisted of Wolseley 6/80s, the Hampshire Traffic car fleet used just one make and model of car. As such, the Volvo 850 T5/V70 T5 deserves to be recognised as one of the landmark cars.

It wasn't just Hampshire that was using them either, with just about every Police force in the UK now using the Volvo, in either saloon or estate variants, it really was becoming one of the most successful Police Traffic cars of all time. As its fame spread, so did the sales to other forces overseas, including Canada and the United States, where the California Highway Patrol, Michigan State Police and others found favour with the car. This was praise indeed, as the Americans in particular have by tradition remained very patriotic towards their own products.

The hugely successful Volvo V70 T5 became the standard traffic patrol car for Hampshire and beyond. This Cosham based car had the call sign MC-07.
Andy Bardsley

Interior of the Volvo V70 T5 showing the much-improved layout and the very neat additional switch panels and radio console.
Note the mobile phone holder.
Author.

Did You Know That.......?
A woman complained that she mistook the new graphics on the traffic cars for one of those red and white chevron boards used to protect road works! To prevent any further confusion a reflective yellow stripe was placed along the edge of the roof and bonnet to show the outline of the car in the dark!

The BMW 325 TDS area car experiment was deemed to be a success and the decision was taken to replace the Rover 820s with the diesel BMW as and when they were due replacement. As with the Nissan Primera, the new issue BMWs were decorated with the new corporate graphics. Equipment levels remained the same.

An accident involving a Fratton based BMW area car made the headlines locally, when it drove through the front window of a hairdresser's in Fratton Road, Portsmouth. Although this was mildly amusing to the local populous, it had major repercussions for the force. The area car driver concerned publicly stated that the BMW was too fast and that the force had failed to train him properly! With the Police service in general looking at all aspects of health and safety at this moment in time, the driver was removed from area car duties and Hampshire started looking at slightly slower cars.

This Waterlooville based BMW 325 TDS area car looks good
in its new graphics. Call sign was JW-52.
Author

In the latter half of 1997, the force took on three very different types of vehicle, albeit in limited quantities, because they were considered the best in their class for the job that the force had in mind for them.

First of the new vehicles was the Daihatsu Fourtrak, a 2.8 TD with selectable four-wheel drive. This tough all-terrain vehicle was a bit basic in comparison with some other off-roaders, but it did the job it was intended for. They were cheaper to buy and run than the Landrover Discovery that they replaced and were somewhat more reliable. Top speed was a rather poor 85 mph, but then it wasn't intended to be used as a performance motor, more a rural work-horse, enabling those officers with plenty of countryside to police, the opportunity of going off-road when necessary. The car was essentially little more than a section vehicle, but only certain driver's, who qualified at the force driving school in off- road driving techniques, were permitted to use it.

The equipment fitted was a mixture of area car and section vehicle. A Premier Hazard Maxim light bar adorned the rear section of the roof, with twin repeater lights set into the grille. Standard section car graphics were placed on the sides, whilst on the rear of the vehicle some attempt was made with providing yellow and orange stripes on the spare wheel cover.

Initially two Daihatsu Fourtraks were purchased, with one going to Alresford and the other to Whitehill. Several more were bought to replace other Landrover Discoverys as and when they were retired.

The Daihatsu Fourtrak TD stationed at Whitehill
gave four-wheel drive capability to rural sections.
Andy Bardsley.

Another Daihatsu to find favour with Hampshire caused quite a stir wherever it went. The Daihatsu Move looked more like an upturned wardrobe on castors, than a Police vehicle. The diminutive Daihatsu was a mere ten feet in length, but still managed to have five doors and five seats. The 850 cc, three-cylinder engine was good for 80 mph and returned an average 47 mpg. But why was it ever used as a Police car? Following a successful trial in the New Forest (see Chapter 8) it was purchased and used by rural beat officer PC Colin Gordon at Ashurst. Like most other rural beat officers he had the use of a lightweight motorcycle to go about his business. The Daihatsu had several advantages over a motorcycle. First and most importantly in PC Gordon's eyes was that he remained dry! Previously, if he had been on an enquiry somewhere and the weather was bad, he would spend the first ten minutes on arrival, removing wet weather clothing and apologising for dripping all over someone's carpet! His paperwork remained dry as well. He was also able to take passengers without the need to call up another four-wheeled unit and as the rear seats folded down, the Daihatsu was also capable of carrying small loads. With typical Japanese reliability, it was actually cheaper to run than a small motorcycle.

A Premier Hazard light bar was fitted by Daihatsu prior to delivery and Hampshire decorated the car in its old Traffic livery, complete with a small amount of rear striping in orange and yellow and believe it or not, it also came fitted with a siren!

The car drew comments from the public wherever it went. Some laughed, some scorned, some shook their heads in disbelief, but all of them talked to the officer who was driving it and it really helped break down some barriers, in particular with adolescent kids who couldn't quite believe what they were seeing. In this respect alone the car has to rate as a success!

The cute little Daihatsu Move turned heads wherever it went.
Andy Bardsley

The final car in the batch of three has to rate as one of the most incredible cars ever to grace the road. The Subaru Impreza 2.0i Turbo 4x4 was a three-times world rally winning car in the late 1990s and the Japanese firm was keen to make in-roads on the Police market. Humberside Police bought two cars and used them as marked pursuit cars in replacement for their Cosworth Escorts. The only other force to indulge at this time though was Hampshire, which purchased just one, an unmarked red model, for use as a video equipped Traffic car.

The two litre, turbo-charged engine was capable of propelling the car to 145 mph with neck wrenching acceleration. But it was the grip and handling from its permanent four- wheel drive system that really got people talking. The vehicle could be driven around bends at an indecent pace and there were few, if any, other normal road cars that could keep with it, or more importantly as far as the Police are concerned, get away from it! The interior was one of the few areas of the car that came in for any criticism because the bucket seats were very cramped, especially with officers having to wear full utility belts as well. The car also had very harsh suspension and it became a tiring car to drive and live with.

Equipment on the Subaru included twin blue repeater lights inside the grille and red and blue repeaters placed on the rear parcel shelf. A hinged Police/Stop matrix board was also fixed to the parcel shelf, with a second reverse unit placed inside the car, facing forward. A new advanced video camera, with liquid crystal screen was placed inside the car, with the actual recorder located in a special bracket placed inside the boot. The screen was housed in a specially made pod, secreted into the top of the dash. This unit housed all the necessary record/stop/pause/rewind buttons for the recorder and the actual screen folded down out of sight until needed to show an errant motorist their driving activities! This was a very neat idea and helped make the car look like any other on the road.

The Subaru Impreza proved to be very reliable, but very expensive to repair when damaged in two separate collisions. A second VW Vento VR6 was purchased around the same time and proved to be just as popular as the first one.

The awesome Subaru Impreza 2.0i Turbo 4x4 unmarked video car, call sign MM-04.
Author

*Interior view of the Subaru showing the flip-top video screen
on top of the dash, with the camera just above.
Author*

By 1998 Ford had introduced the replacement for its most successful car ever. Out went the Escort and in came the radically designed Focus. The new Ford was to prove too expensive and wasn't available in large quantities immediately and therefore a replacement was required for section vehicle use as soon as possible. The MK4 Ford Fiesta seemed like the natural successor to the Escort and now came with five doors, instead of the previously issued three. The 1.8 diesel engine gave a top speed of 96 mph and in almost every other respect was similar to the Escort, although the handling was lighter and more responsive.

A Premier Hazard Maxim 90 light bar was fitted and all section cars now got the blue and white chequered side band and the corporate logo *Working For Safer Communities* splashed across the bonnet.

*The MK4 Ford Fiesta 1.8D
section car.
Author.*

A replacement program for the multi-role vans was started in 1997 and these started to arrive in 1998, with one or two modifications over the previous unit. For a start the base model was the updated MK4 Ford Transit and the conversions were carried out to force specifications by either Hawson Garner or Bedwas. The 2.5 Tdi engine remained the same, but the interior of both the cab and rear compartment was modernised somewhat. Outward changes included taller rear door windows, additional side windows and revised rear view mirrors. Better locks on the now Perspex lined rear cage ensured that prisoners could not escape and more storage room incorporated into the central cabin area. One idea borrowed from the ambulance service was the installation of side alley lights to help the crews find darkened house numbers.

The new MK4 Ford Transit multi-role vans were updated in 1998.
Author.

The force's mobile Control Unit got a revamp in 1998, with a new livery and a new name. Now called the *Incident Support Unit*, it received orange side stripes, rear tiger striping, a second blue light on the rear of the roof and the corporate logo on the bonnet. Inside, the unit was updated with new communications equipment capable of keeping the vehicle operational for several more years to come.

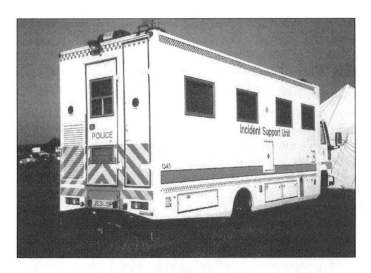

The Incident Support Unit was updated in 1998.
Author.

Meanwhile, the Isle of Wight remained a bastion for the unusual. As has been previously explained, the islands Police vehicles were somewhat different to their mainland counterparts. The island took delivery of two Daihatsu Fourtrak 4x4s and these were decorated in the standard Traffic/area car graphics.

An Isle of Wight based Daihatsu Fourtrak.
Kevin Elliott.

270

The other new arrival on the island was a five-door Subaru Justy 1.3 GX AWD. This rather unusual vehicle, which was basically a Suzuki Swift with Subarus four-wheel drive system added on, was used as a section vehicle. It had a top speed of 96 mph and despite its four-wheel drive was somewhat unstable at speed, although its grip in the wet was said to be excellent. This was basically a cheap, long-term test car from Subaru to test the viability of such vehicles for section car use. Needless to say, it didn't catch on.

The AWD Subaru Justy.
Kevin Elliott

Following an extensive look at other vehicles capable of carrying the area car tag, but in a slightly slower guise, Hampshire opted to continue using the BMW 325 TDS, but in its Touring version and with an automatic gearbox. The estate variant was a bit heavier than the saloon and the auto box also marginally slower than the manual. With the addition of slightly more equipment in the rear, the new BMW was altogether a slower car than the original manual saloon. It was still good for 120 mph but took a touch longer to get there. All the equipment and graphics remained the same as on previous issue area cars.

Overall, the force would reap the benefits as the slower cars would hopefully result in less accident damage and as had already been proved with the automatics used by the Traffic Division, there would be less engine wear. Drivers too would eventually appreciate the difference in comfort and the greater control during a pursuit.

The slower BMW 325 TDS Touring with automatic gearbox.
Andy Bardsley.

The Southern Crime Stoppers logo was replaced in 1998 by a new national Crime Stoppers sign with a uniform telephone number. The new sticker gradually replaced the old one as new cars were liveried up.

The national Crime Stoppers logo.
Author.

Peugeot updated the 306 XLd in 1998 and Hampshire followed up its purchase of one of the early cars with a batch of 1.9 diesel engined cars, for use as section vehicles. The five-door hatchback was good for almost 100 mph and the handling was much improved over the old model. Twenty were purchased altogether as section vehicles and some also found their way into use as CID units.

The MK2 Peugeot 306 XLd section vehicles were a big success.
Author.

'Going green' was the buzzword in 1998, when it was decided that the force would use a series of environmentally friendly MK4 Ford Fiestas, converted to run on LPG. Following the successful trial of the LPG powered Vauxhall Astra and Ford Transit van, Hampshire's Fleet Manager John Bradley, approached the Department of the Environment's Energy Saving Trust to help finance the conversion of 15 Ford Fiestas to run on the green fuel, which produced 75% less emissions than their petrol equivalents. Hampshire entered a three-year trial with the Energy Saving Trust, Calor Gas, Powershift and Vauxhalls Special Vehicle Operations to evaluate the conversions. Huge savings were predicted on the annual fuel bill, which was now the force's second biggest expenditure after manpower.

The new vehicles were posted to Southampton Central, Totton, Shirley and Fratton. Each station was also supplied with the necessary refuelling tanks. Those officers that got to drive the Fiestas could not tell the difference in performance between the new cars and a petrol engined unit. The cars were decorated in the same way as any other section car, except for the addition of various sponsors stickers, which made the cars look more like a mobile advertising board!

The new LPG powered MK4 Ford Fiesta.
Author

Another sponsorship deal between the force and the McCarthy Foundation saw the formation of the *Call Bobby* scheme. This excellent idea saw the McCarthy Foundation sponsoring a range of vehicles across the UK, to assist the elderly victims of burglary in getting their house repaired and re-secured in the event that damage was done by the intruders. The Hampshire based units used Vauxhall Combo vans, diesel of course and manned by retired Police officers with a good knowledge of DIY skills. The vans were equipped with all the necessary tools a handyman might need and decorated with a special *Call Bobby* logo on the sides, together with the McCarthy Foundation signs.

Vauxhall Combo van used in the 'Call Bobby' scheme.
Author.

274

The Accident Investigation Unit at long last managed to get rid of their old and very slow Ford Courier vans and they were replaced by MK3 Vauxhall Astra 1.6i vans. These were identical to the Dog Section vehicles and were decorated in the new corporate livery. These vehicles proved to be so much better for the task they were required to perform and meant that an Accident Investigator could attend the scene of a serious accident that much quicker.

The new Accident Investigation Unit vehicles were
a lot less embarrassing to drive than the old units!
Tony Johnson.

Following the force's success in the *Law and Order* magazines competition in 1997, it entered again in 1998, with the slightly revised graphics used on the fleet of Traffic and area cars. It won first place in the *Agency Not in the USA* category of the International Best Police Vehicle Design competition. The win brought the force a cheque for $400 which it donated to the Hampton Trust charity.

Two photos, taken by Media Services photographer Nick Scott were used for the contest.

Both featured a Traffic Division Volvo V70 T5. The first showed the Tactical Firearms Team in full and dramatic pose, whilst the second highlighted the graphics reflective ability, whilst stationary at the side of the M3 motorway late at night.

This dramatic photo shows the Tactical Firearms
Team and the Volvo V70 T5 to full effect.
Nick Scott/Hampshire Constabulary

This excellent night time photo shows the reflective qualities of the new force graphics.
Nick Scott/Hampshire Constabulary

By late 1998, the Landrover Discoverys used by the Traffic Division were well past their sell by dates and were duly replaced with the new Range Rover Pegasus 4.0i V8 4x4 automatic. In total, three were purchased at a cost of more than £40,000 each. This expenditure was justified in that the diesel power of its predecessor just wasn't up to the job of hauling all that extra kit around and the power had to come from a V8 motor.

The new Range Rover was a vast improvement over the old model, with far better handling thanks to its very sophisticated air suspension set up. Performance was better to, with a top speed approaching 115 mph, although this was reduced somewhat by the addition of all the equipment the car was expected to carry. Its thirst for fuel didn't alter much though and could be as low as 10 mpg if pushed! With better build quality and reliability than before, the Range Rover was a better option than in the past, although it was still plagued with over-heating problems. The need for an internal role cage was dispensed with because the car had to pass stringent role over testing in the USA, prior to it obtaining the necessary safety certificate for export.

The new flagship of the Hampshire Constabulary was packed with a range of equipment. A Whelan Advant-Edge stem light and blue light system adorned the roof, with additional blue repeaters set into the grille and red and blue repeaters placed inside the tailgate. Inside the rear load area, the workshops staff had again built an excellent racking system that could be rolled out on wheels to access items like cones and signs. Other rear load kit included additional signs, tow ropes, Stinger and Stop Stick tyre deflation devices, safety helmets, major incident box, blue lights, torches and a comprehensive first aid kit.

Inside the cabin was the Cleartone radio set, Tracker stolen vehicle system, Vascar 5000 unit, Whelan matrix information control panel and the unit incorporating the lights and sirens. Other minor equipment helped complete a very impressive package. The three cars were based at Cosham, Eastleigh and Farnborough Traffic Sections.

The new Range Rover 4.0i V8 4x4 was a vast improvement over the old model.
This Cosham based unit had the call sign MC-01.
Author.

The last year of the 20th Century saw little in the way of great change, with the emphasis still on value for money, health and safety issues, together with financial constraints. As such, Hampshire still lead the way on so many vehicle fronts that others quite literally followed.

One irritating subject did keep raising its head in 1998 and again in 1999 and that was the pressure exerted by the Home Office for forces to adopt, what it described as the new national motorway livery, in other words, the dreaded battenburg! Most of Scotland, Wales and much of northern England had now succumbed and the hideous graphics were spreading south like an unstoppable plague. Hampshire's intention was to stay firm, politely informing the Home Office that it had spent thousands investing in its award winning design and it wasn't about to change and lose much of its identity.

Interior of the Range Rover shows an array of sophisticated equipment.
Author.

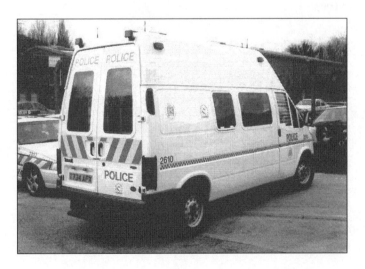

Ford Transit multi-role unit showing off its new rear end striping.
Author.

In an effort to alleviate the pressure, Hampshire starting to add yellow and orange tiger stripes to the rear of most of its front line fleet of vehicles. This included multi-role vans and section cars to aid safety for all concerned.

The Poole's Peugeot 206D used by Gosport Police. Hampshire Constabulary.

Gosport Police were at it again in 1999 and managed to obtain a sporty looking Peugeot 206 to help promote the new *Crime and Disorder Act* in the area. The smart blue 1.9D was again sponsored by Pooles Peugeot and was decorated with some excellent graphics. It was used by PC Andy Sparshott, an *Enforcing the Peace Officer* at Gosport and was the subject of various local newspaper and magazine articles in the six months that it was used.

The Daihatsu Fourtrak went out of production and Hampshire was again left with a problem. It eventually settled on the MK2 Nissan Terrano LWB 2.7 Tdi 4x4. It managed to obtain the first couple of cars at a vastly reduced rate as they were ex-demonstrators and were already over a year old.

The Nissan Terrano was a good replacement for the Daihatsu.
This unit, which was one of the first, was posted to Stockbridge.
Author.

279

The Nissan was an extremely reliable workhorse and was a better car than the Daihatsu. With a top speed of around 95 mph it was a lot quicker, much more comfortable and had plenty of interior space. As with the Daihatsu, each of the Nissans was equipped as a section vehicle and only those officers with four-wheel drive passes could drive them. As a rural vehicle, they were hard to beat.

Not to be outdone by their four wheeled compatriots, the Traffic motorcyclists got the new corporate graphics in 1999. The livery was applied to a BMW K1100LT as an experiment and trialled for several months, before the decision was taken to apply it to all new Traffic motorcycles, which were to be Honda Pan Europeans anyway. The decision on the livery had been delayed, because of the long awaited *Motorcycle Review* report, which had been rumoured to have recommended sweeping cuts in the Traffic motorcycle fleet. It transpired that only a few bikes would be lost through natural wastage and that the wholesale demise of the section would not be brought about by the report.

The BMW K1100LT showing the new graphics. This bike was unfortunately written off during a 'Blue Lights' display. Christopher Taylor.

Light-weight motorcycles however didn't fare quite so well. A decision was taken to scrap the idea of rural motorcycles altogether, as it cost almost as much to run a bike as it did a small, fuel efficient car. A gradual replacement program then took place, with car sharing and some re-distribution of area's taking place.

A novel vehicle was purchased at this time to help with the recovery of motorcycles. With health and safety issues uppermost in the force's mind, it was decided that lifting a motorcycle up onto a standard recovery truck or van was definitely in the high-risk category! A VW Razor Back van was therefore the answer. This incredible vehicle had the ability to drop its rear load deck to the floor on hydraulics, to enable the stricken bike to be wheeled straight in, without the need for any lifting.

The unit was fitted with twin amber beacons, orange side stripes and rear tiger stripes to aid roadside safety. It was based at Bar End, Winchester.

The amazing VW Razor Back motorcycle recovery unit.
Author.

The new Traffic motorcycles arrived in mid 1999 and the entire fleet was now made up of Honda ST1100 Pan Europeans, complete with anti lock brakes, traction control and heated handlebar grips. These were Honda's 50th Anniversary models and looked terrific with their gold wheels and new graphics.

The 50th Anniversary Honda Pan European looks splendid in its new outfit.
Christopher Taylor.

A fully armoured Volvo V70 T5 was shown at the 1999 Police Fleet Managers Conference at Devizes. The car was shown in full Hampshire livery and it was next to impossible to tell the difference between the standard car and the new armoured unit. With fully armoured 21mm glass and between nine and eleven layers of Aramide Composite material in the doors, bulkhead, tailgate, roof, wings and other vulnerable areas it certainly added a lot of extra weight to an already heavy car. The cars certainly go on a long journey prior to delivery. Each V70 is manufactured in Belgium, shipped to Sweden for Police package items to be fitted, then shipped to L'abbé in France, who take it all to pieces again to fit all the armoured parts and then ship it back to Sweden for further preparation to be carried out.

Although Hampshire has yet to purchase a fully armoured, standard looking Traffic car for first line response to an armed incident, it continues to work very closely with Volvo and L'abbé to develop the product further.

The L'abbé armoured Volvo V70 T5 seen at Devizes.
Author.

Various methods of speed enforcement have been tried and tested over the years and the latest weapon came in the shape of a laser speed detection unit linked to a video camera. This was set up in the rear of a fully marked Nissan Vanette 2.3D van. This unit would then remain stationary at a known accident site for a period of time and record those offenders breaking the speed limit. The video would then be down loaded at the end of the day and summonses would be automatically sent to the errant driver. Things had moved on a bit since the days of the Wallop speed trap! Three such vehicles were purchased by the force in 1999.

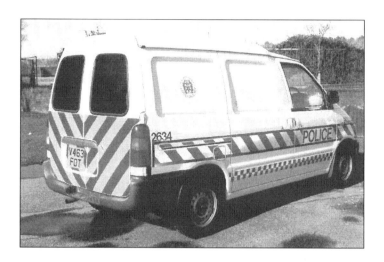

Nissan Vanette 2.3D speed enforcement unit.
Author

The Incident Support Unit got yet another change in style in 1999 and was brought up to date with the new force livery and corporate graphics.

Incident Support Unit shows off its latest look.
Christopher Taylor

Another vehicle to have been given a make over, albeit a major one, was the old Mercedes Benz detention unit. This vehicle had all of its interior load area ripped out and replaced with an exhibition area, all fully carpeted, complete with display units and video. Large side doors could be swung out to reveal the exhibits and additional awnings could be erected to create more space. The work was carried out by Hawson Garner of Andover and the smart graphics adorning the unit really made it stand out. The Mercedes was designed to replace the ageing Leyland Atlantean bus which was now retired.

New life was given to the old Mercedes Benz detention vehicle
by transforming it into this impressive exhibition unit.
Christopher Taylor.

The last 'new' vehicle of the millennium wasn't really a new one at all, but was actually second hand. Following recommendations from the Health and Safety Executive and the Civil Aviation Authority, a former Royal Navy Range Rover Carmichael 6x4 foam crash tender was purchased for the Air Support Unit. The CAA wasn't satisfied that a fire extinguisher in the back of a Landrover was sufficient to assist should the aircraft catch fire. You can see their point!

The 3.5 V8 unit was a familiar power plant, as were the inherent problems associated with the old Range Rover. However, the force spent several weeks stripping the vehicle down and rebuilding all its vital components in the hope that it would last the course. The new fire-fighting unit was fitted with an array of equipment to deal with most airfield incidents. This included foam extinguishant, coupled to a 120-foot hose, first aid kits, large searchlight, ladders and cutting equipment. All the officers engaged in duties at HMS Daedalus were trained to fight an aircraft fire using this new unit. Not since the days of the old Portsmouth City Police Fire Brigade have we seen that!

Front and rear views of the Air Support Units fire fighting unit,
a Carmichael Range Rover 6x4.
Author.

As was stated at the beginning of this book, the Hampshire Constabulary became quite famous at times because of its choice of vehicles. But it could also be argued that it is just as famous for some of the vehicles it didn't use, vehicles that other forces bought as their first choice but Hampshire didn't. No Morris Minors or Ford Anglia's for panda car use, no Vauxhall Vivas or Astras for later termed section car use either. The Vauxhall Cavalier, the Austin Metro, Maestro and Montego all failed against the Volvo 240 in the area car sector and on Traffic there were no MK2 Jags, no MK1 or MK2 Ford Granada's, no MK1 Vauxhall Senator and no MK2 Rover 827s, so beloved of the Met Police. And in the carrier class the force has always stayed loyal to the Ford Transit, leaving the likes of the Leyland Daf 200 and 400 Series vans to others. Without doubt the Hampshire Constabulary has been served by people who know a thing or two about cars and who have always adhered to the policy of buying the best car for the job. Long may that continue.

As the force moved into the new millennium its vehicle fleet stood at almost 750 vehicles, three marine launches and one aircraft, covering nearly 15 million miles a year on a budget of £4.7m.

CHAPTER 8

The Police market is now so important to the manufacturers that they even produce their own door crests for the trial vehicles. Here we see examples from Ford, Volvo and Honda.
Author's collection

HAMPSHIRE CONSTABULARY TRIAL CARS

As has been mentioned a couple of times in earlier chapters, the Hampshire Constabulary has tested and will continue to test various different vehicles, to evaluate the best vehicle for the job. In the early days this didn't happen. A Chief Constable might have a particular favourite make of car and he would choose that as the mode of transport. As time progressed and vehicle design improved, so the competition amongst manufacturers increased. To begin with the Police market was very small and not of great importance to the makers of cars. However, this has now all changed, the Police market is a hugely valuable one in terms of actual sales and the prestige that it can bring. If your car is good enough and tough enough to become a Police vehicle, then you are doing something half right. In the 1960s the force had to ask local dealers if they could borrow a certain car to test. By the 1990s the manufacturers were almost giving them away in an effort to win sales.

Test cars, trial cars or demonstrators are all the same thing, but what is it that the Police service looks at when they are being evaluated? It depends on what role the vehicle is required to do, but generally speaking it has to be reliable, economical to run and that doesn't just include fuel consumption, but actual costs of purchase, depreciation, service, parts cost and resale values. It has to be comfortable to work in and safe to use. Performance cars have to have the right balance in terms of speed, handling and practicality. A Ferrari might be fast, but it wouldn't exactly be practical. Every aspect of the vehicle is now looked at very closely and the Hampshire Constabulary will only ever buy the right vehicle for the job.

Some test cars are only on trial for a day, others for a week, with serious contenders for a month or more. Officers tasked with testing them in everyday situations are required to fill in test reports at the end of the trial, to assist the Fleet Manager with the assessment. He and his staff will look at other aspects like ease of servicing and repairs. Others will look at how and sometimes if a car can be fitted out with all the necessary equipment. Costs are taken into account and this sometimes rules out certain vehicles. A complete package is therefore put together, before a final decision is taken.

Nowadays, Police Fleet Managers even get their own motor show, held annually at the Wiltshire Police Headquarters in Devizes. The Police fleet market is now considered so important by vehicle manufacturers that they will pull out all the stops to ensure that their latest product is ready in time for the show. Equipment manufacturers are also represented so that the entire spectrum of Police fleet management is housed under one roof.

In this chapter we will have a brief look, in year order at some of the vehicles tested by the Hampshire Constabulary. Some made it, most didn't! No records exist as to why certain cars failed to make the grade and no attempt will be made here to second-guess why either. But the sheer variety of vehicles tested has to be seen to be believed and just goes to show how important that market is.

The first ever-recorded trials were in 1965, when the Volvo 120 estate was tested against the Humber and the Citroen. This has already been covered in detail in Chapter 4, but it is worth remembering here the value of comparing certain products in unison, so that the best overall package can be obtained. This was clearly the case during these trials, where the big Citroen lost out fairly early on and the extended test was then between the Volvo and the Humber. Testing such vehicles in everyday routine patrols is very important of course. There could be nothing worse than realising that a vehicle isn't up to the job, when you have a yard full of them!

Chief Superintendent Gordon Gates aboard the Bell G4 Sioux helicopter having just taken off from the grounds at HQ Winchester. Hampshire Constabulary.

In 1967 Hampshire took part in a Home Office experiment to provide air support for the first time. Under the direction of Chief Superintendent Gordon Gates, the force hired a Bell G4 Sioux helicopter from the Army to conduct the trials. They were largely successful but it was decided at that time that the use of a helicopter would have limited scope operationally and the Home Office put the idea on hold.

In 1969 Hampshire started looking at bigger, more powerful cars to patrol the new M3 motorway and tested the Rover 3500 V8 P6 saloon. This was in direct comparison to the new Volvo 144 DL that the force had recently taken on. For all its virtues, the Rover wasn't taken on at this time and it would be another three years before it was. The test car, EXC 975G was obtained direct from Rover and was unmarked.

*The Rover 3500 V8 P6 seen at the rear of Basingstoke Police Station
with PC Roy Ford from the force driving school.
Roy Ford.*

The Rover lost out to the MK2 Triumph 2500 Pi, which was tested at the same time. Four of the new Triumphs were purchased the following year and used on the motorway for another three years and were then replaced by the Rover V8.

*The test Triumph 2500 Pi is seen in the
middle of this photo taken at the old
Aldershot Police Station with PC John Prince.
John Prince.*

By the end of the 1960s and the beginning of the 1970s, the panda car was at its height of course and Hampshire had settled in with the Mini 850. But there were plenty of other candidates that were tested, including the Hillman Imp, the Triumph Herald and the Vauxhall Viva HA. Strangely though, there is no record of Hampshire ever having tested the archetypal panda car, the Morris Minor saloon. Just about every other force in the country had them except Hampshire, although a few of the vans were used as Dog Section vehicles.

One car that was doing the rounds in 1970 was a Volkswagen Beetle 1303. With a suitable registration number of AYM 999H it was passed from force to force, in an attempt to push it onto the panda fleets. The two door, rear engined car was already a firm favourite as a Police vehicle in countries like Switzerland, Austria and Germany of course, but it really didn't inspire anyone in the UK. The car was finished in Bermuda blue with white doors and came with an illuminated Police roof box and a second Police/Stop box positioned above the rear registration plate. Although the records do not show how long the car was tested for, they do suggest that it was trialled at Basingstoke on the 21st June 1970. The car obviously created a lot of interest and became the subject of official force photographs.

The VW Beetle panda never caught on in the UK. Hampshire Constabulary.

Other vehicles that were scrutinised during the 1970s included the Hillman Avenger, the Triumph Vitesse 6, the MK3 Ford Cortina, Vauxhall Viva HC and the Saab 99. Of these the Cortina was taken on as an area car and the others were disregarded.

In 1977 BMW arrived with the first of the 5 series cars, the 525. Hampshire had tested the earlier version, the 2500 in 1972 and for reasons not recorded it wasn't taken on. But the newer car was considered to be much better and following the trial Hampshire took the plunge and bought the German cars the following year. The test car was fitted with a single blue light, an illuminated Police sign on the front grille and a Police/Stop box was positioned on the rear parcel shelf.

The BMW 525 test car in the rear yard at Gosport Police Station.
John Jackman.

In 1979 Renault jumped on the bandwagon and offered the Renault 30 TS as a traffic car. The 3.0 V6 had a good reputation for durability and Renault made a serious effort at tempting the force with a complete package car. It came with a single blue light, twin roof mounted spot lamps, Police/Stop box and two additional flashing rear fog lamps. On the front grille the car sported twin blue repeater lights. It was tested in the northern Traffic area of Hampshire, but failed to make the grade.

The Renault 30 TS on trial with Hampshire in 1979.
Kenneth Porter

292

In 1980 the force tested a rather unusual car that is still remembered with fondness today, by those that got to drive it. The Saab 900 Turbo was one of those rare cars that got instant cult status, due mainly to its excellent performance. It was very quick, with excellent handling and a reliability record some manufacturers would have killed for! It was tough enough for the job, but the thought of expensive turbos going wrong put the force off and Saab withdrew the car. The car came equipped with twin blue lights mounted on a roof rack bar. In-between were two spotlights and the siren. On the front grille came twin blue repeater lights and it was one of the most modern looking Police cars of its era.

The brilliant Saab 900 Turbo didn't make the grade because of fears over the reliability of turbo chargers, which in 1980 were still relatively new on production cars.
John Prince.

In 1981 another Volkswagen arrived for testing, this time it was the widely acclaimed MK1 Golf, for use as a panda car. Sadly, no photos exist of this particular trial car. In 1982 Fiat arrived with the 132 Super Mirafiori, a 2.0 litre saloon car with a fantastic engine, but very poor build quality. Tested by the Traffic Department, it was said to be great around town with excellent acceleration, but wasn't up to long-term motorway speeds.

In 1982 Hampshire tested the Jaguar XJ6 Series 3 Police Special saloon for use as its next generation

Supplied direct from Browns Lane, the 4.2 litre car came with automatic transmission and vastly improved suspension, to enable it to be used on twisty roads. Pressure was being applied to the force by the Home Office to buy British cars and to give the car its due, it passed the trial period with flying colours and an order for 16 cars was tendered, including one for the Chief Constable. As has already been documented, the batch of new Jags arrived with manual gearboxes, taken from the Rover 2.6 SD1 and standard limousine suspension, which was alright on the motorway, but more than useless anywhere else. Somewhere along the line there had been a large-scale break down in communication and the test car exceeded the performance of the actual car by a mile.

The Jaguar XJ6 Series 3 test car came with an automatic gearbox for the first time.
John Prince.

Give Jaguar the credit for trying to make amends though, because in 1984 it came up with one of the best looking Police cars of all time, the 3.8 litre XJS Police Special. The sleek Jaguar didn't really fit the criteria as a patrol car, but nonetheless looked beautiful with its red stripes and full width light bar. Hampshire tested the car for a week, said thanks, but no thanks and handed it back. One force did persevere with the XJS though and that was the Met, who had one for several years, clocking up more than 250,000 miles before Jaguar bought it back off them, in order to strip it down to examine how the component parts had stood up to the rigours of Police life.

Jaguar XJS PS would have made a lovely looking, but rather impractical patrol car.
Jaguar Cars Ltd.

Ford was trying desperately hard in 1985 to get a firm grip on the upper end of the Police market. They had already cornered the section car and van market with the Escort and Transit.

294

Now they introduced the Ford Sierra XR 4x4 with a 2.8i V6 engine and because it was permanent four-wheel drive, it had handling to match. As a traffic car it certainly had the performance, but was cramped inside and failed to make the grade. Fords own new livery was interesting and bore a striking resemblance to that of Essex, where of course the Sierra was made. And as if to show just how important the Police car market had now become, Ford even had its own Police style door crest made, with the words Ford Police Demonstrator on.

*The Ford Sierra XR 4x4 handled very well and is seen here
parked in the yard at Fareham Police Station.
John Prince.*

In 1986 Ford went one step further and introduced the MK3 Ford Granada 4x4 Concept Police Car, to give it its full title. The car came with a unique roof mounted fibreglass pod, which housed a fully integrated blue strobe light in all four corners. Across the front was an illuminated Police/Stop sign and at the rear was a raised spoiler, which had a similar Police/Stop sign inside. On top of the pod was a hinged door to give access to all the radio antennae and this was covered in an orange spot to aid identification from the air. A full Ford RS body-kit and wheels was fitted to the car, together with the most outrageous graphics ever seen on any Police vehicle in the UK at that time. The blue and saturn yellow diagonal striping was very radical and the whole package looked wonderful, especially when the all-new strobe lights were put into operation. It turned a lot of heads. It didn't make much noise though, because Ford forgot to add a siren to the car!

The MK3 Ford Granada 4x4 Concept Police Car in Portsmouth during its test period.
Barry Juchau.

Official Ford photo of the Concept car.
Ford UK.

Renault came back into the fight in 1986 with the Renault 25. This 2.5 litre V6 car was a powerful motor in its day and was very smooth to. Renault thought they had a winner on their hands and gave it to Hampshire saying 'break it if you can'. It has to be said that certain officers did try, but they all failed! Renault had delivered a nice package to the force and the car came ready striped and with a Premier Hazard Olympic light bar and a Police/Stop box on the rear tailgate. There is no record as to why it wasn't taken on.

*The Renault 25 was a smooth looking and powerful car in its day.
It's seen here in the rear yard at Kingston Crescent Police Station.
Author.*

Volvo thought it might be onto a winner in 1986 with the introduction of a Police spec 740 Turbo. This large, 2.3i turbo-charged car was only on test for a couple of days though and as with the Saab 900, the thought of unreliable turbo-chargers, as many of them were in those days, was probably enough to put the force off buying any. The car came with a rather bland looking single orange stripe and single blue light, mounted on a roof rack.

*On test for just two days was this Volvo 740 Turbo, seen here
outside the old Southsea Police Station, in Victoria Road South.
Author.*

In 1987 Hampshire obtained an Audi 80 for a two-week trial period. This sleek looking, four-door saloon was pitched against the BMW 3 series in civvy street and although it was a competent car it was never going to outdo the Bavarian motor. In Police guise it was difficult to decide where to pitch it. As a traffic car it wasn't fast enough or big enough. As an area car it was too fast and still too cramped! It therefore failed to make the grade, not because it wasn't a good car, but because it didn't quite fit in anywhere. Audi fitted it with a standard looking orange and blue stripe and a Premier Hazard light bar.

The Audi 80 didn't quite fit in.
John Prince

Another new Volvo entered the arena in 1989 in the shape of the 460 GLEi, a medium sized four-door saloon with a 1.8i engine. Striped in red and blue and complete with a Whelan light bar, the car suffered the same identity crisis that the Audi 80 did. The car was used for a couple of weeks as a supervisory unit, but in real terms it was very similar to the ill-fated 360 area cars, which were never really suited to full time emergency work. The addition of a glass sunroof looks like a good idea though!

This Volvo 460 GLEi was used as a supervisor's car and is seen here in the rear yard at Cosham Police Station. Author.

By 1990 the Volvo 240s days as an area car were numbered, when Volvo ceased production of the evergreen saloon. Whilst the search commenced for a replacement, new European Union guidelines required that all emergency response units were to be fitted with fully enclosed, full width light bars. Hampshire therefore fitted a Premier Hazard Maxim 90 light bar to the roof of a Volvo 240 GL and trialled the system for several weeks. It was a resounding success and the new Ford Sierra Sapphire area cars purchased the following year were all fitted with them.

This rare photo shows the new style Premier Hazard light bar being tested on a Volvo 240 GL. Note also that the boot mounted box has been removed as the Police/Stop system is incorporated into the light bar.
Clifford Gray.

In 1991 Rover revamped its 800 series cars and gave it a much rounder looking body, new interior and a better all round performance. Hampshire got the new 827 SLi with a 2.7i, 24-valve motor on test as a Traffic car. As with the previous MK1 version the car was very fast, handled reasonably well and was very comfortable to live with. Unfortunately it suffered from the same complaint as before, with no traction control to keep the front driven wheels in order and a build quality, that although improved was still a little suspect. Still the electric glass sunroof was a nice touch. It would be another couple of years before the 2.0 litre version would find approval as the next generation of area car.

The MK2 Rover 827 SLi on test at Cosham.
Author.

The year 1991 might also be remembered for the car that no one was allowed to drive! Unless that is, you were an instructor at the force driving school. The car was the Lotus Carlton, a vehicle so fast that the driving school deemed it too fast to be driven by mere mortals. Based on the Vauxhall Carlton saloon, Lotus didn't compromise when it came to playing around with the mechanicals to come up with a car to beat the Cosworth Sierra. An all new 3.6 litre, straight-six engine with twin Garrett T25 turbo-chargers gave the car an incredible 377 bhp. It came with a six-speed manual gearbox, taken from the Lotus developed Chevrolet Corvette ZR1 and power was laid down by some of the largest tyres ever to roll on British roads, with 265/40x17's on the rear and 235/40x17's at the front. Top speed was 174 mph! The car was awesome. It was tested at Netley for a week and despite some desperate pleas from certain Traffic officers, that's where it stayed. Finished in Imperial Green, as all 300 British registered Lotus Carltons were, the car was just not a practical idea in terms of Police vehicle use. Shame!

Oh a driving instructor's lot is not a happy one, unless of course you happen to be driving the 174 mph Lotus Carlton!
Ross Fuller.

A rather strange vehicle arrived for testing in 1991 and like one or two others, it was difficult to see just where it would fit in. The Suzuki Vitara JLX 1.6i 4x4 was one of a new breed of small, four-wheel drive cars, aimed at the younger *upwardly mobile set* with an active lifestyle. The car was great fun to drive and very responsive. It did suffer from a rather plastic interior that wasn't really considered to be policeman proof and it probably wouldn't have lasted the course in terms of Police use. It came striped in the usual way and had a full width light bar and twin repeater lights placed on top of the front bumper. Although Hampshire didn't take the Suzuki on, Wiltshire Constabulary did and purchased a small number for its rural patrols.

The Suzuki Vitara 1.6i JLX with four-wheel drive on test at Cosham.
Barry Juchau.

In late 1991 Volvo tried to tempt Hampshire with its replacement for the 240, with the introduction of the 940 GL. Powered by the same basic 2.3 litre engine, albeit in an upgraded state, the car was simply too big and heavy to be considered for area car use and no-where near fast enough to compete against the BMW. It was a lovely car, but like several others suffered the indignity of not quite fitting in anywhere.

The Volvo 940 GL on test at Cosham was just too big for area car use.
Kevin Angus.

In 1992 another new motor manufacturer to enter the fray was Isuzu. Leicestershire Police had used the earlier MK1 Trooper 4x4 for a couple of years and had found it to be both reliable and robust. Hampshire was now looking at long-term proposals to replace and update its four-wheel drive capability, without going back to the Range Rover. In doing so it tested a number of four-wheel drive cars, including the new MK2 Isuzu Trooper. Unlike some other big off-roaders, the Isuzu didn't suffer from too much body roll on corners and drove more like a large estate car. It was quick too, with a top speed of 110 mph, with a good turn of acceleration. Where it suffered was in fuel consumption, where if pushed really hard on the motorway, the driver could actually watch the fuel gauge move! In the end Hampshire went back to Landrover and bought the Discovery TDi.

The Isuzu Trooper 3.2i V6 4x4 on test at Cosham Traffic.
Barry Juchau.

Peugeot also arrived in 1992 with their top of the range 605 Sri. This big 3.0 V6 saloon was aimed directly at the Traffic Department but just wasn't capable of mixing it with the BMW 5 series. It was too slow with suspect, high-speed stability and a gearbox that was very difficult to use at speed. Consequently it failed the test. Like many other test cars of the period, Peugeot had equipped the test car with a decent light bar, siren and graphics.

302

The big Peugeot 605 Sri was the French manufacturer's attempt at getting in on the Police traffic fleet. Author.

In 1993 a test car arrived that really did get the pulse racing. Volkswagen introduced the Vento VR6 and Hampshire was one of the few forces in the UK that took the plunge. This compact car came with a big 2.8i V6 engine, giving it a top speed close to 140 mph, with acceleration to match and the most amazing road holding. The test car was striped in yellow and even sported a VW Police Test Car crest on the rear pillar. A full width Optimax light bar from Premier Hazard was fitted and it became one of those rare cars that everyone wanted to drive. It got rave reviews from all that got the chance and it wasn't long before Hampshire ordered one as an unmarked video Traffic car.

In late 1994 Hampshire tested the Subaru Legacy 4x4, which was written off when it overturned during a pursuit with a stolen Ford Fiesta! And Volvo tempted the force again with its new 800 series car, the 850 GLT which was tested by Traffic, but only thought capable of being an area car.

The VW Vento VR6 test car on trial at Cosham. Christopher Davies

303

Motorcycles are also tested in the same demanding way of course and in 1994 Honda produced a Police specification ST1100 Pan European. The 1100cc V4 bike with shaft drive came fully equipped and ready for Police patrol, complete with all the necessary electrics, lights, sirens and luggage already bolted on. All the Police force had to do was put a rider on it! This was in direct competition with the BMW K series machines, which didn't come equipped at all and it was put to BMW that perhaps they should take a leaf out of Hondas book, now that there was a genuine challenge to their supremacy. BMW ignored the threat and eventually lost out in a big way. Even though on this occasion, most riders actually preferred the BMW to ride, the overall package offered by Honda was too good to resist.

The test package Honda ST1100 Pan European was given a long-term evaluation and was even treated to a Hampshire crest. Bob Wheeler.

1995 will be remembered for just one thing. The T5. Volvo's bullet arrived and changed the face of British Traffic cars for the rest of the decade and beyond. No one could have predicted then, just what sort of an impact the car would have. Just about every force in the UK was handed an 850 T5 saloon, with manual gearbox and no traction control. The car was a sensation, pure and simple. With a top speed of 145 mph it easily beat the Vauxhall Senator and its replacement Omega, BMW 5 series and all other large capacity saloon cars of the period. The car was originally on test at Cosham, and then went to the force driving school, before doing the rounds of various other Traffic offices, before being returned to Cosham. Hampshire didn't really take much in the way of persuasion, given its previous links with Volvo and opted to buy the test car at a reduced rate of course.

The Volvo 850 T5 test car in the livery supplied by Volvo. This was later removed when the car was purchased and Hampshire's own livery applied.
Kevin Angus.

But it wasn't saloon cars that Hampshire opted for in the end. Volvo also supplied estate variants in Police package form and it was these that eventually won the day. Hampshire's Traffic cars were being forced to carry more and more equipment and the cars were already up to, and in some cases, over the manufacturers recommended weight limits. Estate cars could carry more and distribute the weight better. The rear load area could also be racked properly to assist with storage of equipment. But it wasn't the fact that the cars were estates that caused the biggest stir, but the gearbox. For the first time, Traffic patrol cars were to be issued with automatic gearboxes. This was a radical step and required some training to assist with the idea. The decision was taken because in Sweden the Police there used automatics and cut maintenance costs by 4%. The auto boxes also cut down on tyre wear and there were far fewer gearbox problems. It was also thought that Swedish officers preferred the automatics because it was less tiring than a manual and left the driver free to use both hands on the steering whilst travelling at high speed. The overall package of estate car with an automatic gearbox then became the number one choice as the Hampshire Traffic patrol car.

The test Volvo 850 T5 estate complete with automatic gearbox, seen here in the rear yard at Cosham Police Station.
Author

In 1996 Saab decided to rejoin the Police vehicle circus and offered the Saab 9000 Cdi. This test car was almost as popular as the old 900 Turbo. It was quick, comfortable and pleasant to drive. It came equipped with a Premier Hazard light bar and Saabs own livery, complete with Saab Police crest. For reasons unknown, the car was not taken on, despite an extended trial period. Other forces, including the City of London and Kent did purchase the cars.

The Saab 9000 Cdi seen here in the yard at Whitchurch Police Station.
Author.

Later that same year Vauxhall tried to reclaim the initiative from Volvo by releasing the new Vectra 2.5i V6 with an automatic gearbox. The four-door saloon was aimed at the Traffic fleet but it was one of those cars that was too slow to be a Traffic car and too fast for an area car. It's trial period lasted two weeks, during which time it was past around various Traffic offices. The car came with a very basic single blue light and enough Police signs to identify it as a Police vehicle.

The MK1 Vauxhall Vectra V6 seen at rest on Portsdown Hill.
Author

Volkswagen hoped to capitalise on the success of the Vento, by gaining a foothold in the section car market with a MK3 Golf 1.9D. Hampshire had already tested the MK1 Golf back in 1981 and although it was a popular car it wasn't taken on. The MK3 Golf though was seen as a good choice for a section car and was offered at the right price. Only one car was purchased and it is seen here sporting a single blue light prior to it being fitted with a Britax unit later in its life.

The MK3 VW Golf 1.9D was a one-off purchase and used very successfully as a section car.
Andy Bardsley

The year 1996 was to prove a busy year for testing vehicles and included the new Pegasus Range Rover 4.0i V8 4x4. Hampshire had plenty of experience with the old Range Rover of course and this trial period was to prove to be the first of several before the force decided whether or not to buy them again. The car came equipped with an automatic gearbox and seemed all the better for it. Reliability was always going to be the key to whether or not the force bought them again, which is one of the reasons why the cars were tested on several separate occasions. They each came in Landrovers own yellow livery, complete with full Whelan light bar and siren system.

The new Range Rover Pegasus with 4.0 litre V8 engine on test at Lyndhurst.
Simon Rowley

And now for something completely different! The Multi Purpose Vehicle (MPV) or People Carriers as they became known, really took off in the mid 1990s. Although Renaults Espace had been around for several years it was some time before the rest of the industry caught up. When Ford released the Galaxy, few would have even dreamed of using it as a Police car. But Ford did just that and came up with a 2.8i V6 motor taken from its tie in with VW and issued it as a full Police specification Traffic car, with a multi purpose role. It could be used as a people carrier, a motorway back up unit or a combination of both. The rear seats had been removed and in its place was a wooden racking system capable of holding a huge amount of equipment and there was still room for five adults. It was very quick and had excellent road holding for a vehicle of this size. In short it was far better than the Landrover Discovery currently in use at that time as a motorway back-up unit and there were those who were dismayed when it didn't make the grade. For reasons unknown it was rejected. The combination of the big MPV and Ford's own Police graphics meant that it turned plenty of heads.

The Ford Galaxy 2.8i V6 was a strange looking, but highly versatile Police vehicle.
It is seen here overlooking Portsmouth from Portsdown Hill.
Author.

Undaunted by their earlier failure, Suzuki hit back with an updated Vitara range in 1996. This time it came with a 2.0i V6 engine and four-wheel drive. Inexplicably it wasn't as quick or agile as the 1.6 unit and felt sluggish and heavy. The rather strange bronzed treatment to the bumpers and sill area wouldn't have lasted five minutes either and the car was returned to Suzuki.

The Suzuki Vitara was pretty but not up to the job. Author.

In 1997 Ford tried tempting Hampshire with the MK1 Mondeo 2.0 Si estate as an area car. It failed, but was used as a general supervisory unit in the New Forest area until it was written off in an accident prior to the end of its full evaluation.

This MK1 Ford Mondeo estate's life as a Police vehicle came to an abrupt end! Simon Rowley.

Another new manufacturer to British Police forces was Daihatsu who arrived with the MK1 Fourtrak 4x4. This robust and reliable diesel powered, four-wheel drive car looked like the ideal vehicle to be used as a rural area car, in replacement for the Landrover Discovery's, which were proving costly to run. The trial was a long one and proved to be successful. However a decision on purchase was delayed because Daihatsu were about to release a MK2 model, which was slightly bigger than the original. Once the force was happy that the new one was basically as sound as the original, it went ahead with an initial purchase of two followed by several more in the next two years.

*The early MK1 Daihatsu
Fourtrak with diesel motor.
Simon Rowley.*

Some trial cars only get the briefest of tests, with the following two only looking in on Hampshire for a couple of days. The Mercedes Benz 412D came as a multi-role unit capable of doing just about anything! It was armed with full internal body protection, windscreen protection, a prisoner cage, twin light bars and a whole host of other extras. The trouble was it was too big and the chances of it getting into most Police station yards was extremely remote.

*The huge Mercedes Benz 412D multi-role unit.
Author*

Another large vehicle not to have been given an extended trial was the Ford Explorer 4.6i V8 4x4. This all American off-roader certainly looked the part but received little more than a passing glance. Some other forces like Surrey and Essex did find favour with the Explorer as did many American Police agencies.

The Ford Explorer 4x4 at Bar End, Winchester.
Author

BMW attempted a fight back with the new R1100RT. This saw the return of the horizontally opposed Boxer engine, albeit with modern valves and other updates that gave it a much smoother ride. The bike, although rather strange looking, won many friends amongst those who got to ride it. So impressed were they that the bike was granted an extended test and was even liveried up in Hampshire's own graphics. BMW had learned its lesson from Honda the hard way and offered the motorcycle as a fully equipped Police specification machine. But in the end it proved too little, too late. Hampshire was now fully equipped to maintain the Pan European and the impressive BM was sent packing.

The BMW R1100RT is seen at an incident on the M275 flyover in Portsmouth.
Author.

311

One of the strangest looking vehicles to be tested was the Ssang Yong Musso GX220 4x4. This Korean made off-roader was fitted with a 3.2i Mercedes Benz engine that gave it an excellent performance quota. It was quick, handled like a car and had as much room as the Range Rover. It did suffer from a rather poorly made interior and bits did tend to either break or just fall off. The car was tested in 1997 over a period of four weeks, mainly at Whitehill Traffic Section. It was given full Hampshire graphics because of its extended test and even received a fleet number. But the car failed its overall test for unknown reasons. It was later tested by Humberside Police still in Hampshire's livery!

The Ssang Yong Musso GX220 had a strange name to go with its looks! It is seen here in Farnborough. Author.

But the prize for the strangest car of them all has to go to the Daihatsu Move. The full story behind its purchase by Hampshire can be found in Chapter 7. It remains as one of the weirdest Police cars of all time, but actually a very practical one too. It was on trial for two months prior to purchase and can be seen here in its original livery, prior to receiving the Hampshire treatment.

The Daihatsu Move on show at the force open day at Netley in 1997. Andy Bardsley

The following year Daihatsu tried again with the introduction of the Terios 4x4. This was another of those cars that didn't quite fit in anywhere and was basically outdone by its own Fourtrak model that was somewhat larger.

The Daihatsu Terios 4x4 outside Bar End workshops, Winchester.
Andy Bardsley

Another car from the Far East that didn't last too long on test was the Proton Persona 1.3 LS. Aimed at the section car market, its quality in terms of durability in Police use was questioned when bits fell off the car.

The Proton Persona at Winchester in 1997.
Andy Bardsley.

Landrover tried again in 1997 with an updated version of the Discovery, this time with an automatic gearbox. An already slow diesel powered car wasn't helped by the introduction of an auto box and it was considered too slow even without a full range of equipment and a heavy stem light being fitted.

*The Landrover Discovery
on test at Cosham.
Author.*

One car that came very close to making the grade in 1997 was the Volvo V40 fitted with a 2.0 litre engine. It had all the attributes of previous Volvo patrol cars but lacked the overall performance of the latest BMW 3 Series Touring that had found favour as the current generation of area car. Volvo had equipped the car to a high standard and gave it more stripes on the rear tailgate than any other Police vehicle in history!

*The Volvo V40 came close to
stealing the area car title
away from BMW.
Author.*

In 1998 another Japanese manufacturer, not previously noted for its Police vehicles arrived on the scene. Mitsubishi's much admired Shogun was trialled as a rural response unit, in direct competition with the Daihatsu Fourtrak, which looked like it was going out of production. Although the test was quite long term it wasn't taken on in the end and the Fourtrak was eventually replaced by the Nissan Terrano 4x4.

The Mitsubishi Shogun on test as a rural response unit.
Simon Rowley.

The MK4 Vauxhall Astra was launched in 1998 and it wasn't long before Hampshire acquired one on test for use as a section vehicle. Unfortunately for Vauxhall, Hampshire's use of LPG Ford Fiestas was just taking off and the prospect of having to re-tool and re-train mechanics was enough to relegate the new car to the briefest of testing.

The MK4 Vauxhall Astra was
tested as a section car.
Andy Bardsley

Other vehicles tested, but not photographed during the last couple of years included the Honda Civic, the Honda CRX, Jeep Cherokee 4x4, Mercedes Benz C Class, Subaru Forester 4x4 and the Mitsubishi Galant. BMW meanwhile did Hampshire the honour in 1998 of lending it the only Police specification BMW 525 TDS in the world. This diesel powered all new 5 series saloon was fitted with an automatic gearbox and was initially designed just for show at the 1998 National Police Fleet Managers Conference at Devizes. Thereafter, it did the rounds of various Traffic offices to gauge the reaction to it being used as a Traffic car. Nice though it was, it was too slow in comparison with the Volvo. It still looked good in Hampshire's livery though.

A unique car, the only Police spec BMW 525 TDS in the world is seen in Hampshire Police livery at Port Solent, Portsmouth in 1998. Note the fleet numbers!
Andy Bardsley

The following year BMW released the new 3 Series saloon and another one-off car was given Hampshire livery, again for display purposes at the National Police Fleet Managers Conference. Only this time it really was for display purposes, because not only was it left-hand drive but it was still sporting German number plates!

This BMW 3 Series appears to be suffering from an identity crisis,
is it from Hampshire or Hamburg?
Author.

Another huge multi-role vehicle came from Renault in 1999, with the introduction of the T35. Badged as a *PSU Demonstrator* with Coleman Milne armoured bodywork, it also sported

316

two Federal Signals Vector light bar units and a windscreen grille big enough to fence the average Police station yard with! As with the Mercedes Benz 412D the Renault was simply too big for everyday use.

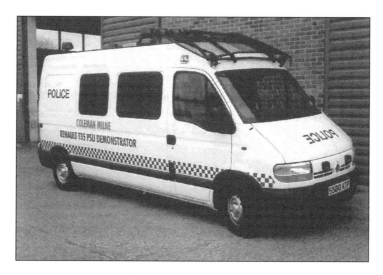

The rear yard at Bar End is about the only Police premises in Hampshire big enough to accommodate the Renault T35.
Author.

No doubt Hampshire will continue to test a variety of vehicles and equipment in the future, to obtain the best product for the job in hand. In doing so it will obviously test vehicles which might otherwise not get a second look by most people, but as we have seen in this chapter, some of the strangest looking cars have found a place at the Police dining table. The Police vehicle market continues to expand and can be a very lucrative one for the manufacturers in terms of prestige and no doubt they will do their best to tempt the Police still further into the 21st Century.

And what about the future as far as Hampshire Constabulary's transport is concerned? If somebody else writes a book in a hundred years time and looks back, what will they find? Will county Police forces disappear in favour of large regions or even a national force? Will battenburg become the recognised national Police livery?

No doubt these and many other issues will come to the fore sooner or later. The force continues to experiment with different fuels in an effort to reduce costs and be kind to the environment. Other ideas include the fitment of black box flight recorders to all Police vehicles in an effort to assist in accident investigation should there be a collision with that vehicle.

Technology is available now to make the roof mounted blue light a thing of the past. Blue light manufacturers are already experimenting with fibre optics being placed across the top of the windscreen and in other prominent places. Although emergency service vehicles will still

317

have blue lights being emitted you won't actually see them until they are operated. There are two very good reasons for travelling down this road and both of them are on cost grounds. The new technology will be cheaper to buy and with no wind resisting blue light mounted on the roof, so fuel consumption will be reduced.

Information technology consoles fitted to patrol cars have been talked about for years. The Americans have had them for a long time and a direct link to the Police National Computer would be a real bonus to frontline officers. Lap top computers (or Lap Cops as they have been called) with the ability to undertake all manner of tasks are another project that could soon be seen in our patrol cars. Volvo has already pioneered the manufacture of a revised dash and gear lever assembly to accommodate a lap top computer into its V70 patrol car.

And a new national radio system is already in the pipeline. Called the Public Service Radio Communications System, or Tetra it will link all Police radio using digital technology.

Who knows what the next 100 years will bring in terms of vehicle manufacture, combined with computer technology and the needs of the frontline Police Officer?

CHAPTER 9

DIECAST MODELS, MEMORABILIA AND

RESTORED CARS

There have been several diecast scale models of vehicles used by the Hampshire Constabulary over the years. In comparison with many other forces, Hampshire has faired quite well.

In 1988, an unknown company that produces those wonderful scale models of commercial aircraft that you see in travel agents windows produced a beautiful model of the Hampshire Constabulary Optica Scout spotter plane. It came complete with full Hampshire markings as per the real thing and as far as can be ascertained only three were produced. Two were given to employees at the Optica factory whilst the third was donated to the force. It spent some time on display in the force exhibition bus, but its whereabouts now are not known.

Creaks of Camberley Crossley lorry, issued to help celebrate Hampshire's 150th anniversary.

Creaks of Camberley

In 1989 the force celebrated its 150th anniversary and commissioned Eric Creak, the proprietor of Creaks of Camberley to produce a model to help celebrate the event. At this time Creaks were producing a range of Police related models called the Alternative Collection. Model number AC115 was the Hampshire version and consisted of a 1918 Crossley lorry with a canvass back. This in turn had the Hampshire crest depicted on it and the words Hampshire Constabulary along the sides. The model was actually a Matchbox based Y26 from the Models of Yesteryear range which was refinished by Creaks. It bore a Hampshire registration number OH 1839 and was a certificated, limited edition of 1000, costing around £20. The model, as far as can be ascertained, was not based on any particular Hampshire Police vehicle of the time and is not therefore considered to be an authentic replica.

Corgi

We had to wait a few more years for the first authentic replica car to arrive. In May 1996 Corgi issued number 57801, the BMW 525 in full Hampshire livery. This car came with the registration number K795 NCR and roof number 15 and was based on a car used at Cosham Traffic Section, with the call sign CM-06 (see chapter 7). For the eagle eyed, you might notice that the fleet numbers used on the model are 1055 and not 1554 as per the actual car. There is a reason for this. Somehow, Corgi managed to confuse the photographs of CM-06 with photos of an Eastleigh based BMW, which had the fleet number 1055. These photos had been submitted to them some two years earlier, but got mixed up with the later submissions!

Basically the model was quite good, but there were those who weren't happy with the fact that the car was left-hand drive (a Corgi policy at that time) and came with a sunroof and alloy wheels. But then it cost less than £6 and was basically aimed at the toy market and not the collectibles area. That said, the model was extremely popular, especially in the Portsmouth area, where it even obtained coverage in the local newspaper, following the real cars demise during a pursuit where it sustained considerable damage. This led to another article appearing in Police Review magazine, complete with cartoon by John Witt!

The famous BMW 525 made by Corgi

Caption; Now it looks realistic!
The cartoon by John Witt that appeared in Police Review magazine about the same model

In September 1997 Corgi issued number 08004, a twin model set that was aimed at the more serious collector. The boxed set consisted of the Hampshire Police Bedford S Type Control Unit (see Chapter 4) and a Portsmouth City Police Morris Minor dog van (see Chapter 1). The models were very accurate and had the correct registration numbers on and a detailed history was provided on the limited edition certificate. The set was limited to 4,800 world-wide and also came with a nice tie tac style badge depicting the Hampshire crest. Price was about £18 a set.

Corgi set number 08004 was labelled as the Hampshire Police Set.
John Alderslade Models

Also in 1997 a real collector's item was issued in the form of the first ever foreign Police vehicle, the Volvo 120 estate, CHO 621C. The model was based on a Brooklin model, but like the Creaks lorry, was finished by another modeller John Alderslade, who specialises in replicas of Volvo cars. It was produced in white metal and was hand finished to a very high standard. The model was limited to just 150 pieces and was priced at £50.

In late 1998 a second model was issued, this time an early Volvo 144 DL saloon, with the registration number UAA 788H (see Chapter 4) and this again was finished to the same very high standards. Limited to just 150 pieces it too sold for around £50. These two models were to be the start of a whole series of Hampshire Police Volvo models, but to date no further cars have appeared.

Two of the early Volvos modelled by John Alderslade.

Lledo Vanguards

Prior to being bought out by Corgi, the old Lledo factory produced a twin car set in 1998 that had a Hampshire model in it. The set was numbered PC1002 and was labelled as *Police Panda Cars of the 1960s*. The Hampshire car was an Austin 850 Mini panda, based on one of the original cars issued to Basingstoke, KOU 136F (see Chapter 4). The other model was a Metropolitan Police Ford Anglia 105E panda. The limited edition set of 5000 showed the Hampshire Mini on the box, complete with correct registration number, but the actual model, although beautifully made came with no registration plates (a Lledo policy at that time). This set is now quite difficult to obtain.

322

Lledo set PC1002 with Hampshire Police Mini panda.

In early 2001 the new Vanguards range saw the release of a Hampshire Police MK2 Lotus Cortina, model number VA 04101. This model was taken from the photos shown here in Chapter 4 and was based on the car used at Aldershot, registration number TOT 802H. It was an excellent model and limited to just 5700. Price was around £10. In late 2001 another model was issued by Vanguards showing the *royal* Rover 3500 V8 in its full traffic livery. The model number was VA 06503 and it was limited to 5100. This model was originally going to be issued as a two model set with the second version showing the same car in its gloss black paint job, but was withdrawn prior to release.

Lledo Vanguard's MK2 Lotus Cortina and Rover 3500 V8

RPM Models

In early 1999 RPM Models produced two Hampshire Police model cars. The first was a white metal handbuilt of the Series 3 Jaguar XJ6 Traffic car, A812 POT (see Chapter 6). This very good model was finished to a high standard and even featured the unique white boot spoiler and an excellent reproduction of the Jet Sonic light bar. It was a very heavy model with an equally heavy price tag of over £100.

The second model in the range was a Volvo 850 T5 estate, P114 LTP which was originally based at Cosham but ended its days at Fareham. The model was actually resin cast and was therefore that much lighter. It was an excellent model and came complete with all the emergency equipment on show in the rear load area. It was priced around £85 and was very limited in number.

RPM Models Volvo 850 T5

Castlehouse Models have ensured that the old Portsmouth City Police crest is remembered forever.

Castlehouse Models

Castlehouse Models from Birmingham specialise in the promotional side of model collecting and have produced a fantastic range over the years, depicting the crests used by various old forces on a basic range of Lledo models. In 1999 they issued a set of 24 models that included one from the Portsmouth City Police. The model was based on a Model T Ford and depicted the Portsmouth City Police crest on the sides, together with the old headquarters address. Each model was a certificated limited edition of just 200 and was priced at £9.50. At the time of writing it is believed that a second model will be released depicting the crest of the old Isle of Wight County Constabulary.

Crossway Models Riley 2½ litre RMB of the old Portsmouth City Police.

Crossway Models

The last model produced in the 20th Century is actually based on one of the earliest of patrol cars. A Riley 2½ litre RMB of the Portsmouth City Police has been beautifully recreated by Crossway Models in white metal. This superb 1:43 scale replica is perfect in every detail, right down to its chrome bell and blue P light, together with its authentic registration number of DBK 956. The overall detailing is just as impressive with vinyl roof and door handles that look good enough to work. Limited to just 100 pieces and priced at £80 they were a bargain in terms of shear quality.

The various tie tacs produced in the 1990s.
C9-P13

Tie tacs

For many years Police officers throughout the UK have bought little enamelled tie tacs, usually depicting a teddy bear or other comic character, wearing a helmet or riding a bike. These tie tacs were usually sold on behalf of Police charities and officers would wear them on their uniform tie. The idea originated in the City of London Police and members of the Police Insignia Collectors Association (PICA) were enthusiastic buyers.

In the late 1990s, Sgt Steve Blake from Portsmouth Central Police Station who was a collector of such tie tacs, decided to commission a series himself and based them on cars used by the Hampshire Constabulary. A total of eight were commissioned and the pictures from which the tie tacs were produced were taken from the author's collection, some of which you might recognise. The first was of the Volvo 850 T5 estate, followed by the Austin Westminster, the famous BMW 525 (K795 NCR), Vauxhall Senator, BMW 325 TDS, MK3 Ford Granada saloon and two Volvo 240 area cars, including one from the Isle of Wight. Considering their diminutive size they had incredible detail and came with authentic registration and fleet numbers.

Each tie tac was limited to a production of just 500, with 50 special gold trimmed versions made available to special customers on four of them. These were the Austin Westminster, Vauxhall Senator, BMW 3 series and the BMW 525. Each tie tac was sold for just £1.50, with a percentage given to charity. The collection came to an early end when dozens of other like-minded officers across the country hit on the same idea and the market became flooded with them and officers like Steve Blake had difficulty in selling them all.

Other tie tacs commissioned at this time were station crests, including Portsmouth Central (Steve Blake), Portsmouth South (Mick Smith) and Portsmouth Fratton (Dave Burgess). The Air Support Unit also got in on the act and produced a very nice badge with Boxer-One-Zero flying above an outline of the Hampshire and Isle of Wight coast. Again two versions were issued, one in silver and one in gold at £2 each.

Slightly larger button badges were produced around the same period for the Traffic Division and showed a Volvo 850 T5 in old livery and the Blue Lights Motorcycle Display Team had thousands produced to give away to the kids at the various functions they attended. They produced two different badges over the years; the first showed three BMW K1100LTs in the old livery. The second had three Honda Pan Europeans in the new livery with the words I've Met The Blue Lights on it.

Restored cars

Restoring classic cars has been the favourite hobby of many people for years. Restoring classic Police cars on the other hand is something relatively new and only really came to the surface in the late 1990s. The public love looking at any restored vehicle but always seem to have a story to tell when it comes to looking at a restored Police car! But why would anyone want to restore one in the first place you may ask? History is the simple answer and we should be thankful that there are people around with the foresight to preserve our heritage.

At the time of writing there are actually eight ex-Hampshire Constabulary cars and two motorcycles that have or are in the process of being fully restored to their former glory. The oldest of these is a 1954 Portsmouth City Police Riley 2½ litre RMF, registration number JBK 244 (see Chapter 1) and this is the sole surviving car of that era. It has been restored by Riley enthusiast Steve Kinch from Norfolk who under-took a complete nut and bolt rebuild, costing thousands of pounds. The car made its public debut at the Hampshire Constabulary Family's Day at Netley in June 2002. The car's former driver Sgt Sidney Booth (who assisted the author greatly during his research) sadly passed away prior to the cars completion, but his daughter Mrs Pat Stallard, attended the event and gave the car an emotional seal of approval. The following day the Riley was transported back to Portsmouth where it was photographed in the grounds of its former home at Byculla House, Southsea.

One of the two original 1965 Volvo 120 estates, FOR 298D (see Chapter 4) has also been rescued. For many years it was left to rot in an outbuilding, half way up a Welsh mountainside, before being restored by an enthusiast from Enfield in Middlesex. This is a major restoration job as can be seen from the photo and even Volvo UK declined to take on the task, despite being very interested in the project.

A sad sight, but at least this car has been saved for future generations to admire.
Author.

This same enthusiast was also responsible for restoring the Rover 3500 V8 that was removed from Basingstoke Traffic Section and posted to the Isle of Wight to be used by the Earl Mountbatten (see Chapter 4). He found the car in a terrible state on a pig farm (honest!) and it was only when he started researching the cars history that he discovered its Royal connections. The car has been superbly restored and after being sold on to another enthusiast, is quite often seen at classic car shows around the country, including Hampshire's Family's Day.

The Royal Rover V8 after restoration.
Christopher Taylor

One of the hundreds of Mini pandas has also been saved and is in the process of being restored. The car was a Portsmouth based Austin 850 Mini variant, LOU 884L and it will be finished in the familiar blue and white colour scheme reminiscent of the period. Although no photographs exist of this particular car whilst it was in service, there is enough written and photographic material available to assist with the restoration.

One of Hampshire's MK2 Lotus Cortinas, TOR 756H has also been saved and this to is under going a major refit and will be returned to full Traffic car spec. This car was originally purchased by a Ford enthusiast in Gloucestershire in 1998 but who then sold it on to a couple of enthusiasts on the Isle of Wight in 2002. Graeme Farrar and Andrew Light purchased the car because it was a former island Traffic car and were fascinated by its history. They placed a small article in the local County Press announcing the cars return to the island and were delighted that its former driver, PC Peter Hillier not only contacted them to assist with any questions they might have but supplied the superb photo of the car seen in Chapter 5.

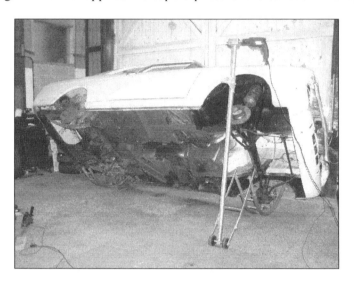

A Norton 750 Commando and a BMW R100 have been restored and are quite often seen at various shows around the country. The Norton was saved and restored by Hampshire PC Hans Taylor and the BMW by former Hampshire Chief Inspector Nick Carter.

Volvo 240 Police Special (as seen in Chapter 6) is also in the process of being restored (by the author) and this too will be shown to the public when finished. When found the car had completed more than 250,000 miles and was in a poor state of repair. One of the old series 3 Jaguar XJ6 saloons has also been rescued and this is also the subject of a major restoration.

Former Southsea area car awaits restoration
Author

And finally Hampshire's last ever Range Rover Classic, K539 NTR has also recently undergone a minor cosmetic restoration and has been returned to its former self, complete with internal roll cage, light bar and full graphics. Although some may question the idea that this car is far too young to claim classic car status, at least it has been saved and can be enjoyed by many at the classic car events that it attends. This car also featured in the excellent *Police Range Rover Handbook* by Peter Hall.

Last of the old Range Rovers has been saved for the future.
Andy Bardsley

Lightning Source UK Ltd.
Milton Keynes UK

172123UK00006BB/6/A